Dear Reader:

Dr. XYZ is a gem. She is a practicing physician in urban areas who grew tired of witnessing people playing Russian Roulette with their lives. Thus, she decided to pen *Nasty*, about a group of people whose situations collide. Extremely nasty things happen when a rich divorcée, an ambitious music mogul, and an extremely horny high school virgin all cross paths in a delicious web of insatiable lust, obsession, and revenge.

This book means a lot to me personally. I feel that the wide spread of HIV in the minority community has to be taken under control. As a mother, I am cognizant daily that my children will have to seek love—and ultimately affection—in a society that could lead to them becoming victims unknowingly. Practicing safe sex is essential and we must protect ourselves. Even now, when I do events and ask the women in the audience, how many of them have been tested lately for HIV, less than two percent raise their hands. Yet, the majority of them are sexually active. There is something seriously wrong with that picture. Please take precautions with your life.

Since it is not my intention to turn this into a public service announcement, I will stop there. *Nasty* is an entertaining thrill ride that can also serve as an educational tool for many.

Thank you for supporting Dr. XYZ's efforts and thank you for supporting one of the dozens of authors published under my imprint, Strebor Books. I try my best to bring you cutting-edge works of literature that will keep your attention and make you think long after you turn the last page.

Now sit back in your favorite chair or, better yet, chill in the bed, and be prepared to be tantalized by yet another great read.

Peace and Many Blessings,

Zane

Zane
Publisher
Strebor Books International
www.simonandschuster.com/streborbooks

ZANE PRESENTS

Nasty

A NOVEL

DR. XyZ

SBI

STREBOR BOOKS

NEW YORK LONDON TORONTO SYDNEY

Strebor Books
P.O. Box 6505
Largo, MD 20792
http://www.streborbooks.com

ISBN 978-1-59309-262-7
LCCN 2009932082

First Strebor Books trade paperback edition September 2009

Cover design: www.mariondesigns.com
Cover photograph: © Keith Saunders/Marion Designs

10   9   8   7   6   5   4   3   2   1

Manufactured in the United States of America

For information regarding special discounts for bulk purchases,
please contact Simon & Schuster Special Sales at 1-866-506-1949
or business@simonandschuster.com

The Simon & Schuster Speakers Bureau can bring authors to your
live event. For more information or to book an event, contact the
Simon & Schuster Speakers Bureau at 1-866-248-3049 or visit our
website at www.simonspeakers.com.

DEDICATION

To Mrs. M, who warned me to never
write about "nasty" things…
and her daughter JM,
who told me to ignore everything
her mama said.

ACKNOWLEDGMENTS

I want to thank the Eternal spirit for all my creativity, discipline and passion for this project. RT, you were my muse and without you, I couldn't have finished. Bee-Maw and Pop-Pop, thanks for supporting every dream or whim I've had over the past ten years. Thanks to all the wonderful folks at Strebor Books who made my dream a reality: Zane, Charmaine and Anita. Keith, your cover was jammin'! Beau, thanks for the intro. To my best friend, JM, your reading of that first "butt-ugly" draft helped to keep the ball rolling. To FS for all her advice and listening to me "whine" about the edit. Dr. ND, for reviving my career, you deserve a special award. To my niece LJ, thanks for keeping me "stylish" during that long writing period. To my brothers, J & W, for the loan and family newsletter (you know who did what). To all my family and friends for their love and support during my years in the "valley."

$\mathcal{A}$UTHOR'S NOTE

The tale you are about to read is a collage of stories and characters that all meet up at one Nasty ending. Many of these stories are true…but names and details of events have been well hidden to protect identities.

PROLOGUE

The pains are bad, real bad. This alien baby is coming out of me now! Oh my Chief...My sweet love. Those bastards stole our baby and put their demon inside me. I remember now. It was that fat, greasy white one. Crusty boils all over his face. When they oozed and dripped out that green slime...that sick pervert made me lick them. If that wasn't bad enough, his breath stank of old whisky and stale garlic. I can still see those boils and smell that godless odor now.

But that wasn't the worst of it, Chief. What grossed me most were those nasty, probing experiments. That's when he switched our baby. Night after night he'd insert his hard alien dick inside me and release his thick fluids. Sometimes he'd yell at me to suck it...suck it real hard. Then he kept slamming it down my throat...choking me when he came. That's when I knew he wasn't human. He didn't taste human. More like an alien from Jupiter...Yeah, he was from Jupiter, all right.

When I found out he switched our baby...I stabbed him.

Stabbed him dead! That was the end of that bastard. But Chief…it was too late. He'd already taken our love child.

That was three months ago. No…it was last week. A month ago? Oh God! They've taken my memory. I don't even remember when it happened…or…or…if it happened.

But one thing is for sure, my darling Chief, he left me with this alien baby. Look at this creature. And there's so much blood. The brightest red I've ever seen. The cord's connected to me. Got to cut the cord like Mama showed me. Umm… no knife. Hey…I'll bite it off. Yeah, that's it. Make a knot, too. Yeah. Good! Oh no! It's moving and crying. STOP CRYING, you beast…STOP CRYING! Why's it crying so loud?

I know. It's sending transmissions to the mother ship. That's what all this crying is about. I know it. Stop crying now! It must be quiet or the head aliens will send their people down here and come and get me and their baby. Probably need me to breastfeed. They'll kill me once it's weaned. That's how they do it on Jupiter.

It must be silenced. I'll take this stick…shove it down its throat. Keep shoving till it stops.

Good…it's only gurgling now.

The aliens are here! I didn't stop the transmissions in time. They're trying to knock the door down. Oh Chief…what can I do? They want their alien baby bad and they're going to take me, too. Can't let that happen. Got to get away. Tell the government about their plot to destroy the earth. I can't let them catch me.

There's a window here.

Perfect.

Got to leave New York now. Just fly back to my Chief…I love you, Chief…I'll be there soon. Safe from the aliens. It's a good thing I have my wings to fly. I knew it was right to stop taking those poison pills they were giving me. Made me forget I have powers…forget about my angel wings. I can fly back to you, Chief…back home to safety.

Here I come, baby! Here I come…

NEWS HEADLINE

A sad New Year's Tragedy. The body of an escaped mental patient, Lizette Odinga, was discovered in front of the Nicola Building in the early hours of the New Year. After allegedly shoving a stick down the throat of her newborn infant, she apparently jumped out of the tenth-floor window of this historic Brooklyn building. Paramedics on the scene rushed the seriously injured infant to Kings County Hospital. Doctors performed emergency surgery on the infant girl, currently listed in critical condition.

CHAPTER ONE

"*So this is where it all happened.*" Nicola stared up at the dilapidated pre-war building. This ten-story monstrosity was her birthplace. Only a few letters of their shared name had survived the unforgiving forces of neglect and time. A once bustling factory, the city's approval for condo conversion was the only thing that blocked its path to rebirth.

A week had passed since she'd last met with the private investigator she'd hired to track down her biological parents. Initially wanting nothing to do with the information he'd gathered, Nicola had awakened that morning, determined to see the building where it had all begun.

Oblivious to the cold winter evening, she'd tried to enter and go up to the top floor where the shameful deed had taken place. All the entrances were boarded up. Frustrated, she'd banged on and repeatedly kicked the front door, stopping only when she spotted blood trickling down from her knuckles.

Nicola hung her head as low as it would go. It didn't take a rocket scientist or years of psychoanalysis for her to figure out that her real purpose for coming all the way to "do or die" Bedford-Stuyvesant was to, in some way, punish the building for providing her mother sanctuary on that fateful night twenty-two years ago.

Now that her plan to do God knows what to the building had failed, Nicola paced back and forth. She needed to perform some ritual to help dim the sadness growing inside her. And then it hit her. Fire! Fire had always helped her in the past.

Armed with a new, quickly forming idea, Nicola bolted across the street and opened the passenger door of a salmon-pink BMW sports coupe. She reached inside the glove compartment and pulled out a cigarette lighter and the old news clipping that revealed the tragic details of her birth.

Slamming the door behind her, Nicola walked over to the nearest garbage can. Hands trembling, she tried to ignite the article. The wind kept blowing out the flame.

"Just burn, dammit!" she yelled out loud.

The few people, who were still out on an evening that promised to be the coldest night of the year, looked at the beautiful woman and how she desperately tried to encourage the flame from her cigarette lighter. Some brave passersby even stopped to ask if anything was wrong. Nicola couldn't hear or see them. The only thing that concerned her, at that moment, was the news about her parents.

She could still hear the portly private investigator with the funny high-pitched voice beg not to make him reveal all of his findings. He'd even offered to return the cash.

"You sure you wanna hear all of this, Ms. Martin? It ain't a pretty story."

But she had insisted. She was marrying Harrison James, the love of her life. A man who believed that family meant everything. Though he had gone out of his way to convince her that she'd become a member of his clan with full privileges, she still wanted her own. How bad could her parents have been? At the worst, they'd been a couple of teenagers who were too young to cope with the responsibilities of raising an infant.

She had listened intently as the PI talked about her father, a brilliant chemist from Kenya, who had met and married her mother while he was teaching at New York University. Nicola could still feel the pride of knowing her father had been an accomplished individual. All her fears about a tragic beginning had been in error, she had thought. But just as she was about to stamp her parents as "normal," the PI's story took a dismal turn.

Her mother had been pregnant when her parents tied the knot. She had been enjoying an uneventful second trimester when she learned that her husband had been killed in a freak laboratory accident.

"Well, that's kinda when things got, uh, confusing for your mother."

"Confusing?"

"Yeah, well, they had to send her to the 'G' building."

"'G' Building?"

"Sorry; you gotta be a Brooklynite to know what that means. Uh, well, what it means is your mother lost it. You know, mentally, and, well, the 'G' building is for the mentals. You know, when you lose it."

"So she went crazy?"

"Yeah, and that ain't the half of it."

The PI reluctantly pulled a news clipping out of a manila envelope.

"This is the last info that I have on your parents, and it's not great; not even a little bit."

Nicola's heart beat wildly. How bad could this information be? Anxious to know the entire story, she grabbed the article out of the PI's hand. Her eyes filled with disappointment and horror as she read the details of how her mother had committed two despicable acts: suicide and attempted infanticide.

Something snapped inside of Nicola. She wanted nothing to do with this newly discovered past. She hurriedly wrote out a check and threw it at the investigator. Never comfortable with giving people bad news, he tried to soften the blow by revealing information about her other relatives.

Uninterested in anything but amnesia for the entire story, she yelled back at the PI as she stormed out of his office. "Throw that info in the garbage. I have no one, no one, but Harrison James. You hear that. Nobody! Just throw it all away!"

"*At last*." Nicola smiled when she saw that the winds had died down enough to let the weak flame ignite the newspaper article. The orange glow intensified, causing the corners of the page to curl up. The slow moving flame destroyed all the information in its path. When the trail of burning embers met up with the picture of a pretty, smiling student nurse holding a tiny baby in her arms with the caption: "Infant survives near-fatal attack at the hands of her late mother." Nicola dropped the clipping into the garbage can.

"It never happened."

She watched the flames dance and engage in a wild, tribal ritual. Her smile broadened across her chiseled face and totally replaced the gloomed hopeless expression that had inhabited it since she'd left the PI's office. She loved watching fires. They calmed her down. She took pleasure in how the flames destroyed everything in their path; especially the bad things.

Watching the fire build, Nicola massaged her neck, caressing the ever-present scarf she wore to cover the thick linear scar that was her only physical imperfection. Neither her adopted parents, nor the counselors at the residential unit she'd lived in after they died, could ever explain exactly what had happened to her. The best explanation was that it was a rare birth defect that had destroyed her voice box. The scar, they all guessed, was probably a result of corrective surgery performed when she was an infant.

She now understood that the real defect was having an insane lunatic for a mother. Using the deep, sultry voice that she had cultivated after years of speech therapy, a voice that drove all the men she had ignored in college wild, Nicola yelled out unanswerable questions into the freezing night.

"God, why me? WHY ME?"

The smiles had all vanished. Staring at the fire, Nicola now felt terribly alone. It was almost as if she missed parents she'd never known. All week long she had tried to hate the woman who'd attempted to kill her. But even she could figure out that her mother's only crime had been loving a man way too much.

What if her dad had lived? What if her mother hadn't loved her father so intensely? What if she hadn't lost her mind? For all the what-ifs in her life, Nicola began to sob like a brand-new baby. She collapsed on the ground. The freezing air hugged her tightly in a bear-like grip. Through the tears, Nicola's body trembled with epileptic fervor.

And then, as if Mother Nature wanted to console her, Nicola could no longer feel the sub-zero blistering

January winds. Instead, she felt bathed in a gathering of cleansing, healing spirits. Almost immediately, an exhilaration of courage swelled within her deepest core, warming her soul.

Liberated, she pulled herself up and ripped off the pink Hermès scarf that hid her scar and the horror of a past that had recently revealed itself. Into the fire it went, joining the newspaper clippings. Hot red sparks spit out at the freezing night as flames consumed the silk fibers.

Since her adolescence, thoughts that she was not good enough often haunted Nicola. Blessed with dark creamy cocoa, flawless skin, she had amazing brown eyes that sparkled so brilliantly, jealous stars in the skies hated it when she came out at night. She'd been told by many that she was exquisitely beautiful. She chose to ignore these compliments and, instead, saw only an ugly, dirty, unfit young woman staring back at her whenever she looked into the mirror to adjust the scarf around her neck, trying to hide what she felt was a hideous scar.

It wasn't until she'd met Harrison that she began to doubt her self-assessment. Her fiancé had spent the last year coaxing her out of a shell of lies that had become her emotional prison.

Well, thought Nicola, *the turtle has finally emerged.* She'd never try to hide or cover her neck again. Never entertain thoughts that she was less than anyone. The lesion would forever be a reminder to her that she was not only a beautiful woman but a strong, beautiful black woman. She had survived her mother's unfortunate attack. And with Harrison by her side, her best friend, the love and light of her life, she'd never be a victim again.

Nicola flipped her thick, waist-length hair out of her face and hopped into the car Harrison had surprised her with on her birthday. No longer a casualty of events she had no control over, she now focused on the future.

Pushing down heavy and hard on the accelerator, she pulled away from the bad memories that lay in the ashes behind. Nicola was glad she'd ordered the PI to trash the information about her Southern roots. She had no desire to contact her grandmother. Pleased with the decision, she glanced at the rearview mirror and smiled as the image of the burning garbage can quickly morphed into an indistinguishable red dot.

Like a queen exiles the malcontents in her realm, the protective muses within Nicola banished the memory of her family to a place her conscious mind never visited. It was the same site she put all of the other horrors she'd encountered in her short life.

She could actually hear a door slam shut as the picture and story of her insane birth were safely tucked away in the "never to be opened" section of her brain.

Blessed and cursed with the gift of selective amnesia, from that moment forward, Nicola had no active memory of her birth.

Nicola headed for the Fifty-ninth Street Bridge. This would be her last night working at Riker's Island jail, or anywhere else, for that matter. Her short career as a medical technologist was about to end. Harrison had insisted that she retire and stay home after their honeymoon, to supervise the renovation of the Harlem brownstone he'd purchased for them. Never happy about her chosen profession in the health field, she'd eagerly agreed with Harrison's plan.

Content and happy about her future, she thought nothing of volunteering to stay and help out when a large group of incoming inmates arrived at the end of her shift. Her colleagues tried to encourage her to go home. They begged her. She smiled and ignored them. It was her last time.

I'll never have to work like this again, she thought. *A few extra hours won't kill me.*

Exhausted and drained from the previous events of the day, she pitched in and helped the crew draw blood.

"Hey, Nicola! I got one of your people! Can't get this man's blood! A junkie! You know you're the only one who can get their damn veins working! I don't know what we're going to do when you leave!"

Nicola looked up at the new inmate her soon to be ex-coworker had dragged over to her station. She could tell that he'd been on the streets. He was scruffier than most. He had that "I live in a cardboard box home and ain't had a bath since I was a baby" kind of smell. "Her people," the folks called them. Just because she volunteered at the homeless shelter every now and then.

He held his head low, avoiding all eye contact. Nicola knew this man was ashamed. His voice barely audible, it was obvious that he was educated.

"What's your name, sir?" Unlike her colleagues, Nicola always spoke to the inmates with respect.

Never lifting his head, he responded, "Eli...Eli Griffith."

She glanced at his sheet and saw that he was in for larceny and murder. Nicola shuddered. She had a soft spot in her heart for folks down on their luck. That was why she had volunteered. But murder? That was where she drew the line.

Drawing his blood was impossible. He had so many old scarred tracks on his arms and legs, he didn't have a single viable vein in his body. She tried everywhere: arms, feet, hands; even his neck veins.

"Uh, sir, where do you, uh, shoot up? What veins are you using?"

He looked at her face for the first time and smiled when he saw how beautiful she was and remarked, "Pretty lady, you don't even want to know."

She tried his foot again. This time she was successful.

"I'm impressed. The lady is not only beautiful, but extremely talented."

Accustomed to inmates' compliments, and usually ignoring them, for some reason she took exception to this one. Though accused of a heinous crime, Nicola smiled back at Eli. It was a smile that he'd never forget. It was the last one he would see for many years to come. She placed a Band-Aid on his foot and motioned for the officer to drag him back to a line where other inmates awaited their fate.

Before she had a chance to catch her breath, they put another inmate in Eli's spot. She picked up his sheet and saw that he was a notorious bigamist. Nicola had had enough.

"Hey, that's it, guys. I'm out of here. I can't do this one."

Overwhelmed with fatigue and a desire to get the hell off of Riker's Island and back to her new life with Harrison James, she hastily labeled the blood specimens, dropped them off at the laboratory, and said good-bye to her colleagues.

When the guards let her pass through the steel-gated doors, she ran out with all intentions of never looking back. Never realizing that, all night long, she had mislabeled several blood specimens, including Eli Griffith's.

CHAPTER TWO

Eli's body curled up into itself. Images of the son he hadn't seen in years haunted him. His beloved ex-wife, Ophelia, taunted him as the waves of withdrawal swallowed every cell in his body and regurgitated back in to the belly of the one toilet bowl in the cell. This was the worst withdrawal he'd ever experienced, but then again, that's what he said every time he couldn't get a hold of Lady H. It always seemed as if the devil had finally successfully chased his Godless, worthless soul to hell.

Where was that methadone? He'd been there for over a week and he had missed more than one of his doses because of administrative glitches. Sweat poured out of his pores, creating tiny mud puddles in the cracks and crevices of his skin folds. He was so funky, he couldn't stand his own damned self. This was nasty. He hadn't had a shower since he'd arrived there. He was scared of the showers. Terrible things happened to men there.

For a split second, the waves of pain subsided. He sneaked a look at his arms and legs. They were covered with swollen tracks. He checked out his penis. He had used it more times than a few to bring his beloved heroin closer to home. Thick, musky smelling, rusty-tinged fluid seeped out of the newest injection sites. Funny, he never had infected tracks before. Seemed like his body was turning against him in his old age. Yeah. Imagine that. Old and he wasn't even fifty yet.

The last time he had picked up his methadone, the nurse had counseled him about HIV and prevention strategies. She'd also told him that he didn't have it in his blood. He had been so relieved. It was the one thing he was afraid of. The last couple of years, he'd gotten a little sloppy and had started sharing needles with his buddies. He realized that he should've taken the free city needles, but sometimes they weren't always where he needed them.

Times were getting hard on the streets for him. He wasn't as young or as resourceful as he had been. He remembered the days when crowds would come from all parts of the city, to see him paint on the canvases he set up in Washington Square Park in Greenwich Village. His specialties were portraits and landscapes. Though he was definitely talented, he was infamous for rarely finishing a painting. Before drugs had completely consumed him, folks with money, especially white Bohemian women with thick fat trust funds, had been so impressed with his skills, they'd invite him to stay in their New York City pads, hoping he'd develop great works of art.

Over the years, he had lived in some of the most exclusive addresses in Manhattan: The Dakota, the building where John Lennon was murdered; multi-million-dollar converted lofts in Tribeca, and his favorite hang, the Hamptons. Back in the day, he could always get an invite to bring his paint supplies and stay a month or two in the summer playground of New York's obscenely wealthy residents.

His freeloading with the rich was always a short-time stay. Drugs always seemed to corrupt his ability to stay focused. When patrons discovered his talent was limited and his need for drugs unlimited, even the women who kept him for sex had soon grown bored with him. Eli was never discouraged when they tossed him out. There were always new people who spotted him at his village "gallery" who were convinced they could tame the un-disciplined artist.

But that was then. Seemed like now that he was older, folks with money didn't want a down-and-out junkie around who couldn't even complete a child's paint-by-numbers project. Nobody thought he was special.

A correctional officer walked past his cell. He yelled out at him through the bars, as if testifying to the world. "Hey, officer, listen! Listen up!" The C.O. briefly turned around. "Look, look here. Now I'm gonna kick this habit, but send me some methadone now before I *die*!"

The officer looked at him in disgust and spit out, "Fuckin' junkie, you'll get it when the nurses call your good-for-nothing ass and not a minute before. Now shut the fuck up!"

He felt like screaming a million obscenities. But he just moaned to himself. Nobody cared about junkies. Even he didn't care about junkies. Eli had long ago resigned himself to the fact that he had chosen a life-style that would eventually kill him. He was too chicken shit to use the old, tried and true, "bullet to the head" method.

If he'd only taken Alan Montana's offer of money and a crack at a decent rehab facility two years ago, he wouldn't be in jail. The wealthy comedian had been so grateful when Eli had helped him find his teenage daughter, he'd offered him the moon. But Eli had always admired him. He wanted to be on equal footing; man to man. To look Alan in the eye. He refused the offer. Alan, impressed by how he clearly needed help, had insisted. But Eli had his pride. The more the comedian begged, his conviction to refuse grew exponentially.

He had bragged about his experience with the come-dian later that night when he was getting high with a musician buddy he'd known for years. The saxophonist shook his head as he injected heroin, wondering why Eli refused the cash. "The biggest tool for a fool is his pride. Ain't you never heard, pride goeth before a fall, and shit, nigger, junkies always falling." Still shaking his head at Eli's foolishness, waiting as the drug took effect, he leaned into a junkie nod.

Two months ago, when his own habit had him living out of cardboard boxes under the Manhattan Bridge, the young girl Eli and her father had tried to save died from an overdose. All the money in the world couldn't keep her from crack and the streets. He wanted to attend the funeral, and maybe ask Alan Montana for help. Once again, the demon pride intervened. He could not ask for assistance, especially since his life was in such a despicable condition.

Now he was in jail. For stealing. In all of his years as a junkie, he had never stolen. He had truly hit rock bottom. He'd fallen from a high of organizing creative art projects in African villages when he was with the Peace Corps to a new low of conspiring with common criminals.

He couldn't help it. He needed money. Dope wasn't free and the waiting lists for drug rehab centers in the city were longer than all the tracks on his arms combined. With a big hit of cash, he could buy his last stash and then enter a good clinic. He wanted a clear exit out of hell. He was getting too old.

The irony of the whole affair was that on the day he committed the crime, Al Montana had opened a new drug treatment center in memory of his daughter. If he'd only set pride aside, he could have been in that first group of patients in the new state-of-the-art drug rehabilitation facility, instead of a Riker's Island prison cell.

Damn that Badheart, he thought. It was supposed to be a simple robbery. Nobody was going to get hurt. He told him to leave his crackhead brother, DJ, out the plan. He hated crackheads with a real passion. They weren't cool at all. Garbage fried their brains or something. With Lady H, you just get mellow; not so with that wacky smack.

Why did DJ bring the gun? It wasn't part of their plan. And why did he shoot the Arab in the neck? Why? Because he was a fuckin' crackhead, that's why.

Even though he didn't pull the trigger. Even though he stayed behind to help the dying Arab out. Even though the store's video camera substantiated all his claims, the court-appointed attorney could not get the self-righteous, junkie-hating judge to set bail at a reasonable level. A hundred thousand dollars! Hell, if he had that kind of money he wouldn't have had to hold up the damn store. But if bail was a dollar, it wouldn't have done him any good. He didn't have that either. Nor did he have a place to stay. On second thought, mused Eli, the judge had done him a righteous turn.

Finally, they gave Eli his methadone. He swallowed the liquid and smiled to himself, knowing that soon, very soon, the razor scraping his insides out would soon be so dull, he wouldn't feel anything at all.

CHAPTER THREE

After a month of regular methadone and nutrition, Eli started feeling human again. Eli eventually ventured into the showers. He might as well get used to them. This would be his second time in jail and his public defender told him to expect some real hard time. Ten years or more. Why so much time? He quickly learned that the combination of robbery, homicide, and drugs made all the difference.

As he became more aware of his surroundings, his personality returned. His natural outgoing nature forced him to try and make small talk with the mostly younger inmates. It sickened him to know that the prison population could have doubled for a huge dormitory at any of the predominantly Black universities. Instead of spending time learning and expanding their minds to do something truly revolutionary and positive, society and the power elite had imprisoned his brothers and sisters when they were in the prime of their lives. Imprisoned like animals. The best and the brightest could be behind this wall, and nobody would know it. Nobody cared.

But who was he to look down on society's corruption and its oppression of his people? He had a college degree. Was only a thesis away from a Masters. How many of his brothers and sisters had he inspired or helped to do better? He had spent the last twenty years of his life looking for money to support his drug habit. The fact that he had had an opportunity to travel a better path was never lost of him.

Eli often looked at his only prized possession, a pocket-sized portrait of his family. The one he abandoned when he couldn't conform to his wife's world. Looking back, there was nothing wrong with that world. Especially when he compared it with the one he currently resided in.

The day the prison barber finally got around to cutting off Eli's lice-ridden dreads and his even nastier beard, a spectacular-looking, distinguished man emerged. Unfortunately, his new look attracted the attention of Sebastian La Roux, a male prostitute from the Bronx who was by far the most brutal inmate at Riker's.

At twenty-six, Sebastian towered over most men at six-foot-five. A disciplined body builder with python-like muscles, he loved to corner HIV-negative inmates and, with the help of his gang, sexually brutalize them.

Terrified of contracting the disease, a snitch in the lab gave him the results of all the men he considered as targets. When he discovered Eli was negative, he eagerly awaited an opportunity that would lead to an intimate liaison.

As prison food put much needed pounds on Eli's six-foot-two-inch frame, Sebastian was mesmerized and completely turned on by his lean body. He had a thing for older men. He especially liked the idea of turning them out. It was the least he could do. After all, an old Catholic Priest had raped him when he was nine. He'd only be returning a favor.

He gazed at Eli with wanton lust whenever he could get a glimpse of his nude body in the showers. He dreamt of Eli's mocha-colored skin and fantasized about the junkie tearing his ass up. Usually a "bottom-man," he didn't mind playing "top," as he was pretty sure Eli would never participate willingly. What he did know for sure was that he wanted to have sex with him; any time he wanted it; any way he wanted it.

Eli was aware of Sebastian's intentions. Walking through the exercise yards or sitting in the prison cafeteria at mealtime, he could feel those steel gray eyes tracking him. Rarely taking glimpses at him, he was intimidated by the multiple, thick keloid, imbedded scars that stretched across Sebastian's forehead, back, and abdomen. They each shouted tales of battles he had been in. Battles where one could only imagine the violent fate the 'other guy' had experienced. He looked like a man who regularly battled Satan and, Eli figured, Sebastian La Roux usually won.

For as long as he could, he tried to avoid the body builder and his two equally menacing cohorts, Jerome and Lady P. His time ran out the day they cornered him in the yard. Guards not around, Sebastian and his crew gagged Eli and dragged him to an abandoned building in a secluded area of the yard. The guard responsible for the old storage unit winked at them as they entered.

"Don't take forever; you only paid for fifteen minutes."

"Don't worry, officer. We'll be as quick as we can!" promised Sebastian.

Eli fought, clawed, and kicked as hard as he could. The white rag they shoved in his mouth prevented his screams from escaping. His mind filled with terror, knowing what they were about to do to him.

"He's a tough one. He ain't gonna give in easy," squealed Jerome. The smallest in the gang, he had sustained quite a few bruises trying to subdue their victim.

"Don't like it easy. Hold the bitch still!"

They pinned Eli against the wall. He tried to jerk his body to avoid his attackers.

"Lady P, you bring the Crisco this time like I asked you?"

Lady reached in his pocket and pulled out the stash of lard he had stolen from the kitchen. Sebastian grabbed it from him.

"Gonna grease this pole good. Won't hurt that much if you hold still, dammit. Hold still; your ass might like it." Sebastian, growing weary of his resistance, hammered Eli's head with his powerful fist. Dazed, confused and with blood trickling from gashes in his face, Eli finally had no fight in him.

Sebastian ripped Eli's pants and underwear down, and slathered the white shortening on his cheeks and anus.

"Gonna hurt me more than it hurts you; believe me. JUST HOLD STILL!" The monster zipped open his pants and released, stroked, and lubricated his eight-inch long, rock-hard dick, preparing for penetration. He stooped down to position himself against Eli, forced his cheeks wide apart, and jabbed his prick up his anus. He thrust his huge member as deep as Eli's anatomy would allow him to go.

"Damn, this shit is good and tight!"

Intense pain shot through Eli's rectum. It traveled up his spinal column and hit his brain like a nuclear explosion. In epileptic style, his body violently bucked back and forth.

"Keep him still. I don't wanna hit him again; might kill him." Lady P and Jerome tightened their hold on Eli.

A rapid knock at the door reminded them that time was of the essence.

"Gonna have to speed this up."

And speed it up, he did. Like a jackhammer tears through city streets, he thrust his steel-hardened penis into Eli's uncooperative body repeatedly without remorse. The sound of flesh pounding against an unwilling body echoed throughout the metal-lined room. Torrential sweat poured over Sebastian's curly hair and banana yellow skin. His beady eyes bulged out as his massive chest heaved rapidly. He was approaching climax. Riding Eli like a stallion, every muscle in Sebastian's body tightened as he prepared for what he knew would be a fabulous orgasm.

He cried out, "Papa coming soon! Papa coming real soon, Daddy! OOOOOh!" An electrical discharge of pleasure exploded throughout his pelvis. He released his load and ripped his dripping penis out of Eli, totally satisfied with the experience. A trail of blood-tinged stool and thick semen seeped out of Eli's anus.

"That shit was GOOD!"

"What about us?"

"This tail is mine!"

"But you ain't never been an ass man!" shrieked Lady P.

"I am now, so just get your own. Come on, let's drag him outta here. Don't want nobody to find out about our little chalet here, now do we." They carried Eli out and dropped his limp body beside the dumpster in the back of the prison yard.

Eli's moans were audible to no one but himself. He tried to move. His body would not obey his commands.

Sebastian had escorted his soul to hell. He'd never be able to look at himself in the mirror without feeling the demon entering him. Tortured by a pain he never knew existed, he fainted...more from not wanting to be mentally present for the mentally degrading ordeal he had experienced, than from the actual physical discomfort.

When Eli came to, guards had surrounded him, demanding he reveal his attackers. He refused. After a brief stay in the infirmary, authorities assigned him to an isolation cell. Honoring strict prison code, he still never revealed the identities of the vicious crew that had violated him.

For three months after his release from isolation, Sebastian had his way with him on an almost daily basis. Eli never gave in easy. He fought each time and tried to escape. His battle only turned on the beast within Sebastian and intensified his sexual needs. Eli was no match for him and his crew.

The rituals ended when they finally released the savage from jail. Sebastian returned to New York City to work as a bouncer at the Rusty Nail, a popular gay bar in Chelsea. Eli breathed a sigh of relief when Jerome and Lady P, who fortunately no longer had an interest in him sexually, informed him that their leader sent his love and regards.

Finally free from that monster, Eli completely immersed his abused soul in the glory of what it felt like to walk through the yards, take a shower, or sit in the common area without having to look over his shoulder. But his joy was short-lived. A week after he got the news about Sebastian, his old friends "Bad Luck" and his evil twin "Fucked-up Luck" decided to pay him another visit.

A guard pulled Eli out of his cell and escorted him down to the infirmary. Once there a nurse explained that on his first day at Riker's someone made a terrible mistake. Several specimens were mislabeled. They had to repeat his test. As the nurse tried to coax blood out of his scarred veins, Eli's mind raced backward to that first night. The vision of the beautiful young technician haunted him. He prayed she was as competent as she was lovely.

But his prayers weren't answered. More bad news came the following week. Repeat tests showed he had full-blown AIDS. He immediately started laughing when he heard the results. The irony of his predicament was not lost on him. One of the main reasons Sebastian had chosen him for his "girl" was that he was supposed to be AIDS free. Laughing uncontrollably, just to keep from crying, Eli knew that he'd been screwed not once, but twice.

Four months later, he was sentenced to ten years with a possibility for parole in five. On the day he transferred to Attica State Prison, he packed his only belongings, a picture of his son, Tarik, and an old newspaper clipping with a picture of his wife, Ophelia. She was a student nurse holding a young infant who had survived a vicious attack by her birth mother. He and Ophelia had fallen in love with the beautiful brown baby girl with the big sparkling eyes.

They applied to be her foster parents, hoping to adopt her one day. When they were finally accepted, Ophelia rushed home to share the good news with Eli only to arrive and find him so high from drugs he had almost killed their son, Tarik.

Knowing that death from AIDS was waiting for him right around the corner, he had only one wish; to see his ex-wife, Ophelia, and their son, Tarik, one last time. He prayed that he could stay alive long enough. But five to ten years in prison was a long time and, with AIDS, the odds were definitely stacked up against him. All this to do and so little time; so very little time.

CHAPTER FOUR

"Ooo-Wah-Shay-La-La...oh, Harrison, baby!" Nicola was so close to coming, she moaned out the chant she learned from her Tantric sex guide.

"Ooo-Wah-Shay-La-La...Ooo-Wah-Shay-La-La...."

He's there. He's on my spot. Good GOD ALMIGHTY HE'S THERE!

Nicola's body and soul enjoyed the complete rapture of all the sensual flavors that Harrison's powerful tongue lathered over her most sensitive area.

"Oh, baby...I'm gonna come. I'm gonna come. You at my spot. YOU AT MY SPOT!"

It had been so long. Harrison hadn't gone down on her in months.

"Ooo-Wah-Shay-La-La...Ooo-Wah-Shay-La-La...OOO-WAH-SHAY-LA-LA!" Knowing what was coming next, she clenched her teeth and held her pelvis still, afraid he'd lose her spot. Her body tensed up tighter than a drum, waiting for the command from his tongue. Any second now, the dam would break and the flood gates of her inner moistness would release ALL her good stuff. Any second. ANY SECOND!

And then, without any warning, he pulled his precious tongue off her clit, lifted his head up from between her legs, and said the worst thing she had ever heard.

"Damn, baby. You take too long. I've been down there for hours. My jaw hurts. We'll do this; we'll do this some other time. There's trouble in the office that I must address tonight."

Harrison raised his pudgy naked body off their California king-sized bed and fled to the bathroom. He slammed the door behind him. Nicola was in shock.

NO HE DIDN'T! No he did not stop. Not when I was so close.

"Harrison, baby, come back! Come back, baby!" she yelled out. But he didn't respond.

She could hear the sound of Harrison spitting and gargling his mouth out with the English herbal rinse he so adored. All hopes that he'd return back to bed and finish his business were destroyed when she heard the noise from the shower.

Damn his British ass to hell, she thought. Frustrated in an exponential fashion, she didn't know if she wanted to kill him now, or kill him later. How could he? And she had done the pole dance for him. Even let him have her from behind. It wasn't something she was too crazy about, but it surely rocked his world. Everything or anything to please him. All she needed was a little more time; she was so close.

Harrison came out the bathroom and dressed quickly. The silence in the room was thick as pea soup. Nicola was still on the bed naked. She stared at him with loathing, "I'm gonna get you sucka'!" eyes. Knowing he had disappointed her, he gave her a quick, dry peck on her forehead.

"I'm sorry you didn't come, love. We'll do this again, soon; honest. Cheery-OH."

And he left her. He left her unfulfilled and horny as hell! Needing release in the worst way, she rummaged through her nightstand and took out her cute little pink electric buddy. She switched it on and let it do what Harrison didn't have enough time for.

She had her orgasm, but it was empty. She wanted him. She liked to hold him when she came. The pillow just wouldn't do the trick.

As the vibrations subsided, Nicola began to cry. What was wrong with her and Harrison? They'd been married more than five years and she could feel him slowly drifting away. And it scared her, for she still loved him as much now as she did in the beginning. In fact…she loved him more, if that was at all possible.

In the beginning, it was all good. It was the best.

They first met over six years ago, at a McDonald's on 125th Street in Harlem. Nicola was sitting alone, totally engrossed in a laboratory science magazine and a bag of fries when she was summoned back to earth by a crisp, proper, British-accented voice. "I hope you enjoyed your meal. Miss, I'm sorry to interrupt but I just wanted…"

Nicola looked up at a pair of the warmest caramel-colored eyes she'd ever seen. They hypnotized her from the first moment she made contact.

"I just wanted to introduce myself. I'm Harrison James, the new owner of this restaurant. I signed the papers today."

From that quaint meeting, they slowly began dating. Nicola was initially unclear about her warm reaction to Harrison. Men had approached her over the years that were far more attractive. In fact, at just five-foot-seven, with a reddish brown complexion and being slightly overweight, he was barely cute. But what he did have, and what these other "gorgeous" men would never have, was a kind, giving, and loving spirit that was more beautiful than merely being "handsome" could ever be.

Harrison was a devout Catholic and very old-fashioned about the mating ritual. This suited Nicola very well. She enjoyed the slow, non-threatening pace of their relationship. It was two months before he attempted to kiss her, and petting didn't enter the picture until six months after they met. Nicola was comfortable with

Harrison leading their way into the intimate aspects of their relationship.

She was in love with him from the very beginning. He was kind, industrious, and thoughtful. Born and raised in London, England, his mother, originally from Jamaica, relocated the family to New York City when Harrison was in high school. A brilliant student, he easily obtained a college scholarship to Columbia University.

At the time they met, she was twenty and he was thirty-two years old. Thanks to investing a large payout from a lottery win into a McDonald's restaurant eight years ago, he now had sixteen restaurants and several properties in New York and Florida to call his own. He was a millionaire who took great care of his mother. His two sisters and several other relatives were now in college, thanks to his financial support.

Nicola loved his devotion to family and religion, and chose to convert to Catholicism. This pleased Harrison. When she had completed the process, he surprised her with a trip to Rome to visit the Vatican. He told her, every Catholic should go there once in their lives.

Rome was a wonderful holiday for them. He proposed to her after they attended a prayer session led by the Pope. Nicola was beside her self with joy. She hugged him and accepted. That moment firmly erased all the pain and joylessness that had been her constant companion since she was born.

After their Roman holiday, they flew to the beautiful Seychelles Islands in the Indian Ocean. They boarded the private yacht, Nicola's Beauty. Under Harrison's direction, the owner had temporarily changed the name. She squealed with delight when she saw the trouble he went to in order to please her. She was in heaven.

The day after their arrival, under a bright sunny sky with the calmest ocean breezes, the captain married them. Harrison said they would repeat their vows in a proper Catholic ceremony in the States, but he'd always dreamt of marrying a beautiful woman on a luxurious yacht at sea.

The crew completely pampered the newlyweds. When they weren't waited on hand and foot, the two snorkeled in the crystal clear waters off the coast of the Seychelles, swam with the dolphins and ended every evening dancing under the black velvet sky. They had so much lobster, caviar, and champagne that they grew weary of it. When Harrison longed for a McDonald's Big Mac, they both knew it was time to go home. It was a breathtaking month at sea. It was more than romantic. They were living in a beautiful dream.

In the beginning months of their union, they enjoyed cuddling and talking long hours with each other. When they did have intercourse, Nicola found it hard to relax. Frigid, she was never comfortable. She preferred the generous back rubs Harrison administered and the long shared soaks in their Jacuzzi tub. If she could avoid sexual intercourse the rest of her life, Nicola would do it without any regrets.

Harrison sensed her indifference and made improving the intimate aspects of their lives together a shared goal. He wanted his wife to experience full carnal pleasure and enrolled them both in a journey to discover true sexual intimacy. Nicola, always willing to please Harrison, agreed with his plan. They devoured illustrated sex manuals, hired a Tantric love guide, viewed sexually explicit tapes, and purchased a countless amount of sex toys.

After a year of experiencing all the sexual positions from the Kama Sutra, studying Tantric sex and using all types of vibrators, dildos, oils, and sensual massages, Nicola became a fully sexually aware, multi-orgasmic woman. Harrison had successfully turned on his wife's freak button.

She installed a pole in their bedroom. An exotic dancer taught her how to use it. A quick learner, she soon performed for Harrison like a pro. He was never bored. Nor was she. In fact, Harrison slowly realized that he had created a monster. Nicola wanted sex all the time. And so did he. They were the perfect couple.

CHAPTER FIVE

After three years of marital bliss, Nicola wanted a child. Harrison agreed. Unfortunately, his sperm count was not cooperative. Disappointed, and more than a little upset about his infertility, Harrison channeled his energies into expanding his business into other cities. Nicola found herself alone more than she liked, as he was often on business trips out of town. She often complained and he promised to slow down, but he never did. If anything, the trips out of town increased.

In the last eighteen months of their union, sex slowly disappeared from their marriage. Nicola, always eager, was frustrated and bitched constantly. Harrison accused her of being preoccupied with sex and believed that her obsession with it was bordering on abnormal.

He explained that her passions were immature and unbecoming of a mature woman satisfied with a loving marriage. He convinced her that the frequency of sex naturally declines with "old married couples." Despite the fact that she was still in her twenties and nowhere near elderly, Nicola, always eager to please her husband, agreed to slow down.

In an attempt to tame the sexual wild beast Harrison found so unattractive, Nicola signed up for meditation seminars. She attended the classes religiously and devoured a library of metaphysical books, hoping the information would help re-channel "abnormal" sexual energy into positive spirituality. The books and classes did not help. If anything, Nicola was hornier than ever.

Thinking she had too much free time on her hands, she decided to take more interest in their businesses. Harrison supported her efforts and found a good partner in his wife, yet he continued to leave her behind when he went on business trips. On the rare occasions that Nicola joined him, she often found herself alone in the hotel suite, waiting for him to return. More frustrated than ever, Nicola poured all her time into rehabbing three distressed Harlem properties the couple had recently purchased.

So after all her work, Harrison was now accusing her of taking too long to respond sexually. She couldn't win with him. Maybe he was right, though. Harrison usually was. She probably had oversuppressed her sexual drive with all those meditation exercises, and rehabbing buildings was no picnic. Even with a crew of ten who actually did the hands-on work, she often ended the day totally exhausted.

A month after Harrison had abandoned her in the bedroom, Nicola's brownstone refurbishing project ended. She tried to lure her husband away for a vacation, but all he said was, "You go on without me, lovey. You deserve a break." Sensing her disappointment, he added, "I know what, I'll send you to Monte Carlo. You love it there. You haven't been in over two years."

He was right. She did love Monte Carlo. The luxurious hotels; the gambling; the beaches. But she loved Harrison more. Not at all happy with his decision, she reluctantly agreed to a month-long stay at the five-star spa resort in the silver mining town of Taxco, Mexico. *Maybe*, she thought, *it'll revitalize my tank*.

Once there, Nicola enrolled in their popular regimen of activities created especially to de-stress busy, wealthy women. After three weeks of daily massages, healthy gourmet meals, and long herbal soaks, she began to feel like a new woman. The only disturbing things at the spa were the buff young men on staff whose only job was to cater to the client's every whim. Some were quite brazen in their attempts to tease her into serious sexual activity.

Nicola ignored their advances. She was, after all, a one-man woman. Harrison was her one man. Besides, she could still hear him complaining about how long it took her to reach an orgasm. *If my own husband doesn't have patience for me, these fine young waiters won't either,* thought Nicola.

A seminar at the spa given by Dr. Ana Perez, an Argentinean reconstruction gynecologist, changed her mind. Her talk, "The G-Spot…Everything you need to know but were afraid to ask," was enlightening. She was especially interested in the intra-vaginal injection that promised to heighten a woman's sexual response. She called it the "G-Shot." After the talk, Nicola literally attacked the doctor. Dr. Perez agreed to perform the simple procedure at her clinic.

"Hold still, *señora…por favor…*hold still…relax!" pleaded the doctor. With both legs resting in stirrups, Nicola squirmed and jumped every time the doctor tried to position the needle into her vagina. She hated injections and the G-shot was given in a spot that she just couldn't fathom wouldn't hurt. Though the doctor explained it was nothing…her mind told her it was something. Dr. Perez pleaded again, "I cannot do if you move!"

"I'm so sorry, doctor, I hate needles; and in my VAGINA!!!"

"I know. I put you to sleep. *sí?*"

Pleased with her decision, Nicola looked at the doctor and smiled, "*Sí!*"

When she woke up from the procedure, as the doctor had promised, she had a new pussy. One, she explained, that would respond effortlessly to even the slightest provocation. She joked, "You'll need a little hombre in your pocket now because you will want amor all 'de time, señora!"

And the doctor was right. She could feel that warm sensation when she walked, when she ran, and she swore on the Bible whenever she breathed too deeply. Her pink little electronic buddy, that she was happy she remembered to bring on the trip, never left her side. Nicola decided to cancel the last week of her spa visit, and make a surprise visit home to her husband. There was no way he could complain about her taking too long to respond now.

CHAPTER SIX

When the limo pulled into their tree-lined block located in the famous Hamilton Heights section of Harlem, the sound of John Coltrane's "My Favorite Things," was blasting in the street. She knew Harrison was the culprit before she stepped out the car. Nicola smiled. Though the man was a virtual saint, he did have one bad habit…he played music way too loud. He was like a teenager. She opened the front door with her key. The driver carried her matching Gucci luggage, and set all four pieces down in the foyer. She tipped him generously and he left.

The house was pitch dark, except for a flickering light peeking out from the den. *Oh*, thought Nicola, *my baby's chilling by the fireplace listening to his music*. Feeling lucky, she hoped he was relaxed and ready for action. She sneaked over to the liquor cabinet, poured brandy into two large glasses, and quietly entered the den to greet her man.

What she saw, she would not have been prepared to see in a million years. In front of the fireplace, facing away from the door, Nicola discovered Harrison ramming his penis into someone's ass. She watched the scene for what seemed like an eternity. The couple was not aware that she was there. She was in shock.

As Harrison's pumping action intensified, he yelled as he had never yelled with her. "I'm coming, baby! I'm coming!"

She watched as her husband thoroughly enjoyed what appeared to be an extremely intense orgasm. He had never responded with as much passion with her as she now witnessed. She was hurt and jealous. When his pleasure subsided, he spun his partner around and they engaged in a deep kiss. The light from the fire increased fully for a second, just long enough for Nicola to see and realize for the first time that Harrison's lover was a man.

And it wasn't just any man. It was Sebastian La Roux. She remembered him from her days at Riker's Island. He was a notorious prisoner that had stricken fear in all the staff whenever he came to the clinic for a visit. Which, unfortunately for them, was far too often. In shock, all she could think was, *How could he betray me, and with such a low-life! HOW COULD HE!*

The flames from the fireplace seemed to jump out at Nicola. She immediately transferred back into time. Back to when she was a little girl, watching the house she lived in burn down. They were both the same flames. They both destroyed something equally powerful in her life: the evil she unfortunately grew up in as a child and the love she had for a man she worshipped almost as much as she worshipped God.

The flames pulled all the horrible memories of her tragic life into the forefront. She screamed as thoughts of her earlier abuse mingled with the pain and disappointment she now experienced because of Harrison's betrayal.

Harrison yelled at his lover, "Sebastian, leave! I'll deal with you later!"

"But why I gotta go? Send her away!"

Harrison looked up at the towering giant, and decided to deal with him less aggressively. "Please, just go down to the Rusty Nail. I'll be there later."

Sebastian looked at Nicola with disgust. She was oblivious to both of them.

"That bitch ain't even here; she so in shock. But… I'll leave…uh-ruh…" He held his hand out, waiting for a donation. "Forget something?"

Harrison looked for his wallet, snatched out several hundred-dollar bills, and threw them at him. Sebastian made a face at Nicola and left.

Harrison tended to his wife. She was hysterical. He never knew about the abuses in her life. Nicola was now rambling off details of what happened to her as if she were a reporter giving a biographical rundown of a victim. She spoke of her childhood in the third person, never admitting that it had actually happened to her.

Nicola finally stopped the endless chatting about her childhood. She sobbed uncontrollably throughout the night. She never yelled at Harrison. He was so disappointed and ashamed of himself. He had never wanted his princess to discover his extracurricular activities. He rocked her in his arms all night long.

He left home as the morning sun was rising.

CHAPTER SEVEN

"Nicola, I never wanted to hurt you." Harrison mixed chicken gravy into the grits, and while waiting for them both to cool, he stuffed a small piece of cornbread in his mouth, and added, "I love you completely."

Why did she meet him at T-Lilly's Place? It was his favorite soul food restaurant. They were sitting in his favorite booth. It should have been a neutral location… a place she didn't have to watch him eat. Knowing what she now knew about him made looking at Harrison pack his face with food a disgusting event. But curiosity and something called stupid compelled her to meet with the man she would have given up her life for.

Nicola spat out with vengeance, "You mean like a real 'man' loves a woman? I don't think so." Her lawyer had advised her not to have any contact with Harrison. She was now really mad at herself for not listening. The divorce was only two weeks away and there was really nothing he could say that would change her mind.

"I know, in my heart of hearts, that I am a man." Squirming in his chair, uncomfortable, he looked around to see if anyone could hear his declaration and added, "I am not a homosexual. I just…just…" Harrison looked at Nicola and whispered, "I just need a little variety every now and then."

"Oh, so that's what you faggots call fucking now? *Variety*? Umm, interesting; very interesting." Nicola coldly stared at the man she had once thought could replace the Pope in the Vatican; he had been that pure of heart.

"Before I met you, I only flirted with it, curious like. I went to the bars every now and then. Maybe had one or two or…"

"Or three thousand homo-dates or whatever you call them!"

Breaking the tension, the waitress arrived and set a cup of hot tea, lemon and honey in front of Nicola. "Anything else, Miss?"

Nicola shook her head and the young girl, grateful for the opportunity to wait on other tables, left them alone.

Harrison looked at his beautiful, soon-to-be ex-wife. Her contempt for him was palpable. "When I met you, Nicola, *it* all stopped. You were my world. You rocked it completely. I never needed anyone but you. You have to believe that."

With cold eyes ready to spit fire with the slightest

provocation, she lashed out, "What the hell changed everything then?"

"It was not being able to give you that baby."

Pissed at his flimsy, self-serving excuse, Nicola blurted out, "Give me a fucking break…"

Ignoring her dismissal of his explanation, he continued, "At any rate…that's when I started hanging out at the Rusty Nail."

Nicola looked at him, puzzled. "The Rusty what?"

"It's a gay bar in Chelsea. At first it was to have a drink and listen to the music."

"I know….'just a Coke and smile.' Yeah…right!" Her sarcasm was biting. She poured honey and squeezed lemon juice into her cup of tea. A few drops squirted into her eyes. She wiped them away, wishing that wiping away the memory of Harrison's betrayal could be just as simple.

"At first it was for a…'Coke and a smile,' as you call it. But then I met Sebastian La Roux."

"That beast!"

"He's not a…well…I guess…" Harrison stopped defending his lover as images of how, as part of their foreplay, Sebastian had repeatedly lifted him up and "playfully" slammed him against the wall. "…well…yes… he is kind of a beast. It's probably why I was attracted to him."

Nicola rolled her eyes. "I remember his demon-ass from Riker's."

"Nicola, I never wanted my downtown life to mix with my uptown life. But, I had vowed to myself that afternoon in the den that it would be my last time. And, darling, I've never been back with him, or anyone else. You are still the love of my life." He looked at her with pleading eyes, knowing that it was all futile, but somehow hoping that she could forgive him.

She looked long and hard at Harrison. For the first time in all their years together, she got a real good look. He was not a saint. He was just a man; one who wanted life his way and on his terms. And sexually, well, he obviously wanted goodies from both sides of the aisle. She thought about how he had manipulated her. He had made her think her demands for sex were abnormal. Made her go all the way to Mexico to get collagen shots in her vagina; just to make sex easier for him. Dammit, every time she got that warm feeling between her legs, it made her gag and run to the bathroom to vomit up any desire she had ever had for this selfish creature who now sat across from her.

Angered and embittered by his adulterous behavior, Nicola rose up, knocked her chair down and screamed out loud, without any regard for the other customers in the packed restaurant, "But that last time was the bitch, now, wasn't it? Didn't expect to have an audience for your last performance…NOW, DID YOU?"

Nicola, sickened by him and his deed, and wanting to hurt him as he had hurt her, looked down at the steaming hot tea, picked it up, and threw it in his lap.

Harrison jumped up from the table and tried to dry himself off.

He yelled, "Have you lost your mind? ARE YOU CRAZY?"

"Yep! I'm the crazy bitch that can't stand looking at you. Seeing that monster's nasty hands on you...just... don't ever... don't ever call me again! I'll see your ass in court!" She ran out of the restaurant.

Two weeks later, Nicola stormed into the top hair salon in Harlem, wearing a skintight black Jasmine Lee suit and a pair of diamond-studded stiletto heels designed especially for her by Stu Evans. She ordered Tia, the Dominican head stylist to, "Cut it off; just leave a little peach fuzz."

The beautician had cared for Nicola's long, black, thick hair for years. She could barely perform the deed. In a thick accent, as locks of hair fell on the carpeted floor, Tia pleaded, "*Mija*, you sure? I can stop now."

Impatient for the deed to be completed, she yelled at Tia, "Goddammit, it's just hair! Speed it up!"

The hairdresser pleaded, "But, *Mija*, all of it? I know; I'll give you a nice bob or..."

Angry, Nicola rose up from the chair, and stared the petite Tia down. "I've got to be in court in less than two hours. If you don't cut this shit all off and soon, I'll go right on down the block to the barber. He won't have any trouble."

Thirty minutes later, Tia gave her exactly what she

asked for. Never looking at the mirror, Nicola left the beautician a two hundred-dollar tip. Tia called after Nicola as she quickly exited the shop, "*Mija*! Mommy! 'Dis…'dis…is too much!"

Nicola never looked back. She hopped into a waiting limousine and ordered the driver to take her to the courthouse.

Her soon-to-be ex-husband had loved her long black hair. She remembered how he had enjoyed playing beauty shop. He had assumed the role of the gay beautician as he plaited her hair. She would laugh uncontrollably for hours, never suspecting that he was not acting.

Harrison gasped as she strutted into the courtroom with her new look. Sitting in the chair next to her high-powered attorney, Nicola smiled. Witnessing his expression was worth every penny she paid Tia.

The proceedings went quickly, without any complications. Harrison was extremely generous. Nicola now owned half of his empire, which included several McDonald's franchises, three apartment buildings on the West Side of Manhattan, the Harlem brownstone, beach houses in Miami and the Hamptons, and 1.5 million dollars in alimony every year.

Later that day, Nicola leaned against the railing of her rooftop garden. The setting sun had toasted the Northern sky a reddish-orange glow. It was chilly outside. Trembling, Nicola pulled a mohair shawl over her shoulders. It was spring, but like relatives who did not know when to leave, winter was still hanging around.

From this spot she could hear her next-door neighbor chant his Muslim prayers. His melodic almost haunting voice soothed her in a strange and exotic way. It reminded her of the time she and Harrison had spent in Tunisia.

That was three years ago. They were so happy then, or rather, she was happy. She doubted if he had ever really loved her. She remembered how Harrison had always made mysterious disappearances on those trips. Always under the guise of, "Just taking care of business, lovey." Some business? *BULLSHIT*, thought Nicola. He was more than likely slipping out for some gay rendezvous.

She felt so stupid. How could she have not known? How could she have been so blind? Now that she was divorced, she had time to deal with the issues of her childhood. Since that night when she had discovered Harrison and Sebastian together, she had found it impossible to decipher if the scenes from her past were real or imagined. They were so horrible. She had heard about false memories and had prayed that it was so with hers. She needed a way to pick out the truth of what had happened back then.

The private investigator, thought Nicola. The one she had hired years earlier to find her birth mother. That's who could help her. She decided to contact him. He would help link the dots of her memory. For the first time in months, Nicola smiled and mused, *soon the whole truth will emerge...then maybe I'll get a chance to start my life all over again.*

CHAPTER EIGHT

"Carlos…I'm gonna come, baby….I'm….OH YES… SWEET BABY JESUS!"

Carlos lay on his back as the two-hundred fifty-pound, light-skinned Amazon rode his dick like a jockey rides a stallion in the Kentucky Derby. Her pendulous tits flopped in all directions. Her nostrils widened large as the expression of her freckle-laden face changed into a pleasure-seeking alien, hell-bent on getting the best orgasm on the planet.

Beads of sweat shot out from every pore of her body. Carlos guided her butt up and down, repeatedly ramming his enormous twelve-inch pole through a maze of juicy flesh. Wanting to speed up her "race" to an ecstatic finish, he rubbed the ultra-sensitive tissues on her love knob back and forth. He could feel her insides spilling out juices in joyful response. She was ripe. She was ready. She was 'bout to come.

"CARLOS…It's here, baby…YOU DOING IT… YOU DOING IT, BABY!!!"

Carlos almost had another orgasm from merely watching the performance. He loved watching women come. Especially the big ones. They put all their weight into it. And this one came hard.

"OOOOOOH, Carlos…Carlos…OOOOOHH… BABY!!!" Almost tearful, she collapsed on his chest and held him like life depended on it. And then she went and spoiled everything for Carlos. She whispered in his ear, "I love you, Carlos…baby…I love you so much…"

Later that morning, Carlos could see the 'What the fuck?' look on the young women's chubby face when he pulled his jet-black Jaguar sports car away from the curb and, more importantly, away from her and her clinging ways.

She said she wanted breakfast. I dropped her off at McDonald's. Why's she upset?

Navigating midtown Manhattan traffic, Carlos knew that after a morning of hot, torrid lovemaking, women expected you to be so smitten…so grateful… so indebted…he was supposed to love and worship her dirty drawers, or at the very least take her out for a fine breakfast. But, if he did that, she'd think she was special. When women think they're "special" their commitment genes activate. Pussy never feels the same after that.

Carlos wanted no parts of attachment with women.

He was the pin-up boy for fuck 'em and dump 'em. The music business was his only passion. Building the new record company with his brother, Tarik, took all his focus and attention.

But that wasn't the real reason.

In all his twenty-five years on the planet, Carlos had never had a crush or the slightest desire for what the poets or crazy R&B songs called romance. When puberty had set in and his loins had demanded something other than his hand for pleasure, he had felt betrayed. He knew he had to be with the opposite sex or he would explode in a million different pieces.

At six feet, he was considered tall, trim and terribly fine. With his clean-shaven head, an ever present diamond stud in his left ear, and designer suits that showed off his lean muscular build, women came easy to him; way too easy. He quickly figured out early in the game that females would let him have his way with them. He was even upfront about his non-intentions and still they laid down, still thinking that wrapping his dick up in their tight little juicy vaults of desire would make him lose his mind.

But all it ever did was make him come hard and dump the woman as soon as he detected even the slightest inkling that she wanted more than he was ever going to give. And he always wrapped it up tight; real tight. He wasn't bringing any baby Carloses into the world. One was enough.

And that's why the cute plus-sized freak had gotten her walking papers that morning. Not only did she profess her love for him, she had wanted him to meet her mother. *What the hell for?* he thought. He had a mama; he didn't need to know hers. What was he gonna say when he met her? *Hello, my name is Carlos. I only want to fuck your fat-ass daughter's brains out.*

No, there was no reason to meet the family or keep the relationship in "active" status. It was easier to drop her off in front of McDonald's and refuse to answer any of her calls. It was actually the humane thing to do, and Carlos was all about being the humane kind of brother.

He glanced at the clock. *Good*, he thought. There was plenty time to run some errands in Greenwich Village and pick up his brother, Jonathan, at JFK airport. His seven-foot sibling was returning from a trip to California, where he had visited the college he was attending in the fall. A star athlete while in high school, Jonathan had won an opportunity to participate in an elite NBA summer camp held in Harlem.

After Pops died, Carlos had made a special note to spend extra time with Jonathan. This summer was the time to do it. It would take some serious schedule juggling, but he had made a graveside promise to Pops to take care of him.

Pops and Mama Ophelia had adopted Carlos when his parents died. He was only seven when he moved from Florida to Brooklyn. From day one, they had treated him just like their natural son. They had made him feel right at home. The added bonus was that Carlos had always wanted brothers, and both Tarik and Jonathan fit the bill.

Carlos never looked back at his life with his parents in Florida. He loved his new family; his real family. He had no desire to start his own either. A confirmed childless bachelor, he laughed every time Mama Ophelia threatened that one day he'd meet someone who'd change his mind. There was no chance of that happening. As far as Carlos was concerned, there was no need to complicate things and upset what he knew was a damn near perfect life.

Carlos smiled. For once, the traffic and parking spot gods were shining on him. He made it downtown in record time and got a parking spot right in front of the café where he, Pops, and Tarik used to hang out at before they caught a jazz set at the Blue Note. He loved the Village; especially in the summer.

He entered a small shop at the corner of Fourth Street where Mrs. Doutrelle, a gifted seamstress from Senegal, greeted him warmly. Close to seventy, she kissed him on both cheeks. She did wonderful things for his clothing. He always looked sharp. She handed him his new suit.

"How's ze record business, Monsieur?"

"Oh, better every day. Better every day."

And he wasn't lying. All throughout his college days he had interned at the university radio station and at Mega Hits, an independent record company. By the time he graduated with a major in marketing and finance, he knew all the music industry's VIPs on a personal level. The label had hired him and made him their VP of Marketing. Two months after Pops died, the company went belly-up and Carlos, still grieving, now had another cross to bear.

It was a blessing, though. Not even in disguise. Instead of trying to get another job in the industry, he and Tarik had cashed in their sizeable inheritance from Pops and started their own record company, Infinity. Besides pushing Tarik's act, they had a few other up-and-coming artists that looked real good. Omara, a rapper with a unique style. Everlasting, a teenaged boy group that had tight harmonies and looks guaranteed to charm the teenybopper crowd. Most recently signed to their label was Katrell, a male vocalist destined to fill the void left by Luther Vandross.

But for now, it was Tarik and his piano playing and Bob Marley-like persona that had their new company on the verge of a big distribution deal with one of the majors. In an industry where the technology was so cheap anybody and their mama could cut a CD and call themselves a record company, it was your distributor's clout that separated little fish from the king whale.

As far as Carlos and Tarik were concerned, their

record company, Infinity, was going all the way up the food chain next to Diddy, Jay-Z and his hero, the big granddaddy of them all, Berry Gordy of Motown.

Carlos put the new suit in the back of his car next to a box of fliers advertising Tarik's big show in Prospect Park. He looked at his watch and decided to give out a few at Washington Square Park.

He had made a good decision. It was lunchtime and the park was packed with folks. He noticed an older, distinguished, somewhat frail-looking man sitting on the bench feeding pigeons. Knowing that he probably wouldn't be interested in the show, Carlos handed the man his last flier anyway and then quickly walked out the park.

Something made Carlos turn around to look back at the man. He was clapping, laughing, talking to himself, and dancing a less than vigorous jig. He looked nuts. Carlos decided he probably was. He shook his head, got into his car, and headed for the airport.

CHAPTER NINE

*E*xhausted from jumping up and down and acting like a complete fool, Eli collapsed back onto the park bench. He was ecstatic. It had been three months since his release from prison. He had spent most of the time hospitalized at Bellevue Hospital in Manhattan for treatment of AIDS-related complications. He could not believe that he was now holding in his hands a flier that revealed the whereabouts of his son, Tarik. In three weeks he was scheduled to perform at Prospect Park in Brooklyn.

Even the bad news doctors at Bellevue had given him earlier that day about the failure of an experimental drug regimen he had initiated during his last hospitalization could not deflate his balloon. No, that couldn't drag him down from the high he was feeling. He would turn down the best dope in the known world just for the information he now had.

Printed on the flier, for all to see, was a picture of his

son, Tarik Singleton. He laughed out loud when he realized that the system's inability to place him in a Manhattan shelter was to his benefit. His new residence in Brooklyn was not far from Prospect Park. On a good day…that is if he had any more good days, Eli could walk there. That's what the social worker had told him the day he was given his placement.

He thought about his latest lab results. So what if his CD-4 count was low or his viral load was off the charts. Nothing could interfere with his joy. Three weeks couldn't come soon enough for him; especially since doctors advised him that the end of the road in terms of his disease was just around the bend. They continued to give him medicine, but no faith, hope, or promise that things would improve. They said he needed a miracle.

Well, making the cabbie stop at Washington Square Park to check out his old stomping grounds and running into that nice-looking young man who had given him the flier constituted a miracle in Eli's book.

All those years in prison, volunteering for clinical drug trials, hoping it would slow down the progression of AIDS or shave off years from his sentence. Anything to get him out and maybe get a glimpse at his son…or even his ex-wife, Ophelia, before the disease claimed his body and soul. And now, at the end of life's road… his dream would soon be realized.

Attica had not really been that bad for him. It was there that he had kicked heroin. He didn't even need methadone anymore. When his health cooperated, he ran both a GED and an arts program for his fellow inmates. The young guys even used him as a life counselor.

Eli shook his head. Imagine him, a total loser, giving out advice. But they sought him out. Asked him questions. He shared the truth he knew best. It seemed to give the young men hope in an otherwise hopeless situation. During his prison stay, he had behaved and done all the things he should have done on the outside but was too pig-headed or too weak of a person to try.

Looking at the picture of Tarik playing at the piano, Eli beamed with pride. He could not help but notice how much they resembled each other. He prayed that physical appearance was the only thing his son had inherited from him. It didn't bother him that he didn't carry his last name. He had signed over his parental rights years ago to Ophelia and her new husband, Richard "Pops" Singleton.

After five years in prison, he hoped that they had taken good care of his son. He had never really doubted that they would. Ophelia was an excellent mother. She wouldn't let anything happen to him. Hell, after all, she was the one who had the good sense to get him out of his own son's life.

In three weeks, Lord-willing, Eli would see his son perform in concert, and maybe get a peek at his ex-wife. He prayed he was alive and strong enough to attend.

CHAPTER TEN

"*I* knew it! When you ran outta this office five years ago, I knew one day you'd want the whole story, and I knew there'd be more to the story."

Nicola rolled her eyes as the private investigator rattled on about her case and rummaged through cold, gray, dusty cabinets.

She looked around Max Whitlow's disorganized, claustrophobic office and sent up silent prayers that he'd soon find her information and that this would be the last time his services were needed. Waiting for the big reveal in his hot office added unnecessary drama. Beads of sweat slid down the curves of Nicola's back. She could not wait to get out of there and put an end to the mystery of her childhood.

After a half-hour of searching through file cabinets and boxes, God answered her prayers.

"Oh yeah, here it is." Max pulled out a thick manila file and handed it to his client.

Eager to leave, Nicola grabbed the file out of his hands and stashed it into her purple leather satchel.

"Aren't you gonna read it now? You might have some questions; it's heavy stuff, Mrs. James." Max knew she would need help. It had taken him almost three months to put all the pieces together and the story was not pretty.

"If I have any questions, Max, I'll call." She wrote out a check paying him a handsome sum, thanked him for a job well done, and left the office.

It was two days before she got up the nerve to read the file. She left it in the third floor library on top of Harrison's antique mahogany desk.

She could not find the courage to face up to her past. But today was different. Armed with a fifth of Courvoisier, she entered the office knowing that she was leaving it a different person. The bits and pieces of her childhood that haunted her since the evening she busted Harrison were about to be clarified. She took a big sip out of the bottle. The liquid warmed her insides and inspired her to face the truth.

An hour later, exhausted from reading, Nicola's brain whirled with details of her childhood. All the disjointed scenes from her childhood were now connecting and finally making some kind of crazy sense as she now remembered how life had been with her adopted parents.

The fiasco with Harrison was not the first tragic event in her life. From Nicola's perspective, on the scale of life's catastrophes, it only scored a three out of a possible ten. No, the big ten belonged to her childhood. Her fucked-up childhood.

The Martins weren't exactly Claire and Cliff Huxtable of *The Cosby Show*. The only decent thing they had done was rename their baby girl in honor of the Nicola building, where officials discovered her at birth. It had all gone downhill from there.

From their rustic secluded cabin in Albany Pond, New York, Hezekiah and Ida Martin had run an ultra successful video business. Their top earner quickly became "Scenes with baby Nicola" series. These were not the cutesy, first steps taken, first words spoken type of home family movies. Her parents were proud, card-carrying sex perverts.

They adopted beautiful Nicola for the singular purpose of casting her in child pornography scenes. From day one, Nicola was the star in their sick videos. The couple filmed Nicola as they and other paying adults performed lewd and indecent sexual acts with her.

Nicola did not have a childhood. Her first memory, at age three, was of her daddy, Hezekiah, ejaculating all over her face. Mommy was directing her from behind the camera to laugh aloud and act happy. This scene was repeated so often, little Nicola grew up thinking it was normal.

When she turned five, the couple made more serious, painful demands of her body. Customers paid more for videos that included both sex and violence. The Martins thought nothing of tying her up and slapping her around. They would thrust objects into her mouth, anus, or vagina. All the time her "parents" would ignore her screams as she pleaded for them to stop. The pain at times was unbearable. The more she screamed, the more the torture would intensify. All the while, the camera rolled.

Successfully isolating her from the world, they home-schooled Nicola. She quickly learned how to read and, at age seven, she could understand the newspaper. By age eight she'd connected all the dots and knew that this "loving couple," the only parents she knew, who had tortured her without mercy, were the devil and his wife. She was desperate to escape.

On her eighth birthday, she ran away. Unfortunately, they caught her in the woods near their cottage. For punishment, her father had chopped off her pet ferret's (that everyone called Little Nicola) head. Her mother forced her to witness the spectacle. As the ferret's headless body jerked in what seemed to be endless spasms, blood squirted everywhere, some splashing on Nicola.

Hezekiah promised if she ran away or called the authorities, she and the animal would share more than just the same name. The next day, he brought home another pet ferret and renamed it Little Nicola. She cared for it as if her life depended on it. They were inseparable.

Nicola needed to find a way out of her hell. The filming sessions had become a loathsome part of her day. She felt nasty and dirty after performing in the scenes. She hated her life as a "child star." Ironically, a video saved her. At age ten, she watched a movie about a pyromaniac. It gave graphic details about how they had burnt down a house, killing everyone in it.

Over the next few years, Nicola was convinced that the only way she would survive was if the Martins died. The thought obsessed her as she made meticulous plans for their "departure." A few months shy of her thirteenth birthday, at the Martins' annual "for perverts only" Fourth of July celebration, alcohol flowed freely throughout the crowd. Wearing a provocative French maid outfit, with her hair stylishly pinned up, it was Nicola's job to serve drinks.

She spiked the Martins' drinks with the same valium they forced her to take to make her more cooperative during filming. She knew from reading through the Martins' medical encyclopedia that alcohol and valium could induce a dangerous coma.

Nicola smiled as she watched her adoptive parents pour the cocktails she'd created for them down their evil throats. By party's end, when the last guest departed, the Martins both collapsed at the kitchen table. Hezekiah still had a half-full glass of Scotch in his hand. When Nicola's potion took full effect, they were both in a deep sleep.

Ready to execute her plan, Nicola, nervous and afraid

they'd awaken before the deed was done, closed all the windows. She placed candles, hoarded for months, all around the kitchen, placing them strategically around the sleeping couple. The Martins often used them in the video scenes to create a relaxed mood.

When she ignited the candles, she looked at the evil duo, both sleeping and snoring peacefully, unaware of their fate. She smiled and had to agree, candlelight did have the effect of chasing away the fear and anxiety that gripped her inside. In its place was a keen sense of justice.

Nicola turned all the knobs of the old-fashioned stove on full blast. Escaping from the top of the stove and the oven, gas rapidly diffused throughout the house. Satisfied, she lifted her pet ferret out of its pen. Carrying the animal with her, stroking its black fur, she walked out of the house and slammed the door behind her, forever shutting out the life she had led there.

She found a spot not far from the house where she could view the event and fell asleep. A loud explosion awakened her. As the only home she knew disappeared in the belly of the red-hot inferno, Nicola felt true peace. Her hellish nightmare was over. For the rest of her life, the sight of flames would always calm her.

Investigation of the fire revealed that the deceased were the leaders of a sophisticated child porno ring. They confiscated videos starring Nicola. Evidence helped to successfully prosecute several members. Luckily, a fire inspector's report listed the official cause of the fire as a gas leak. The insurance company placed a quarter of a million dollars in a trust fund for Nicola.

Immediately after the fire, she was admitted to a regional hospital for observation. Nicola remembered how doctors examined her and tried to coax memories about her time with the Martins; none would surface. After a short stay in the hospital, authorities placed her in a group home in the Bronx. At eighteen, she was considered an adult and discharged from social services.

Nicola used the insurance money from the fire to purchase a tiny studio in Harlem and to support herself through college. Now that she understood the complete story, knowing that she was indeed the arsonist responsible for the Martins' death, Nicola felt no remorse.

She realized now, the experiences in her childhood had damaged her emotionally. All through high school and her first years at the university, she had never even had a close friend. Never responded to a single boy or man who approached her. Even the decent ones. She had never dated. That is, until she had met Harrison.

Ain't that a bitch, thought Nicola. *All that fucked-up life, and the first man that I turn to wasn't a man at all!*

The pain and hurt were too much to bear. Nicola threw her head back and emptied the bottle. Totally out of it now, she and the empty bottle wandered down the hall. Somehow, she made it down the stairs into her bedroom. Forgetting to turn the light on, she walked smack into the pole she had used to entertain her ex-husband.

Rubbing her head, she yelled out as if the house was full of people, "OH SHIT! WHO THE FUCK PUT THAT THERE? OH, THAT'S RIGHT! I DID! I DID IT TO ENTERTAIN THAT FUCKIN' FAGGOT! WHAT THE HELL WAS THAT ALL ABOUT? WILL SOMEBODY, SOMEWHERE, TELL ME, PLEASE! WHAT WAS IT ALL ABOUT?"

Frustrated, Nicola felt her way to the nightstand and turned on the light. She looked up over in the sitting area and spotted the huge framed photograph hanging over the fireplace. It was the one picture of Harrison she didn't have the heart to pull down. It was a photo of them snuggled together on the yacht, *Nicola's Beauty*, enjoying their honeymoon in the Indian Ocean near the Seychelles Islands. She looked at it from where she stood and threw the bottle at it, smashing both the picture and the memories into a million pieces.

"Next…" Nicola pointed toward the pole, as if she was giving instructions out to her rehab crew, "we're getting rid of YOU!" Nicola found her way to the bed and passed out.

The next morning, everything about Nicola hurt; throat, muscles, brain, and bones. She vomited her insides out till all she could do was dry-heave. A high fever kept her body in sweats and chills. Frighteningly ill, her housekeeper called the ambulance. When they arrived, Nicola refused to go to the hospital. Instead, she popped Tylenol and drank the soups and teas that the kind Jamaican woman had prepared for her. On the seventh day of her illness, she awoke without pain or a fever.

That evening, she took a long hot bath and dressed in her most provocative outfit. She found the most dangerous pair of stiletto heels in her shoe closet and strapped them on. With one last confident look in the mirror, Nicola's reflection confirmed that she was indeed a beautiful woman.

Nicola walked out of her brownstone that night a completely different woman. She was no longer the shallow, timid woman that Harrison "saved." No longer the tragic child that two sociopath deviants had had their way with. She would never again be that vulnerable infant who was victim to an insane mother's reign of terror.

This was a new Nicola. She would now be in charge and running the show. *The Nicola Show*. Starring, you got it, Nicola. And she dared any man, woman, or beast to stand in her way. And this time payback would indeed be a bitch. To a society that had stood by and let so much happen to an innocent baby, Nicola was going to tell all...FUCK YOU!

Clicking her heels to a confidant rhythm, she strutted proudly down Convent Avenue. As she walked, she could feel a little warm "itch" from her G-shot. It made her smile, because tonight she was retiring her pink little electronic buddy. Tonight she was in search of the real thing…a real hard, fuck-you-all-night, never-get-tired dick.

When she got to 145th Street, Nicola hailed a cab.

"Where to, Miss?"

"Downtown. Club Zeon." Nicola sat back in the seat as she headed to the hottest club in the city.

CHAPTER ELEVEN

The African drums pulsated at a frenetic joyful pace. Ophelia had problems keeping up with the younger students.

"MOVE THOSE HIPS, OPHELIA! Move them to the right…now left…NOW! That's it, baby! Ooooh… you got it. Now give me some nice belly rolls! Here… like this…" The young, buff, scantily clad instructor slid up behind her and rhythmically rubbed his pelvis against her buttocks, encouraging her body to do the same. He then placed both his muscular hands on Ophelia's abdomen, forcing her to perform the proper movement. "Ahhhh…you got it, girl!" Pleased with his pupil's progress, he moved to the front of the room and continued to lead the class.

Now able to keep up with the class, Ophelia hopped, stomped her feet, and jumped up and down, matching ancient African rhythms beat by beat. Her heart, loving what she was doing, pumped in time with the music.

Sheets of hot sweat poured down her back as the endorphins cascading through her body made her feel good, inside and out. This was a love dance. She was in love with her body and wanted it healthy. It was her way of saying thanks to the Creator.

Later, in the dance school's locker room, Ophelia looked in the mirror and could see that her body was as tight as that African drum! Her reflection revealed a woman fifteen years her junior. No one would have guessed that ten years ago, at three hundred and twenty-five pounds, she could have easily fit into a size twenty-four. Even at five feet and ten inches, that was packing quite a load.

She thought about her poor late husband. Pops never met a bucket of fried chicken or smothered pork chops that he could walk away from. He loved sitting on his four hundred pound ass and when he conducted business for his successful architectural firm, he rarely left his desk.

That's where she found him dead two years ago after a massive heart attack. It took her a long time to get over him leaving her like that. If he had only listened when she begged him to shed the weight and adopt a healthier lifestyle. She was a nurse, after all. She knew what she was talking about.

Pops was a good man though. The best man. Together they had raised three boys. Three men now. Tarik and Carlos were successfully running their record company.

Their youngest, Jonathan, was on a clear path toward academic success and basketball fame. She wished Pops had hung around longer to see the fruits of their labor.

After taking a quick shower, Ophelia rushed home to prepare a big welcome-home dinner. Tonight her boys were coming to celebrate Jonathan's return from prep school.

Tarik and his family were the first to arrive. His wife, Sherry, led the way, carrying a macaroni and cheese casserole. She set it down on the kitchen counter and gave Ophelia a warm hug.

"Mama Ophelia, I followed your directions. I didn't put as much butter or cheese, like I did the last time, even though I know it won't taste as good. But I did what you said."

Ophelia liked her daughter-in-law. She was a tough, sharp-talking straight shooter who was strong enough to handle Tarik and keep him in line. She also knew it wasn't easy for Sherry to change her favorite recipe, so she complimented her and said, "Good. Good, and I'm telling you, it'll be just as delicious."

A four-year-old speeding bullet named Javon ran smack into his grandmother's arms. She lifted him up in one swoop and hugged him. "And how's Grandma's baby doing?"

"I lost my tooth in the car and Poppi said you knew this fairy, and..."

Ophelia kissed the grandson who had stolen her heart the first time Tarik had introduced him to the family over two years ago.

Whispering in his ears, she promised, "Javon, after dinner, I'll get in contact with my buddy." She winked at him and added, "The Tooth Fairy and I are good friends."

Javon smiled; he knew she wouldn't disappoint him. He had Mama Ophelia twisted all around his little brown finger.

"Hi, Ma. How's my best girl doing today?" Tarik gave Ophelia a quick peck on her cheek, and headed directly for the refrigerator. He opened the door and dug around, rummaging for food. He pulled out a roasted chicken leg and happily announced, "This'll hold me 'til dinner."

She looked at her fine son as he devoured the meat. She trembled when it hit her. *My God! He looks just like... just like...Eli*, she thought. She had never realized how much Tarik resembled her first husband. It was those dreadlocks he had started growing a year ago. They were now covering his head, just like Eli's had.

"Ma, what's wrong? If you want me to put the chicken back in the fridge..."

"No...no...eat...eat...don't mind me...I had a...had a senior moment."

Now that she allowed herself to think about Eli, she had to confess that Tarik shared more than his looks.

Like Eli, Tarik was artistic, spiritual, peaceful; a gentle soul. Pops, before he reached four hundred pounds, had tried to "toughen up" Tarik and had taken him hunting and fishing. But the boy had never taken to Pops' ways.

Tarik hated guns and violence of all kinds. They did find a way to bond, in that Pops recognized early that they both shared a love of music. A gifted pianist, Pops had taught the young boy all he knew about the instrument. Despite some of their differences, their relationship had been tighter than a drum.

Seeing Tarik's resemblance to his biological father wasn't the only thing that had upset her lately. Instead of entertaining fond memories of her late husband, Ophelia's dreams now included scenes of the years she had shared with Eli. They were disturbingly erotic, loving images of the man she had made sure Tarik would never know.

It didn't help that in his last years of their relationship, Pops was so out of shape that his performance in bed was just plain unappealing. She faked headaches so she could miss having his fat, sweaty body pound her for the two seconds he could keep his dick hard. Even in the beginning of the marriage, Pops never did rock her world. She had left the man who could do that. Eli's worthless ass absolutely excelled in the bedroom, and that's what her dreams were now all about.

"Hey, Mama Ophelia, I brought you a gift!" Carlos

yelled out as he entered the kitchen. His voice snatched her away from her intense thoughts about Eli. She looked up and saw the person she had been waiting all day to see. At last, her seven-foot baby boy, Jonathan, was home. She called everybody to the dining room. It was time to eat.

"Mama Ophelia, you gonna spoil that boy!" warned Sherry.

Ophelia paid no mind to her unsolicited critique. She hadn't seen her boy since he graduated from high school a few weeks ago.

She piled mountains of macaroni and cheese, smothered chicken, and mashed candied yams, all of Jonathan's favorites, on his plate. He encouraged her. "Yeah, Ma, that's the way to put food on the plate."

"How come he doesn't get the 'portion control' speech?" inquired Tarik. He yelled down at the other end of the table at Carlos, "Hey, brother man, how you like being pushed aside by the baby now?"

Barely coming up for air as he tore up a juicy barbecue rib, Carlos sputtered out, "Long as I get *my* share, I don't care."

Ophelia laughed at her boys. But they were absolutely right; she was doting on her baby. She looked at him across the table as grease from the chicken dripped all over his white T-shirt. Jonathan's dark skin, brown eyes draped by notoriously thick black lashes, and an easy smile that lit her world up like the Rockefeller

Plaza Christmas tree in New York City made him quite a handsome young man.

Ophelia had missed Jonathan more than usual and worried about him being so far away from the family. Sometimes at night, she'd wake up, her heart fluttering, wondering how he was, afraid that something dreadful had happened to him or that he had gotten himself into some kind of trouble. She'd always call him, no matter what time it was, simply to hear his voice.

Looking at him, laughing and joking with his brothers, she realized her mind was working overtime. Jonathan was a fine young man and had never done anything to make her think he wouldn't act correctly. How could she worry about a young man who was an active member of a Christian youth group that was determined not to engage in premarital sex? He was saving himself for marriage. She was so proud of him. Looking at him, trying to wipe the grease spots off his shirt, she decided not to spend another moment worrying about her boy.

After the meal, Carlos came into the kitchen carrying a pile of dishes. She smiled. "You didn't have to do that, baby."

Stacking the dishes in the sink, he said, "You know how I like working in the kitchen with you. But uh... ruh...I can't stay to wash...I have some work to do... but I uh..."

She playfully pushed him away from the sink and

started prepping for the dishwasher. "You don't fool me one minute. You're going out with one of your girlfriends!" Seeing that she had him dead to right, she added, "Which one is it tonight? Hmmm?"

"Let's see. If today is Tuesday and tomorrow is Wednesday, I should be with…"

Concerned by his admission, Ophelia warned, "It's not nice or *healthy* to be with too many different women and you do know what I mean by *healthy*, don't you?"

"Yes, I *do*, and I always protect myself. Besides, it's easier to have lots of women 'stead of just one."

"How the hell you figure that?"

"One girl demands all your time. When they know they're part of a harem, they're happy to get a few seconds with King Carlos." He winked at Ophelia.

She shook her head and pointed her finger in his face, trying not to laugh at his bodacious bragging.

"One day, boy, with God as my witness, you will find the one who will make you lose your mind. Mark my words, young man."

He leaned over and gave her a hug. "T'aint a woman alive could make me lose my mind. I got control of all of this."

Carlos performed a little moonwalk dance, and exited out the kitchen, all the while waving his hand at Ophelia. She laughed so loud and hard she had to hold her belly to keep it from bursting. Ever since he was a boy, he could always make her laugh. It was his humor that had captured her heart so many years ago.

As she placed dishes in the washer, Ophelia's mind drifted back to the time when she had given birth to Jonathan. Pops received a call from the Miami police in the middle of night. His twin sister, Ernestine, had been shot and killed by her husband, Hector Salinas. When the police had cornered him in the couple's home, they had begged Hector, a highly decorated police officer, to release their seven-year-old son, Carlos. Instead, he had turned the gun on himself and blown his brains out.

She and Pops decided, on the spot, that they would raise his sister's only child. Money wasn't a problem. They could afford it. He owned a successful architectural firm and she was a nurse practitioner, adding one more person to their family would not be a problem.

Expecting to see a depressed, solemn, withdrawn seven-year-old boy who had witnessed an atrocious event, she had insisted they schedule him for counseling. Pops disagreed. Though he was a well-educated architect, trained at Tuskegee and Georgia Tech, Pops didn't trust mental health professionals. He thought lots of love and attention would be all Carlos needed. If that didn't work, he promised he'd personally take him to the shrink. Ophelia wanted to push the issue, but she was so busy raising Tarik and her new baby, Jonathan that she didn't have time to fight Pops.

Ophelia didn't have anything to worry about. Right from the start, Carlos did appear to be a well-adjusted boy. With the exception of an almost pathological aversion to ice cream, the handsome little boy had shown no signs of mental instability. He had excelled in school and easily made friends. When they adopted him a year after he arrived, it was as if he had been in the family all along.

The only time he seemed to have trouble with his past, was the day they were looking at Pops' old home movies. Carlos was fifteen years old. Pops popped in a reel that turned out to be footage of Carlos's parents' wedding. Before Pops had a chance to pull the plug, Carlos was confronted with scenes of a happier time for his parents. Tarik, not knowing who the people were in the film, innocently commented that the groom looked a lot like Carlos. Obviously upset, Carlos immediately got up and ran out the room.

And Tarik was right. Carlos was the chocolate version of his Cuban father. It was a resemblance that proved too much for the teenager. The next day when he returned from school, Carlos had cut off all of his curly black hair. In his ear was a tiny diamond stud that had belonged to his mother. He had found it next to her body the day she was murdered.

From that day on, he wore a clean-shaven head and always had his mother's earring in his left ear. He obviously wanted no connection to Hector Salinas. She remembered asking him, then, if he wanted to talk to her or a counselor about his parents. He refused. Wise beyond his years, he remarked that what had happened in the past was behind him. The only thing that mattered, according to Carlos, was now, and he was fine with that. Ophelia left the door open for him to talk about it anytime he wanted to, but in the ten years that followed, he had never once approached the subject of his parents with her.

And it was funny. After seeing Tarik's resemblance to Eli, she truly knew how Carlos felt about not wanting to look like or share any trait or behavior with Hector Salinas. She wished to hell that she could erase Tarik's connection to his father…just like Carlos had hoped shaving his head would destroy his dad's memory.

Ophelia went to bed early that night, looking for a way to sever thoughts of Eli out of her mind. Instead, her dreams betrayed her. A healthy, fit Eli greeted her in her subconscious mind and made sweet love to her all night long.

CHAPTER TWELVE

"*Y*ou lying! You ain't never had no pussy?" Carlos stared up at his little brother with horror and disbelief. "You're a basketball star. I know the babes are throwing it up at you. Don't tell me you're turning shit down. Not my baby brother."

Defending his virtue, Jonathan bragged, "When you're truly in love, kissing is" Visions of his last wet dream flashed through his mind. He added half-heartedly, "Kissing and holding hands is...is special enough!"

Carlos really lost it then. "You mean to tell me that, at eighteen years old, you don't even know what it *smells* like? What the hell is wrong with you?"

"There's...there's nothing wrong with me."

Ignoring Jonathan's claims, Carlos paced back and forth, trying to make sense of what he knew was a sense-less situation. He stopped abruptly and faced Jonathan. "I know what it is. Something's wrong with your equipment. That sports injury you had two years ago. Fucked you up. Right, man?" Carlos desperately searched Jonathan's face for an answer. He was truly concerned. Never had any pussy. He couldn't fathom it. Not in a million years.

Feeling he hadn't handled his position adequately, Jonathan looked Carlos in the eye. "Everybody is not like you, Carlos. In my church group, we're taught that love is…"

"I know…I know…it's *special*. You already told me that before. Boy, you better get that pole of yours good and greased before it breaks off. You do know what they say?" Jonathan shook his head no. Carlos warned him. "If you don't use it, you sure 'nuff gonna lose it."

Jonathan nervously picked up his ball and twirled it on its axis. "There's plenty other things a man can do… like…"

"Jerking off? Shit, all that beating your own meat unnecessarily cuts off oxygen from your balls. Causes all kind of diseases. Makes you sterile."

Jonathan looked at him with an air of disbelief.

"Carlos, you know that's not true."

Carlos would not back down. "I know because I read it in a book."

"You're a crazy man."

"I'm crazy? Shit, you better let one of these freaks at least give you a blow job while you're here."

Jonathan looked up at him with an innocent "what does that feel like" look.

"Don't tell me none of those cheerleaders ever went down on you?"

Carlos had successfully worn him down. His own frustration with the girls he dated in his church group and their ultra-strict "no-touch" policy made him drop his head and avoid all eye contact with Carlos.

Knowing he'd hit a nerve, Carlos continued with his attack. "NO! I thought so. What the hell has up and gone wrong? I hope the fuck it ain't headed for Brooklyn!"

Ophelia called from downstairs, "Carlos, you have company."

He yelled back, "Coming, Ma." Standing up, ready to leave, he looked at his brother. *What a doofus*, he thought. *A genuine nerd.* He couldn't help but feel sorry for him.

"This conversation ain't over. I'm gonna help a brother out. You coming out with me tonight to Club Zeon."

"Carlos, I don't like those places."

"I don't want to hear no protests. Be ready in a half-hour."

Carlos left Jonathan's room but poked his head back in and pointed to a nightstand where a half-empty jar of Vaseline rested. "And throw that shit out. After tonight, you won't need it anymore."

Angry with himself, Jonathan slammed the door behind Carlos. What was wrong with being a virgin? He was handling his sexuality his way. The truth was, he was glad his older brother was taking an interest in his virginal status because he knew he'd get different answers about "doing the nasty" from Carlos, the sexual renegade in the family. The sex talks he'd had with his mom and Pops, when he was alive, had been so sterile and clinical. Talking to Tarik had been worthless. He had avoided the topic entirely.

If he just "looked" and didn't touch, technically, he was still a virtuous man. Hanging out at the club tonight would be safe, if he checked his libido at the door. Knowing that Carlos would handle him right, he eagerly waited for the evening to approach.

Driving to the club, Carlos took advantage of the time alone to school Jonathan. He was going to make losing his virginity a project. If he had anything to do with it, Jonathan was going to college, a man.

"Man, there's a freak I know who will do anything for you. A real nympho type. For just one of your big smiles, she'll suck your dick so good and hard, you won't stop coming 'til it's time to collect social security. I'll introduce you to her at the club and you can go to the parking lot and she'll…"

Jonathan was shocked. He only wanted to look at the women; doing something was out of the question, and in a parking lot? The thought of it made him want to run all the way back to his mama's arms for safety.

In a horrified voice, he exploded, "Are you crazy? A parking lot? Thanks, but no thanks. I couldn't. No! NO!

I couldn't do that thing with a nympho? Not one second...not ever."

Carlos could see that Jonathan was upset and that his
suggestion was a bit premature. He'd have to break
homeboy in a little slower. "Hey, man...man, calm
down...it's okay...it was just a thought...you ain't ready.
I know that. I respect that...I just thought...maybe...
while you were home for the summer...before you started
college and shit...you might you know...experiment...
not go all the way...just a taste...with a pro...you know?"

There was dead silence for the rest of the ride.
Jonathan was upset by the offer, not because he wouldn't
consider it, but because there was a part of him that
seriously wanted to "experiment." Carlos had flipped
his little perfect world of abstinence upside down. No
one had ever challenged his decision to remain celibate
quite as aggressively as Carlos. It made him face one
big fact. He was indeed madly curious about screwing,
fucking, licking, and everything in between.

CHAPTER THIRTEEN

*C*lub Zeon was no ordinary place. Only the rich and famous could acquire the famous phallic-shaped key that allowed entry into the eighteenth-century renovated church. Owners wisely decided to maintain the Gothic exterior. For the interior they hired a top designer, and spared no expense to create an ultra-futuristic space that catered to the tastes and eccentricities of the world's elite crowd.

This used to be a church, thought Jonathan. He gasped when he first entered the club. It was hard for him to believe that babies were once baptized, couples married and blessed, in the place that now displayed nude couples of all sexual orientations in cages engaged in a variety of erotic activity.

Carlos left Jonathan alone to take care of business in the VIP section of the club's lower level. Without his chaperone, Jonathan decided to explore. He drifted toward the main lounge. On a stage that seemed to be suspended in air, an Afro-Brazilian combo performed intoxicating rhythms. Jonathan's blood bounced in rhythm to the music as he glared at the beautiful, scantily dressed women that surrounded him on the dance floor.

They moved their bodies in an enticing provocative manner and generated an enormous amount of sexual "heat." Jonathan, the national vice president of Teens for Abstinence, was immediately overwhelmed. Too young and too inexperienced to handle it all, he "escaped" from the dance floor, moved on to one of the smaller more intimate lounge areas, and decided to order a Coke.

Leaning against a bar that was actually a giant salt-water aquarium filled with exotic fish, Jonathan thought about Carlos's offer of a "teaching session." Thinking about it now, in a club full of desirable women, made him reconsider.

The mental image of luscious lips wrapping around the crown of his manhood, made pressure build between his legs. He whispered commands to himself, hoping the fullness rising beneath his pants didn't expose his thoughts. "Down, boy, just relax. It ain't real. It ain't real at all."

Just as he was getting things under control, a scantily clad goddess slowly slid by him, barely grazing his loins. At five-foot-nine, she stared up at him, capturing his full attention. "Excuse me, sir. Can I pass by? It's so crowded in here."

He was completely hypnotized by her seductive beauty.

His groin ignored all commands to relax and resumed its search for orgasmic release.

Almond-shaped eyes shaded by thick black eyelashes twinkled up at him. She was a natural beauty with just a hint of blush that accentuated dark-chocolate skin. The subtlest of gloss added shine to full mocha-colored lips. She had the kind of lips white actresses paid good money for. A short-cropped hairstyle revealed a long gracious neck that added a sense of regal beauty. A linear scar that draped the front of her neck was the only flaw on an otherwise perfect woman.

She repeated her request. "Can I pass by? I'm sorry, sir. Are you all right?"

And that voice! Whew! It was husky with honey sweet undertones. Jonathan heard its resonance vibrating long after she had spoken. He knew he'd never wash his ears or the pants she brushed her body against.

Under a trance, he heard himself clumsily reply, "I'm okay, I think."

Reluctantly, he freed himself from her gaze and let her go by. She was indeed a knockout. She looked back at him and blew a kiss. He swore he felt it land on his face.

There was something a little different about this woman. He couldn't put his finger on it, but it had something to do with the way her full double-D perky breasts seemed to smile at him through a sheer purple halter. Sweat built up across his brow. He turned back toward the bartender and ordered another Coke filled to the brim with ice. He grabbed the plastic cup and rolled it across his forehead and neck, anxiously waiting for his body temperature to slide back down to normal.

The party was rocking hard and strong. Carlos was working the room as usual, reminding folks to check out Tarik's concert. His eyes swept the club to see if he'd ignored anyone of importance. He discovered a woman sitting alone in a corner booth. Only her silhouette was visible, but it was enough information to let him know she definitely had the kind of shape he wanted to know better.

As her face came into full view, he almost gasped at her beauty. She looked like the statues of the Nubian queens in the lower Nile Valley. He'd seen them when the family visited Egypt five years ago. Gazing at this woman, he was glad Pops had insisted that they take the trip. It was nice to have such an ancient reference with this woman. Plus he had a ready opening line to greet her with.

"So you arrived just on time."

"Come again?"

Her deep voice captivated him immediately. He was instantly smitten. Carlos grabbed her hand and planted a kiss. *Did her eyes sparkle or was that just the house lights*, he thought as he gazed into her golden-brown eyes.

"When we last met in Nubia, you were queen and I was Pharaoh. We promised to meet again in the after-life, and well, goddamn, here we are!"

"A genuine Egyptologist." She lied through her teeth. "I'm really impressed."

"No, I'm no specialist. I did take a trip to Egypt a few years ago, and you do bear a striking resemblance to the statues of the Nubian aristocracy." Carlos was shocked at himself. He was actually using correct grammar with this girl. She had immediately put him in an "impress this chick with everything you got" mode. He knew she was a woman of intellect and character. Something he rarely, if ever, noticed in any of the other females he met.

He offered to buy her a drink, which she politely refused. *Damn*, he thought. He would have enjoyed a more relaxed version of this woman. But they spoke and had quite the conversation. He never noticed he was doing most of the talking. She was expertly inter-viewing him and letting him express all the things that most folks didn't have the time or inclination to listen to. Carlos felt empowered with her. He felt powerful without feeling he had to dominate her. He wanted to know more about her and he realized that he didn't even know her name.

"We've been talking, I mean, I guess I've been talk-ing for over an hour and…please, what is your name?"

"It's Nicola…Nicola James." She looked at her diamond-studded watch and quickly gathered her purse and shawl. "I'm way past my curfew. Look, call me sometime." She pulled her business card out. Carlos looked it over.

"You're an interior decorator?"

"That's what the card says."

"Hey, how old are you, Nicola, if you don't mind me asking?"

She rose up and waited for Carlos to slide out of the booth so she could exit.

"If you have to ask, my dear sweet Carlos, you can't handle it."

He looked at her purple halter and the way her tight curves filled the outfit. He knew then he could not rest 'till he made love to every square inch on her body. He confidently replied, "Don't worry; I can handle the whole thing."

"Really now? So then tell me why you need to know how many years I've been here?"

"It's just that…" He stood up, never taking his eyes away from hers, and held her in his arms. "You have what all beautiful black women have…ageless beauty. You could be jail bait."

Laughing, she gently freed herself from his embrace. Speechless, not knowing what to say next, he joined in and laughed with her. He did not care if he was the subject she found amusing. His only concern was that this woman of indeterminate age was getting to him like no other woman before had. He had to have her.

Carlos could sense he was losing his infamous cool. What the hell was going on with him? He'd only known her for an hour. He commanded his mind to chill out and slow down. He was thinking too stupid and too fast. That was not Carlos's way. Not at all.

He offered her a ride home. She accepted. Guiding her through the crowd, it finally dawned on him that he had Jonathan with him.

"Nicola, my brother is with me. Could you wait here in the lounge while I get him?"

She smiled at him and said, "No problem."

He walked back into the main section of the club and found Jonathan sitting at the bar, staring at a glass of Coke. So eager to return to Nicola, Carlos didn't recognize the despondent look on his face.

"I met a bomb babe. I'm leaving to take her home up in Harlem. I'll drop you off on my way to her crib." Jonathan, still thinking about his mystery woman, nodded absentmindedly and followed Carlos as he searched for his girl.

"Man, I left Nicola right here in the lounge. Where the hell did she—" A tap on his shoulder made both young men turn around and greet Nicola at the same time.

Jonathan yelled out, "It's you!"

Shocked, Carlos exclaimed, "You know her?"

Jonathan started sweating again. She can't be the girl

Carlos was planning to "knock boots with," as he called it. This was the siren he had met. She was his find. Jonathan realized that he was thinking crazy.

This girl Carlos called Nicola was not his at all. She had only brushed up against him for a split second and blew him an apparently insignificant kiss. He looked into her eyes frantically searching for some sign of recognition. Nicola did not respond with anything other than her trademark smile that made all men who met her melt like candle wax in a blazing inferno.

"No, I just thought she was someone else."

Carlos ignored Jonathan's strange behavior. He gently pushed them both outside the club where a uniformed valet waited with Carlos's top-of-the-line, black Jaguar sports car.

"Folks, let's get moving. I know Nicola wants to get home some time this century."

Jonathan smiled at Carlos's time reference, because he knew the short ride home would indeed feel like a hundred years long. He was miserable from thinking that Carlos was going to be with Nicola. Sitting in the backseat, watching Nicola from behind, left him aching inside.

He tried to conjure up images of the girls in his church group back in Boston. That didn't help. They were too stiff, usually too white, and too skinny to generate any real heat. All he could see was beautiful Nicola. He gave up trying to block her out and joined in the conversation. He discovered that she was an intelligent, knowledgeable person.

She was also sophisticated, well-traveled, and even had a keen sense of humor. She told tales that had both he and Carlos laughing several times during the ride. He was disappointed when Carlos pulled up in front of the house. When he reluctantly waved good-bye to both of them, Nicola blew a kiss and winked. He shuddered. The most insignificant of gestures confirmed that she had indeed remembered their brief encounter.

That night Jonathan's wet dream had a new star: Nicola. She was the vixen in a dream that caused his hot rod to explode with sticky wet passion. Surrounded by a packed audience, in the center ring of Madison Square Garden, Nicola lay totally nude on top of a giant-sized, round, red satin-covered bed.

She beckoned him closer to him. Imitating the studs that starred in his stash of porno DVDs, he impaled her creamy center with his wrought-iron weapon, pumping in and out of her with the fervor of a wild beast. When he climaxed, the Madison Square Garden crowd stood up and cheered.

Carlos was relieved when he finally dropped off Jonathan. He wanted this woman all to himself. As if reading his mind, Nicola slid her hands across his groin and massaged him for what seemed like an eternity. He quickly responded to her touch.

"Mmm, I take back every doubt I had about your ability to handle things. You're pretty well packed."

Carlos smiled to himself. He was always upset that, at six feet, he was the shortest male in the family. But as fate would have it, he'd been amply blessed with an enormous, twelve-inch pleasure rod.

Some women even refused to have sex with him, strictly on mechanical reasons alone. He tried to assure them that he could handle his equipment in a fashion whereby all were pleased. Still, some declined. They doubted his technique and it was their loss because Carlos had plenty of technique.

He looked at Nicola and realized that he had picked up a phenomenal woman. She was nothing like the freaks he usually wound up with. He was going to rock Nicola James' world.

Nicola's thoughts were so very different. There was only one man on her mind, the bastard that had broken her heart into a million pieces: Harrison James. Every man she met would pay for his crime. No one was safe. Looking over at an unsuspecting Carlos, just driving his car and ranting about his latest accomplishments, she knew conquering him would be an effortless task.

CHAPTER FOURTEEN

"Now I know you two aren't going to lie up in this basement all day and not help clean it up."

Carrying a bucket in one hand and dust rags in the other, Ophelia burst into the basement clubroom, yelling at her boys as if they were still teenagers. In knee-jerk fashion, both Tarik and Carlos snapped to attention, jumped off the leather sectional, and awaited orders.

"The after party is in two days and I want this place Pine Sol clean!"

Tarik hugged his mother. "That's why I'm here. Just tell us what you want us to do for you."

She looked up at her two angels. She was proud of her boys, though they had sure put Pops and her through many struggles over the years. Nothing too terrible. Just typical adolescent issues that they were able to handle. Except for Tarik's brief brush with the law in his teens, they had managed to avoid the urban pitfalls that slapped crippling criminal records on young Black and Latino men.

Jonathan joined them downstairs. Showing off his skills, he twirled his basketball on the tip of his index finger and then, for added effect, rolled it along his arms.

Only marginally impressed, Ophelia exclaimed, "Oooo! What a talented young man you are! Here." She shoved a rag at Jonathan. "Let's see some of your other skills… you DUST."

Jonathan dropped the ball. "Hey, what's going on here? What did I walk in on?"

Carlos pulled the vacuum cleaner out of the closet beneath the stairs. "Ma's turned me and Tarik into her slaves."

"Ma, I thought you were hiring a crew to help you with Saturday?"

"I did…you, Carlos and Tarik." She turned around to face Tarik as he was cleaning behind the bar. "And don't break my crystal glasses, please."

"Ma…I got primo press for Tarik for this event and there's a good picture of him in the *Amsterdam News'* entertainment section."

"Make sure you get me clippings for the scrapbook, Carlos."

She looked at all three young men. "Pops would sure be proud of all you boys now. Jonathan with the basketball. Carlos, you're doing so well in school and handling Tarik's career so professionally. And Tarik, well, baby, he'd be real pleased to see how hard and earnest you've been working for your dream." She gave them each a hug.

Tarik hugged his mother again. "He'd be proud of the way you're keeping busy helping us and working in the community with your AIDS program."

"Now that I got you guys organized, I'm going up-stairs to finish painting my study. I appreciate all of your help."

A chorus of "Sure, Mother" and "No problem, Ma," followed her as she walked up the stairs to the parlor floor. Upon reaching the landing, she dragged herself to the end of an exquisitely decorated hall, and entered her private study. Surveying its contents, she slapped her hands on both hips and exclaimed out loud, "Finally, I can finish this room!"

It was her latest decorating project. On her desk were several swatches of fabric for window treatments and a new slipcover that would soon rejuvenate the old sofa she had recently purchased at an estate sale. Shelves of books lined the walls, mostly medical texts. She picked up a paintbrush and slapped three different colors on the one wall that did not have any shelves.

On this same wall hung a picture of a yellow rose. It was obviously an unfinished painting as there was a pencil-traced outline of a vase on the bottom left-hand corner of the canvas. Ophelia stepped back, trying to decipher which hue served her decorating purposes. She'd painted the room several times over the past twenty years, and it was always the same demand. Which color best matched the unfinished yellow rose painting?

As if engaging in a forbidden act, she closed the door behind her and walked over to the painting. She tenderly stroked its mahogany frame as if it were alive. A tsunami-size wave of memory whisked her back to the time Eli had started the painting. Thoughts of a love that had come and violently swept away tormented her. *Damn it, Eli! The only thing you ever finished was our love.*

CHAPTER FIFTEEN

"Tarik, how'd you know you were in love with Sherry?"

"Love? Why is the Mack Man so interested in love all of a sudden?"

"Why can't a brother just entertain a little curiosity?" replied Carlos, smiling from ear to ear like an overweight kid who'd just discovered where the candy was hiding.

"Not the way you do things. Like, the way you run through girls. The way you called them 'hoes' and 'tramps' and 'freaks.' Hell, I thought you considered women mere fluid receptacles."

Carlos cringed when he heard his brother's appraisal. It was partially true.

No, hell, it was all true, he thought. He did have a low opinion of women. That was, until he met Nicola. He realized he must have been sampling from the shallow, murky end of the female pool. He was now in the deeper and classier section.

Carlos hadn't bent his knees in a spiritual way since Pops died. Meeting Nicola sent him back to church. Ever since he met her, he constantly prayed he wasn't too far in over his head and that he could keep this refined woman interested in him. It would take much more than his big dick to keep her satisfied.

Carlos now referred to everything in his life as either occurring before or after meeting Nicola. The former ladies' man's first and last thought of the day was now how he was going to live the rest of his life with this woman. He understood fully what Tarik was trying to tell him. Carlos was in love with Nicola James. Little hearts encircling both of their names, covered notepads on his desk.

Never wanting body tattoos before and now wanting anything that represented permanence, he made an appointment at the biggest parlor in downtown Brooklyn. The artist agreed to put a huge tattoo with her name on the left side of his chest, right over his heart. He would have that tattoo forever; just like he prayed he'd have Nicola forever. Carlos's nose was so wide-open planes could fly through it.

What kept blowing his mind was he had only known Nicola for a few days. They hadn't even consummated the relationship. That first night all they shared was a long intimate. They stayed in the car just talking until the sun rose. Nicola made it clear that she was ready for an intimate "visit" and had invited him into her Harlem brownstone.

Not wanting to rush things, he declined the offer. He wanted to take it good and slow with this woman. He wanted their first time to be the beginning of forever for the both of them. Initially disappointed, Nicola eventually agreed with the idea.

He tried to plan the perfect moment for their lovemaking. He asked anyone who listened about advice on romancing a special lady. He was anxious to please Nicola. He knew from their conversation she had seen the world with her ex-husband. She'd led a charmed life and he wanted desperately to prove to her that he could provide the same.

He rarely considered the age difference. She finally confessed to twenty-seven. A two-year difference was insignificant. What was significant was his bank account. After sinking his inheritance into the record company, his cash flow was tighter than he liked it to be.

Carlos bumped up his efforts to make Tarik's concert as large as possible. With a strong audience reception, the record labels would not only sweeten the contract but increase the upfront dollar advance as well. He understood how the dollar bills were generated in the industry, and he worked overtime to make sure it continuously flowed in Tarik's and his direction.

Yes, if all things went according to plan, he'd soon be set financially and if what he thought he could have with Nicola was real, she'd be around to help him spend his cash. Yes, everything was gonna turn out right for everybody.

Carlos's head was stuck too deep in the clouds of romance to notice that Jonathan was trying his best to avoid him. As he was the only one who'd actually met Nicola, Carlos tried to share the events of their developing relationship with him, but the basketball player was never around. It helped though, knowing that someone other than himself had seen her, because he was beginning to think that he'd just conjured her up.

Since that first night, he'd had only short phone conversations with her. She was busy at night with clients. Though it troubled him a little that she was inaccessible, Carlos decided to be patient. He did not want to appear possessive so soon in the relationship. They would spend the whole evening after the concert together. He had planned to take her to a top hotel for the night. If everything went his way, it would be a memorable evening for both of them.

CHAPTER SIXTEEN

"You're doing real good work, Jonathan."

"Oh, thanks, Coach."

Jonathan smiled to himself as he headed for the showers after a particularly grueling early-morning workout. It was the first positive feedback he'd had since he had arrived two weeks ago. He was beginning to doubt his skills. But fortunately, the hard work was beginning to pay off. He could feel that his game had seriously bumped up several notches. When he returned to high school, he'd be a lethal weapon indeed.

The other players were excellent competitors. He was looking at future NBA stars. Still beaming from his first pat on his back, he allowed himself to entertain the possibility that one day he too would don the jersey of a professional basketball team. But that was a few years away. He had a little thing like high school and college to complete before he had to make the decision about what team to play for. Jonathan headed straight for home. He was tired. Tonight was Tarik's concert and he wanted to be well rested.

"Jonathan, man, wake up! Wake up!" Carlos shook Jonathan out of deep sleep.

Half-drowsy, he thought Carlos was asking him to pick up Nicola for him. He woke up fully. "You can't be serious, Carlos!"

"Help a brother out. I'm going to be busy with the concert—you know, politicking with the A&R label folks. That would totally bore Nicola. If you'd do this one thing for me."

But that one little thing would be one thing too many. Since he'd met Nicola, he was having trouble knowing she was in the same city as he was. That was too close. But now this.

"I don't know, Carlos. I just…"

Carlos interrupted. "If you're bringing a girl, well, that shouldn't be a problem."

Jonathan shook his head; there was no way he could get out of dodging Carlos's request. "No, it's not like that. I thought you two would be together, you know, doing your couple thing. I was just thinking about you, man. Sure, I'll uh, pick Nicola up and keep her company." Lying through his teeth, Jonathan covered his nose, hoping that the Pinocchio tale was just a myth.

Carlos was genuinely relieved. He patted Jonathan

on his back. "You're a lifesaver. I didn't want her to be all alone. Didn't want the brothers smellin' new meat and gettin' all horny and shit and tryin' to tap my lady before I got a chance my damn self. You know how treacherous they can be sometimes. Good to have blood around to help protect your property, if you know what I mean."

A cold frost traveled up and down Jonathan's spine. He had betrayed that trust so many times in his dreams with Nicola. He'd have to behave himself completely when they were together at the concert. He didn't know whether to be happy that he'd be near Nicola or sad because he had to control himself with her. He decided to be sad, for truly behaving himself would prove to be a most difficult task.

Carlos took out his keys and wrote down her address, phone number, and directions. "I already told her about the change in plans and she's cool with it." Carlos misinterpreted Jonathan's reluctance. "Hey, I might even make you best man at the wedding. Tarik would be pissed though." He thought about it for a moment. "Fuck, I ain't got to be conventional; I can have two best men. Thanks, man." With that, Carlos darted out the room to tie up last-minute details relating to the concert.

"Jonathan! It's so good of you to pick me up like this. Come on in." Nicola answered the door wearing next to nothing. Embarrassed by its revealing nature, Jonathan tried his best not to look directly at her as he entered her home. Chatting as if nothing was unusual, she added, "I tried to tell Carlos I could have called a limo and travelled to the little concert, but he wouldn't listen."

He flinched when he heard the "little" part. Carlos would have cringed to hear his crowning moment in the industry reduced to a mere "little concert." But, to an outsider, he had to admit, it was indeed a little concert.

Trying to make small talk, he commented, "I made good time on the FDR Drive…no traffic at all." He looked around her tastefully decorated brownstone. It was on equal par, if not more extravagant than his mother's home in Brooklyn. Jonathan walked around her living room admiring her exquisite collection of Haitian and African-American art.

"Your home is beautiful, Nicola. I…what?" Nicola had slid up behind him and totally caught him off-guard. Having her so close was extremely disturbing.

"I'm sorry, did I scare you?" She playfully stared into his eyes. A tremor went through his body that was off the Richter scale.

"Just startled," he mumbled.

"Did you tell Carlos we had met earlier in the club that night?" She was almost on top of him now. Any closer and their bodies would touch. The old "brain-less" one below his waist was about to take off from the launch pad any second. At the first sign of contact, it would be no holding back, and Jonathan knew it. He pulled away from Nicola, and sat back down on a chaise lounge covered with genuine leopard skin.

"I would have if you had said something to back me up." He sounded childish, blaming her for his reluctance to be honest with his brother.

"It was just an innocent meeting, Jonathan." Nicola was wearing a sheer Japanese kimono. She twirled around modeling it for him. "Do you like?" The material easily revealed her body. Of course he liked what he saw. "I purchased this last year when I visited Japan. Ever been?" Jonathan was having difficulty keeping a growing erection from embarrassing him. He shook his head and repositioned himself on the couch.

Trying to refocus, he picked up an ornament off the mosaic-tiled coffee table and asked her about it. Why did he do that? She had to sit next to him and describe it to him as it was indeed a show-and-tell piece.

"It's an obelisk made of pure jade. It has a…" She pressed a button. A secret drawer popped out, startling Jonathan. "Oh, I didn't want to scare you." With that Nicola stroked his thigh. Jonathan did not, could not do the decent thing and pull away from her. He sat there paralyzed with pleasure; unable and unwilling to move away.

She gazed into his eyes, looking for signs of disapproval. Finding none, she traveled to his inner thigh. "That's right; I wouldn't want you to feel uncomfortable with me. After all, I am your brother's little girlfriend, aren't I?" Parking her hands over home plate, she stroked his dick back and forth in a sensuous motion.

Jonathan had waited his whole life for the first time someone would stroke him other than himself. As his penis reached granite-hard status, Nicola patted his leg and smiled the smile that got all men in trouble and asked, "Is your whole family endowed like this? First Carlos, now you. What a terrific gene pool."

What happened next, Jonathan would remember the rest of his life. He decided right on the spot that it would be the last thing he saw flash in front of his eyes the day he died. In one swift motion, before he had opportunity to object, Nicola pulled down his zipper, reached inside his boxers and liberated his cast-iron hard dick. It sprang to attention.

Nicola, Jonathan's high priestess of pleasure, squealed with delight as she surveyed his treasure. "Now isn't this special." Jonathan watched Nicola bend down before him, between his legs, in what he imagined to be geisha-girl style. She took control of his penis as if it was a scepter, stroking it up and down in royal fashion. "So special, Mr. Basketball Man. You're a special young man indeed."

Under his breath, hoping that it would give him strength to pull away from Nicola, Jonathan chanted the Teens for Abstinence mantra…"No Ring; No Sex." He repeated the words over and over, but they had no meaning. The only thing he understood was Nicola's hands kneading his dick expertly, coaxing his hot blood to fill deep, tortuous, cavernous spaces. Then she did the unexpected.

"This looks good enough to…" Without any request from him, she planted gentle kisses along the shaft of his penis. Jonathan's eyes bulged out. He was very near to exploding. When she whipped out her wet tongue and slid it up and down his massive expansion, Jonathan's brain and body seemed to detach from his penis. He was just one big dick, waiting for Nicola to send him off…and send him off she did.

"Stand up," she ordered. Jonathan obeyed. Nicola frowned. "Umm, you are tall. I know what. Bend on your knees and I'll sit on the couch." Like a slave, Jonathan obeyed once again. "This is more like it. Now, put it right here in Mama's mouth. She wants all of it."

He realized what was about to happen. He'd seen enough videos. He placed his missile between her lips. It was tight as a visor.

Instinctively, in piston-like style, he rammed himself into her mouth. She was indeed able to handle all of him. He held on to her head and controlled the rate. Faster and faster. He kept banging his love crown against the far reaches of her throat. His balls slapped against her chin with each thrust. Approaching the inevitable end a scream escaped from his mouth; a blood-curdling primal scream. His first orgasm with a real live woman! It was nothing as he had imagined. It was indeed better than he had imagined.

Swallowing what she could, thick copious fluid erupted from her mouth, dripping over her chin.

"Mmmm…virgin protein…I just LOVE IT!" Not wanting to miss a drop of the precious fluid, she licked the remains off of his penis.

"How'd you know I'm a virgin?"

Her only response was to wink and say, "Little messy here. Let me wipe this up for you." She took tissues out of an attractive brass elephant dispenser on her coffee table. She gently patted his glistening dick till it was dry. Jonathan stood there in a trance-like state. Tiny aftershocks rippled through his penis, causing his body to jerk. Nicola planted a kiss on his crown. "Guess I'll get dressed now."

It was over. Nicola rose and disappeared out of the room, leaving behind a confused and very fulfilled young man. One question troubled him as he stared down at his dick. His penis was still rock hard. What was he supposed to do with it? He'd never had a real woman do what Nicola had just done. He was scared. With great difficulty, he stuffed himself back into his pants. Would his dick ever shrink back to normal? He'd heard about men who had erections that lasted so long they had to go to the emergency room for treatment.

An absurd thought flashed through his mind—to call and ask Carlos, but he knew how that would go over. The vision of Carlos giving him advice and kicking his ass at the same time, did help to cool him down. Finally, his erection faded.

Alone, waiting for Nicola to get dressed, he wondered how he was going to deal with Carlos. The "guilties" were beginning to haunt him. He wanted to blame everything on Nicola. After all, he had not provoked her. On the real side of truth, he was guilty of not pulling away. She hadn't exactly raped him.

What really made him feel lower than the crud between his toes, was that he wanted it to happen again. Not only did he want a repeat, he wanted more from Nicola. He wanted to make love to her. In fact, at that moment, having sex and worshipping at the feet of the one woman he knew to be a genuine Black Goddess Queen of Love, was his only goal in life. Fuck college…fuck basketball…but most of all, fuck the Teens for Abstinence Club. He needed to fuck Nicola.

Nicola's entrance into the room shocked the young basketball player back into the present. Wearing an Edward Williamson original, a snug-fitting, fuchsia-colored pantsuit that advertised her goods without giving them all away, she was nothing short of fabulous. Jonathan, impressed, whistled loudly. Nicola twirled and modeled her outfit.

"You think Carlos will like this?"

Now it was his turn to straighten things out. "Nicola, about what just happened, I don't think…"

"You mean that little massage? That was nothing, Jonathan. Something between new friends. Don't even worry about it. Just act like it never really happened, okay?" With that, she opened the front door. "Time for the concert."

They rode back to Brooklyn chatting about simple, benign, everyday life. Anybody listening would never guess that anything other than a platonic relationship existed between the two. And, as Jonathan regretfully admitted to himself, that was indeed all that they had... that and the memory of his very first blow job.

CHAPTER SEVENTEEN

*E*li looked at the clock. It was 5:30 in the morning. He pulled back the curtain and saw the sun rise up into the sky to start a brand-new day. Today was his boy's show. He reached out and grabbed the Bible off his nightstand. He turned to the twenty-third Psalms and pulled out the meticulously folded news article he'd placed there for safe keeping. In the center of the first page of the entertainment section of the *Amsterdam News*, was a picture of Tarik. Since he got the flyer a week ago, an article about Tarik appeared in the weekly newspaper.

For the thousandth time he read it. He'd memorized almost every word. The journalist had given many details of Tarik's career. He particularly beamed with pride when his boy was described as a "genius poet/songwriter." What really made Eli happy, was that an itinerary of his show dates revealed he'd be performing in Prospect Park. It was only a short cab ride away. He was elated. Nothing in this world would keep him from attending the event today.

Slowly rising from bed, Eli prayed his frail health would hold out. He didn't have to speak to Tarik. He just wanted to see him. He was so proud of this young man. Ophelia and the man who had adopted Tarik had obviously done a wonderful job raising him. He no longer regretted signing the papers that officially cut him out of his only child's life.

Trying to look as presentable as possible, he decided to trim his scraggly gray beard. Completely bald, he'd lost his hair when he participated in an AIDS drug trial while in jail. He looked at his reflection in the mirror. A gaunt, scary face stared back. When Eli entered prison over five years ago, the scaled tipped in at 165 pounds. For a six-foot-two man he was thin then. This week, he weighed a whopping 130 pounds. The disease had reduced him to skin, brittle bones, and according to his last round of tests, a blood profile so abnormal it was damn near incompatible with life.

After five years of fighting infections, the tuberculosis that refused to respond to standard treatment, and the anti-viral meds and their crippling side effects, Eli was nearing the end of the battle. This time, he would not emerge the victor.

Brushing his teeth, a comforting thought visited him and temporarily pushed aside the curtain of gloom that so often darkened his waking moments. There was one thing he had done right. Heroin no longer ruled his life. Didn't even need the methadone either. Life, and the hope he would one day see his Ophelia and Tarik, was enough high for him.

He was close to completing the yellow rose painting he had started in prison. Another few sessions and he'd be through. When he'd arrived at Hilton Arms, an abandoned building the city rehabilitated for residents suffering with AIDS, he planned to one day present it to Ophelia. It was his way of expressing both his gratitude for raising their son and apologizing for his utter failure as a husband and father.

Suspecting there was a slim possibility he'd run into her at the concert, he thought about bringing it with him. He looked over at the painting. Unfinished. He frowned. He couldn't give it to Ophelia in that condition. His inability to complete tasks was one of the main reasons their relationship suffered.

No, today he was just going to see his son perform. Hopefully, one day soon, he'd finish the painting and have an opportunity to meet with her. Realistically, as he assessed his declining energy, the odds were against him. More than likely he'd have to give Ophelia her finished painting when they met on the other side. He smiled. He could almost see glimpses of the "light" some mornings. It was probably his eyes deteriorating, but he spiritually understood it to be divine illumination. One day soon this light would bathe and cleanse him before he reached the other side. The thought calmed him and gave him strength for his day's journey.

The meals on wheels lady dropped off his nourishment for the day. He was not hungry, as usual, but today he forced the food down. He needed fuel for the long journey ahead. This was probably his last trip alone.

*C*HAPTER EIGHTEEN

*P*rospect Park was a beautifully landscaped area located in the heart of Brooklyn. Generations of African-Americans, Latinos and the new crop of gentrifying whites had visited over the years to swing in the swings, play basketball and listen to some of the best music in New York City. For the summer, there was no better place to be.

The place was packed. Surveying the huge crowd of over ten thousand people, Carlos was glad he invited record company executives to the park's annual Fourth of July festival. It was a natural choice to display Tarik's talents at the outdoor amphitheater. His brother had headlined the event for the past two years. Tarik knew what people liked and the crowds loved him for it.

It had been a steamy, hot day that, thanks to a brief shower, had finally decided to cool down. Folks arrived more than anxious for a good time and a slammin' show. Vendors sold everything from incense to Jamaican jerk chicken. Early summer breezes carried the smell of food from all over the world. The unmistakable aroma of ganja weed was so strong most of the crowd enjoyed a mellow contact high.

The sounds of wild fireworks, cherry bombs and other incendiary items popping and crackling added to the festive atmosphere. Families, friends, and lovers sat on wooden chairs, the grass or each other. At twilight, it was time for the show to begin. An expectant hush fell over the crowd.

In the small dressing room behind the amphitheater stage, Tarik and his entourage formed a circle. Always apprehensive before a big concert, Tarik's heart pounded with anticipation. Small droplets of sweat beaded up along his hairline, waiting for the signal to slide down his forehead.

Trying his damn best to kill the colony of butterflies attacking his stomach, Tarik led his fellow musicians in a moment of prayerful silence. It was a ritual that helped him merge with the creative universe. It mellowed him out and prepared him for the job he'd been summoned to do.

The drummer, percussionist, bassist, lead guitarist and three "healthy-looking" sisters who looked like they belonged in the front pew of a gospel choir, were the first to appear on stage. While waiting for Tarik, they performed a sound check.

Back in the dressing room, Sherry gave Tarik the pep

talk he had grown to depend on before his concerts, "Now, baby, look me in the eyes and say, 'I was born to do this.'"

Tarik looked at his wife adoringly and repeated, "I was *born* to do this."

Sherry hugged him and whispered in his ear, "Then go out there and do what you supposed to DO!" Seconds later, warm, robust applause greeted Tarik as he joined his band on stage.

Seated at the keyboards, Tarik dropped his head in a meditative pose. He entered the zone where his hands and instrument reached union. Not classically trained, Pops had taught him just enough piano for him to develop an inimitable style of his own. The solo piece hinted of jazz, blues and classical music weaved with rhythm and blues basics. There was literally something for everybody's listening pleasure in his music.

Increasing the tempo, the other members of his band joined in. In a perfectly planned moment of crescendo, Tarik and his background vocalists burst out in an ecstatic, joyful blend of harmonies that rocked the crowd into a mad frenzy.

Sitting next to Carlos in the front row was Jeff Moses, president of Mo-Sound Records. Jeff was a well-respected, powerful player in the music industry. His label was a major company known for standing behind its artists. Carlos knew, if Jeff liked what he heard, Mo-Sound would be *the* place to park his brother's awesome talent.

"I told you he was bad," Carlos yelled into his ear.

Jeff, a short, well-built Black man, who spoke with a booming commanding voice, said, "From what I've heard, he's sold over fifty-thousand CDs."

"For the record, Jeff, if you factor in the internet downloads, the number is closer to two hundred and fifty thou', but then, who's counting?"

"Very impressive; very impressive. Call me Monday and let's set up that showcase for the suits and get this show on the road. If I have anything to do with it, and I do, you can consider Mo-Sound your partner!"

Carlos worked hard to suppress a strong desire to jump up and down and spin cartwheels all through the park's lawn. Happy could not describe the joy he was feeling. He and Tarik had worked long and hard to hear those words. And now it was happening.

He could not wait to share the news with Tarik and the love of his life, Nicola. After the party at his mother's house, he was going to kidnap her and take her to one of the finest hotels in the city. This was turning out to be the best night of his life.

Turning around and surveying the crowd, he tried to single out Jonathan and Nicola. So absorbed with details of the concert for most of the day, it finally dawned on him that he hadn't seen them that entire evening. A seed of concern the size of a golf ball slowly began to expand inside of him. Where were they? Was she all right? Had she changed her mind about coming?

He pulled out his cell phone and checked for calls. None from either of them. Trying not to appear anxious around Jeff, he forced his eyes and attention to focus on the show.

Nicola and Jonathan stood in the back of the crowd. The little detour to his aunt's house cost them two hours. They arrived too late to get a seat. Why had he mentioned to Nicola that his house would be empty and that everybody would be at the concert? And why did he go against his wisest judgment and bring her home?

Nicola had insisted it was all innocent. She suggested she could help with last minute details of the after-party. Surely his mother needed assistance. Jonathan agreed that his mom had mentioned she'd wished she had an extra person's help with setting up for the occasion. Why not Nicola?

But honestly, the only help he needed was "help" getting his dick sucked and licked as many times as the temptress could handle. Thankfully, there was no one home but the catering crew. Jonathan literally dragged Nicola upstairs to his room. She unabashedly repeated her earlier performance. When he came, it was better than the first time.

Tarik was onstage performing an up-tempo dance number. Jonathan and Nicola rocked back and forth with the enthusiastic crowd. All was going fine until

Nicola deliberately moved her French-manicured hand across his crotch. Jonathan's attention instantly shifted from the stage ahead to the growing bulge inside his pants. Shocked, he could not help but enjoy the sensation and the naughtiness of what she was doing in public. It gave him a rush that caused his intimate flesh to expand and greet her hand properly.

"Jonathan!" Ophelia appeared out of nowhere and scared him so, he almost fainted. Nicola, always cool, always in control, slithered away from him.

"Ma…Mother…Mama Ophelia…uh…uh…it's…it's good to see you." Jonathan's deer-caught-in-the-headlights expression was evident for miles around. Certain his mother had caught him and Nicola in the act, he nervously proceeded with the introductions. "This is Nicola. Carlos's…uh…Carlos's girlfriend. That's right. This is Carlos's girlfriend."

"I know who she is. Carlos described you…uh… perfectly. You are beautiful."

"Why, thank you. It's a pleasure to meet you, Mrs. Singleton."

"I'd love to chat but, I've got to deliver this first-aid kit. Can you believe it? They were short a person on the emergency health team. I volunteered at the last moment. Oh well…better to do that than have the concert cancelled. Well, I'm off. Hope to see you at the after-party, Nicola."

"I wouldn't think of missing it."

"See you, Jonathan."

Ophelia walked away in a trance of disbelief. *Was that woman feeling up my baby's crotch? Was that real?*

It was such an absurd thought. Ophelia shook her head and dismissed it immediately. Not her baby. Jonathan was too pure. He wouldn't let someone do that to him; especially not his brother's girlfriend. No... it was dark...her mind was playing tricks with her eyes...and besides, she was long overdue for a trip to the eye doctor. No, it did not happen.

But why was Jonathan so nervous? The possibility was so disturbing, Ophelia made a mental note to keep her "mama" eyes on Nicola at the after-party.

As soon as his mother was out of earshot distance, Jonathan turned on Nicola.

"Look, you can't be doing to me what you're doing, and where you're doing it!"

Nicola smiled devilishly up at him and playfully squeezed his cheeks. "You are so delightful when you're mad."

"Nicola!"

"My fine, tall drink of comfort, why do you insist on confusing me?"

Puzzled by her line of reasoning, Jonathan inquired, "I...I confuse you? How so?"

"Why, it seems like you were enjoying the whole affair." Batting double-thick, natural eyelashes, she looked up at Jonathan in teasing fashion, and added, "How's a poor girl 's'pozed to know when to do 'what' and where to do 'what' and when and with whom to do 'what,' hmmm?"

Even more confused than before, Jonathan reluctantly replied, "Never mind; never mind." He slowly began to realize two things. He absolutely enjoyed this woman and the things she did to his body. But he could forget about ever being able to control her behavior. Hell, he really didn't want to anyway. An uncontrolled Nicola was far more pleasurable.

CHAPTER NINETEEN

Eli couldn't believe his luck. He had a great spot at the concert, away from the main crowd but close enough that the binoculars he brought along helped him get a good view of the stage. And he liked what he saw through the lenses. His boy was talented. The article had not used enough superlatives in describing what he brought to the stage. He enjoyed himself immensely as his son effortlessly entertained the crowd. Eli even managed to put two of his boniest fingers together and snap them to the rhythm of his son's music.

After sixty minutes of performing to the crowd, Tarik introduced his last song of the evening. It was a tribute to his wife and son. Hearing the news about Tarik's son for the first time, confirming that he was a grandfather, Eli wept. He would never get a chance to meet either his son or his grandbaby. He'd given up that privilege many years ago. A view with binoculars was all he could hope for. It was all he deserved.

Momentarily feeling sorry for himself, he barely noticed that the young man standing next to him had passed out. His body jerked in a typical seizure pattern. Eli yelled for help as he tried to keep the man from banging his head on the ground. As the seizure subsided, the man stopped shaking. A group of curious lookie-loos gathered around Eli and the sick man, all yelling various incorrect remedies that promised speedy recovery.

The medics responded seconds later. Ophelia, a member of the team, took control of the crowd and pushed them away to make room. Two emergency technicians prepped the man for transport to the hospital.

Trying to get information, Ophelia, questioned the crowd. "Did anyone see what happened?"

Eli spoke up...he was so excited he at first didn't realize it was Ophelia. "Miss, I was standing right next to him...and he... he..." Ophelia turned around and looked dead at him. He knew instantly who those dark-brown eyes belonged to. "Miss...Miss Ophelia?"

Ophelia looked at the frail man before her. She knew what she didn't want to know. This was Eli. And just like the first day she had met him at that Hampton University Sweethearts Ball, her heart danced and twitched. It was the tiniest part of her heart that had refused to let the love they once shared die. "Eli...is that you?"

He smiled. "It's me. Old Eli. Yes, I saw what happened." He explained how he had suddenly noticed the man lying on the ground. Ophelia passed the info on to the technicians who were now putting the man in the back of ambulance. With lights flashing and the siren loudly booming, they drove off.

"It's good to see you," commented Eli. He immediately admired how attractive Ophelia still looked. She was close to fifty...but yet she appeared much younger.

"Yeah...Eli, what the hell happened to you?"

"Still shooting from the hip?" Ophelia hadn't changed a bit, thought Eli. She never was one for beating around the bush. But this time he was in control. He didn't want to talk about his health or lack of. He ignored her. "Tarik was wonderful up there. I'm so glad I came. And seeing you, too...what a treat."

He needed his cane to walk. It was time to go. "Well, it looks like Tarik's concert is about over. That's all I came here for. Just to see him. So I must leave you now." He had held up for as long as he could. The strength he'd felt earlier was rapidly leaving him. The shock of seeing Ophelia had drained his battery. He fell back on the bench.

Ophelia rushed toward him. "Are you all right?"

He motioned for her to stay back. "No, I'm okay. Just a little winded. You could help and get me a cab though."

She did that. Helped him into the taxi as well, as he obviously could not do it himself.

Once inside, wanting to shake Ophelia's hand, Eli extended his almost pencil-thin arm. "Well, Mrs....it's still Singleton... isn't it?"

Ophelia gasped to herself as she shook the hand that was attached to an all but wasted body. She could not help but compare it to how Eli used to be when they were both young and he was her handsome, robust lover. She heard herself answer, "Yes, no, well, it's Singleton but I'm...I'm a widow...he passed a year ago."

"Sorry to hear that, Ophelia...well."

The Pakistani cabbie interrupted, "Where to, Mister?"

"Hilton Arms corner of Monroe and Franklin."

Ophelia almost collapsed. She knew then exactly what was wrong with her ex-husband. Only AIDS patients lived at the Arms. She had trained nurse case-managers for their program. Ophelia also knew that its tenants usually were in the end stages of the disease. Eli was dying.

With the same solemnity that one closes a casket, Ophelia slammed the door shut. Trying to sound strong and virile, but failing at both, Eli called out as the cab pulled away. "Good seeing you, Ophelia." As the taxi faded from sight, Ophelia, shaking her head in disbelief the entire way, headed back to the stage.

CHAPTER TWENTY

*T*he after-party back at Ophelia's house was catered by the folks from Makwaba, the renowned company known for providing the best food and service to its customers. Carlos and Ophelia had planned the evening to celebrate what they knew would be the outcome of the concert: a real bite from a serious company. Thanks to Jeff Moses's en-dorsement, they were much closer to their dream.

Over a hundred of their closest family and friends congregated in Ophelia's beautifully restored brown-stone. Ophelia, a lover of African culture, had taken several trips to the continent to collect the furniture and art that was now tastefully displayed in her four-story home that boasted original woodwork, fifteen-foot-high ceilings and a working fireplace in every room.

When Tarik and Sherry arrived at the party, the in-vited guests greeted them in the exquisitely decorated parlor area with robust applause. Nicola forced her way up to the front of the crowd and planted a big, sloppy congratulatory kiss on Tarik's lips. Tarik blushed and Sherry's blood boiled as she pondered: *What the FUCK is going on? We just met this heifer.*

"Nicola, why don't you stand back and give my man some air?" Sherry's request, though delivered playfully, had serious homicidal overtones. Nicola reluctantly pulled away and stared straight down into Sherry's eyes. She could literally feel the claws that Sherry mentally dug into her back. Not the least bit intimidated, all she returned was a smile.

Carlos burst into the foyer to find Nicola chatting with Sherry and Tarik. He was so happy. It seemed that Nicola fit in with his family like she'd known them all of her life. Jonathan looked up to her like a big sister, and Tarik and Sherry seemed cool with her. "Looks like everybody's having a good time here." He pulled Nicola close to him.

Nicola smiled, never taking her seductive eyes off of Tarik. "I was congratulating your brother on his performance. He was simply...," she added in her most seductive tone, "...super."

Sherry gritted her teeth and clenched her fist as the worst thoughts paraded through her mind: *This bitch is fuckin' with the wrong person. She beggin' for a slap down! But I can't do that and face the girls down at the Stop Gang Violence Center.*

Using techniques she had taught her clients, Sherry mustered the courage to channel the rage seeping into her veins into socially accepted behavior. She calmed down completely when she reminded herself that Tarik was hers and she was his and this viper from hell didn't stand a chance.

"Nicola, I so agree with you, girl! My husband is SUPER! Oh, baby, let me get that nasty lipstick off of your face." Sherry reached in her purse for a tissue and cleaned off all traces of Nicola. "There, that's better." She shot a dangerous look at Nicola, rolled her eyes, and commented with much in-your-face attitude, "MUCH BETTER!"

Tarik was proud of his wife. She had handled herself very well with the overly aggressive Nicola. No one would have ever suspected that, at age thirteen, Sherry had nearly killed a girl for just flirting with one of her gang members' boyfriends.

Carlos, oblivious to the potentially vicious catfight, looked around the room. "Hey, where's Jonathan?"

Tarik, pulled Sherry close to him, and answered, "I think he said something about turning in early."

Trying to avoid Carlos, Jonathan had left the party early. Keeping busy, he looked through his e-mail. Most of the messages were from the editor of the Teens for Abstinence newsletter. His article for the "*A Kiss is Good Enough!*" column was long overdue. He'd been a passionate contributor to the newsletter for the past two years.

After his experience that afternoon, writing anything on the subject of "Just Say No" would win him first-prize honors in the "Hypocrite of the Year" contest. Yes, the thought of Nicola made Jonathan's blood boil so hot he was now an official lustful, nasty guy...one who couldn't even fathom stopping at a kiss.

"Yo, Jonathan, why you not at the party?" Carlos burst into the room unannounced. Upset by his entrance, Jonathan made a mental note to fix the busted lock on his bedroom door as soon as possible.

"I was catching up on my e-mails. I'm waiting for uh... ruh...some important messages."

"Man...thanks for helping me out with Nicola. We both appreciate you."

"No problem, she's a...very special lady"

"Special? Hell, she's more than that. She's *the one*."

Jonathan looked at Carlos funny.

"The one! She's got my heart, man. If we keep going like this…"

"You're not talking commitment?"

"The big 'C,' yep...the bigger 'M' word...Yep...I could see me with some little Nicolases and Carloses running all over my crib and making Mama Ophelia a grandma again and shit." Carlos stared off like he could actually see the future in front of him. He jerked away from the scene to confront Jonathan. "Yo, man, look,

I owe you one. I'm definitely checking you out for the game. Okay? Peace, G." Before he left, he added, "One more thing. At the concert, where were you and Nicola sitting? I looked and couldn't find either one of you."

Jonathan's tension rose. *So we were missed*, he thought. He knew it. Never a liar before, he came up with, "Oh, we were way in the back. Got there late. There was a lot of traffic on the FDR, man."

Carlos was satisfied with the lie. "Of course…FDR Saturday traffic can be a bitch. Sorry, man. Sorry you had to go through with that. I *really* owe you now."

Carlos left, as did the part of Jonathan that thought it was "cool" to have an affair with Nicola at the same time she was dating his brother. The "guilties" were beginning to eat him inside out.

Jonathan was determined to make all the wrong things that had transpired in the last few hours right. He had stepped away from his usual code of behavior. After all those years of swaggering around town as the poster boy for squeaky-clean values, he had failed the first time someone had challenged him.

He didn't even give Nicola a good fight. At every point he could have stopped her, but he never did. Pulling away from that luscious mouth and her experienced hands was never a serious option for him. And though he tried to admonish himself for his behavior, he was most ashamed of the coldest fact of all: He didn't really regret his time with Nicola at all.

If truth be told, there was a side of him, one he was unfamiliar with, that was damn grateful for the pleasure he had experienced. He looked at himself in the mirror, and he thought he saw a glimpse of the devil. Shocked by what he thought he saw, he rubbed his eyes. He calmed down when he realized how the mind plays tricks on you…especially when you know you've done wrong.

Playing nasty little games with your sibling's girlfriend was definitely on the list of doing the wrong thing and he didn't want to go straight to hell!

Jonathan made a solid promise to himself that Nicola would never ever get that close to him again. He looked back at the mirror and didn't see the devil. This time he saw a young man, strong in his convictions. In a whispered voice, Jonathan proclaimed, "Yeah, Nicola, just try and suck my dick again. See how far you get." Jonathan struck a pose that even Superman would envy.

CHAPTER TWENTY-ONE

With mellow party music blasting in the background, and the crowd thinning out, Carlos escorted Nicola into a secluded part of the backyard. Walking past a fully stocked koi pond and a massive jasmine bush that, with the help of summer breezes, scented the entire area, Carlos pulled her inside the gazebo near the rear fence. "Good, I got you all to myself now." He pulled her down to sit next to him on the custom-made bench. Carlos softly kissed Nicola on the lips.

"Nicola and Carlos sitting in a tree…"

Nicola joined him in the silly children's song, "K-I-S-S-I-N-G…" Carlos pulled Nicola close to him and they engaged in a deep, full kiss. With no party folks around to see them, Nicola's hands conducted an exploration of Carlos's private parts. She unzipped his fly, breaking through the opening of his treasured BVD's. Her hands stroked the responsive contents.

"Mmmm Nicola, you make me feel ten feet tall."

"And your dick is about the same size. I'm really going to love, loving it."

"Don't you mean loving me?"

"It; you; same same." Nicola reinitiated the kissing, never stopping the stroking motion between his legs. Inspired by her, Carlos slipped his hands past the straps of her top and fondled her pendulous breasts. Nicola's nipples harden in response to his touch. She moaned out ever so quietly, expressing deep pleasure. "Oooh, Carlos, you make me want to have you, all of you, right now." A drop of viscous fluid in total agreement with Nicola's desire, collected at the tip of Carlos's enormous tool as she stroked up and down its monstrous shaft, begging him to climax.

Carlos's cell phone interrupted their "kiss." Always ready for business, Carlos pulled away from her and answered the call.

Frowning, Nicola was visibly disappointed by Carlos's abrupt change in mood and focus.

"Hey, I'm a businessman. I always take my calls. Hello? Yo, Mark, what's up, man?" Nicola tried to distract him by stroking his balls. Carlos left the gazebo to find a "quieter" place to continue his call. Looking back at Nicola, he blew a kiss in her direction.

Feeling slightly rejected by his behavior, Nicola adjusted her clothing and marched back inside the house with all intentions of finding Jonathan to finish what she had tried to start with Carlos.

Nicola wandered upstairs to the second floor. Along

her way, she admired the beautiful Haitian art that adorned the walls. She hadn't noticed the art earlier that day because the hallway had been totally unlit. Disoriented, not knowing where Jonathan could be, she took a wild guess and pushed her way into a room at the end of the corridor.

There to greet her was Tarik all laid out on a daybed, trying to take a nap.

"Look who I've found; the star of the show!" Nicola closed the door behind her and literally attacked the unsuspecting Tarik. He had zero opportunity to refuse the tongue that she shoved down his throat, or push away the groping hand that freely massaged his private parts. No chance to keep himself from responding to her attack, when the door swung open again, he heard his mother shout, "TARIK... NICOLA...WHAT THE HELL IS GOING ON HERE!"

Nicola, smiling, marveling at the chaos she had inspired, disconnected herself from Tarik. She stood up and adjusted her dress. Tarik started talking a mile a minute. "Mama...Ma... This is not what you think it is. Please don't tell Sherry. Don't tell Carlos." He looked at Nicola in disgust and added, "This wasn't nothing. Just a bad, bad mistake."

Clearly disappointed in her son, Ophelia looked into her son's eyes, and then shot a disapproving scowl at Nicola. She shook her head and left the room. Tarik looked at Nicola and spat, "Get the fuck outta here and leave my brother Carlos alone, you hear me?"

"I'm leaving here, but I'm not leaving Carlos." She pulled a solid gold compact out of her purse and refreshed her lipstick. Before leaving the room, she smiled triumphantly and added, "And don't act like you didn't enjoy it 'cause we *both* know that you did."

Tarik was pissed with himself because the crazy broad was dead right.

"NICOLA!"

Nicola gasped as Ophelia, carrying a butcher knife, literally snuck up behind her when she entered the kitchen looking for Carlos. Startled, she almost dropped her purse.

"Mrs. Singleton!"

"I'm sorry; didn't mean to sneak up on you."

Yeah, I bet, thought Nicola.

"That's alright. I'll survive."

Nicola looked at the knife, wondering what Ophelia was going to do with it. Ophelia, who had been busy chopping up a side of beef, preparing it for storage in the refrigerator, saw Nicola's reaction and set the knife down on the butcher block…never taking her eyes off of her.

"Nicola, the men in this family mean a hell of a lot to me. Don't start any trouble between them. Because if you keep messing with Tarik, and Carlos, and my *baby*, Jonathan…" She picked up the knife and for the sheer effect alone, deliberately kept chopping the meat into little pieces and said, "…you are going to have to answer to Mama Ophelia! And it won't be pretty; not one little bit."

Unthreatened by the attractive older woman, Nicola could not have cared less what she thought of her. She wasn't looking for her approval. Not from her. Not from anyone. Ophelia didn't scare her one little bit. Not getting inside Jonathan's pants, now that was a far scarier notion. But he was eager. There would be no problem "deflowering" Mama Ophelia's "baby."

Carlos would be an easy conquest, too. Tarik, she decided to pass on. Though he did look delicious, and she could definitely devour the whole thing, a fight with his half-pint wife would prove far too time-consuming.

Yes, she'd have to be satisfied with Jonathan and Carlos and all the other little conquests she had picked up along the way. As far as she was concerned, both Sherry and the mama could go to hell on a fast plane. Nicola beamed a triumphant smile at Ophelia and walked out of the kitchen, deliberately clicking her stiletto heels rhythmically against the imported Italian tile.

Her eyes literally sparkled, thought Ophelia. A cold chilling memory flashed before her. She had seen those eyes years ago. But where? Had she known Nicola before? No, she couldn't have known her. The only thing she knew was that the wench would be smart not to trespass and make trouble between her sons. Ophelia kept cutting the meat and only stopped when she looked down and realized she had cut the beef into a pile of mush.

As the last guests departed, Carlos could not wait to begin his "special" evening with Nicola. Looking all over for her, he found her sitting out front on the stoop humming to herself. He put his arms around her. "We'll be leaving in a few. Why don't you come back inside with me to say good-bye to my mother?"

Replaying the scene she had had earlier with Ophelia, Nicola smiled mischievously. "I don't think so, Carlos, but you go on ahead. Give me the keys; I'll wait for you in the car."

Disappointed and confused by her refusal, he reached into his pocket, gave her his keys and playfully demanded, "Don't you go nowhere, hear?"

Ophelia was in the kitchen giving final instructions to the catering staff. Carlos gently pulled her to the side.

"Mama Ophelia?"

"Enjoying yourself, dear?"

Carlos slipped his arm around his mother.

"More than I planned to. Well?"

"Well, what?"

"I saw you two talking. What do you think of my Nicola?"

Ophelia smiled politely. Her son was waiting for a full endorsement from her. Not wanting to burst his bubble on an evening he'd worked so hard for, she took the diplomatic route. "I definitely agree with you, Carlos. She's a beautiful-looking woman. Like a model."

Unable to hold back what was really on her mind, she burst out, "But I got to be honest with you, son. Nicola is a pure tramp, and you'd be better off without her. And I ain't got anything else to say on the subject. Excuse me, but I have to do some work here in the kitchen." Ophelia walked away in a defiant "sometimes a mother has to say the hard truth" manner.

Carlos was dumbfounded. His mother was always an opinionated woman, but she was usually a great judge of character. How could she be so wrong about his Nicola? He decided to ignore her. Mothers were always the last ones to approve of their son's choice for a mate. Hell, it had taken forever before Mama Ophelia had accepted Sherry after she discovered that Sherry had done time in jail when she was a gang member.

And now, she and Sherry were both raising Javon together. They were thick as thieves…just like Mama was going to be with Nicola…once she got to know her better. Confident that all would work out eventually, Carlos headed out the door.

"Mama? Mama?" Tarik tapped Ophelia on the shoulder to snatch her from the deep trance she was in. She was standing in front of her Yellow Rose picture, staring at it. "Sherry and I are going home now, but I'm not leaving 'til I explain to you that what you saw tonight was just stupid stuff. That woman attacked me right before you came in the room and I…I…"

"Hush; I know what happened. I've seen that type of witch before. Just stay away from her and keep an eye out for your brother. He's going to need all the support he can get because he's in for the ride of his life."

"She's definitely a piece of work. Well, give me my kiss 'cause I got to go now."

"Tarik. Tarik, baby, I saw him at the concert."

"You saw who, Mama? Who did you see at the…" It didn't take him long to figure it out. His biological father had painted the picture she'd cherished all those years. She finally told him that it was Eli's after Pops died. Even Pops never knew about the real artist. To catch her staring at it now, could only mean that he had been at the concert.

What a hell of a day, Tarik thought. First, the concert turns out perfect, then I get caught in a compromising situation with my brother's woman, and then the excuse I have for a biological father pops up after all these years.

"It was Eli, wasn't it?"

Ophelia looked up at him and nodded her head.

"Figures he'd show up when I'm beginning to make it." Tarik, uncharacteristically angry, paced back and forth in his mother's small office. "He's probably looking to share in the limelight. Get some of the profits. Well, it ain't gonna happen, Mother, not now…not ever…not…"

"Tarik, from what I could see, he's not going to be sharing much of anything with anybody for too much longer." Tarik stopped pacing to look at his mother. "He has AIDS, dear, and it looks like he's at the end of the line with it."

CHAPTER TWENTY-TWO

*C*arlos escorted Nicola into the luxurious lobby of the recently renovated Ritz-Carlton. After a brief check-in, a uniformed concierge and bellman personally escorted them up to the most expensive suite in the five-star hotel. It boasted the best in European-inspired décor. With crystal chandeliers in the dining area, a telescope that magnified a magnificent view of Central Park, and a massive Louis the Fourteenth bed covered with the finest Egyptian cotton to be found on the planet, Carlos was certain he'd spent his five-thousand dollars well.

He had planned this evening to be extra special. He had scheduled breakfast in bed for the next morning and a carriage ride around Central Park afterward, which he hoped would be the perfect way to end their first "sleep-over" together.

Carlos dismissed the private valet. He wanted complete privacy with his lady. Once alone, he triumphantly turned around to Nicola, thinking she had been properly impressed and asked, "Well, how do you like it?"

She went over to the California king-sized bed, sat on it, bounced up and down to check the mattress out, and simply said, "Good solid springs. We should have *lots* of fun on this."

Not getting the response he expected, Carlos shrugged his shoulders and opened a magnum of Dom Pérignon that he had ordered especially for the occasion. He poured the bubbly champagne into two crystal flutes. Interlocking their arms, they sipped the liquid in unison. Room service interrupted and rolled in the finest beluga caviar and a tray of chocolate-dipped strawberries.

He used the pearl-lined spoon to spread the fish eggs on a toast point and popped it into Nicola's awaiting mouth. A few crumbs fell down her décolletage. His eager tongue licked them off. The tiniest of moans escaped from the back of Nicola's throat.

Never taking her eyes off of him, she reached for a strawberry and dropped it into Carlos's hungry mouth. Red, sticky, sweet juice seeped out. Nicola greedily lapped up every drop. Back and forth, they fed each other in an erotically charged "dance."

A half-hour later, the bottle was empty and the food was gone. They were both giddy and seemingly ready to consummate their relationship. Nicola kissed Carlos on the forehead and disappeared into the bathroom to prepare for the evening's activities.

As she shut the door behind her, Carlos scratched his bald head. It was hard for him to read Nicola. With other females, he could always figure out their entire game. It was usually so transparent and weak that after the sex, he was finished with the woman.

Nicola seemed to be impressed by the surroundings. She seemed to be enjoying herself with him but, at the same time, she also seemed bored.

Had she been here before with someone else? Had her rich ex-husband taken her to five-star hotels before? Was this entire scene too blasé? The thoughts gnawed at him as his level of anxiety spiraled upward.

But no, Carlos rejected the notion that she was bored. It was a ridiculous idea. Carlos laughed at his insecure musings. How could she not want him? He had planned the *perfect* evening. Of course she was having a good time. No, Nicola was having a *great* time with him.

Yes, everything was indeed perfect, except for one thing. Carlos totally underestimated the combined effect an entire bottle of champagne and only three hours of sleep in the last two days would have on his body. While waiting for Nicola to come out of the bathroom, he convinced himself that stealing a few moments of REM would be just what the doctor ordered. Poor Carlos. Sleep attacked him like a hungry lion attacks a piece of freshly killed meat.

Nicola prepared for their night together in the luxurious bathroom. It was completely covered with the best Italian marble. The fixtures were all fourteen-carat gold. She languished in the spacious Jacuzzi tub and soaked in water scented with essence of lavender. The hotel had spared no expense to provide only the best bath oils and soap.

She stepped out of the tub and entered the shower stall, where over twenty strategically positioned jets engulfed her in a cool mist of water that immediately reinvigorated her senses. Wanting company, she called out to Carlos to join her in the shower. He never responded.

Nicola emerged from the bathroom covered in a white, thick terrycloth robe and discovered Carlos sprawled out on the bed virtually unresponsive. She tried everything to revive him; took off all of his clothes; even massaged every erotic site on the male body. Nicola knew them all. The only response she got was when she thought she heard him say, "I don't want any ice cream. I don't like ice cream." He was dead to the world.

Staring at Carlos's strikingly handsome face, his six-foot lean muscular body and a limp dick that even non-erect was frightfully huge, she shook her head in disappointment. Pissed and horny as hell, she admitted to herself, *Damn, I should have dumped him for the brother*.

He had tried so hard to impress her with the hotel room. She didn't have the heart to tell the boy that in the first year of their marriage, she and Harrison had virtually lived at the Ritz. Carlos was so full of himself.

She was slowly growing bored with his "mini record mogul" persona. He really needed to score big in the bed if he wanted Nicola to stick around.

She compared him with her ex-husband. Say what she might about him, Harrison never bored her. His entrepreneurial exploits and the life they were able to live because of the fringe benefits associated with wealth, made life exciting for her. The cruelest of ironies was, though she had been thoroughly satisfied with their relationship, Harrison obviously wasn't.

He craved something she could never provide him. Just like Carlos couldn't give her what she so desperately needed at that moment. A good, long, deep screw. Her little G-Spot was throbbing just looking at the lusciousness that lived between Carlos's legs. She smiled. Maybe, just maybe, she'd have to give the boy another chance.

Not wanting to waste a perfectly good night, she decided to get dressed and cruise the neighborhood clubs. There were a few in the area. Maybe she'd get lucky and find a real hunk. She wrote a quick note for Carlos and stepped out into the night. Like a hunter on an African safari, Nicola was out for wild game... the kind that could screw her all night long.

Carlos awoke the next morning with a monster of a headache. He reached out for Nicola only to discover the note she had left behind on the night table: "Sorry we missed our first night together. There will be others. Kisses, Nicola."

Carlos banged his head against the bedpost. "Damn, damn, damn!" How could his body betray him so? What the hell could Nicola possibly be thinking about him now? None of it could be good. He tried to reach her on her cell phone, but she didn't answer.

His only message was from Tarik, reminding him of their early afternoon meeting with Uncle Link, their family's attorney. He'd totally forgotten about the whole affair when he had planned the evening with Nicola. Maybe her "early departure" was a good thing. Quickly chasing away that thought, he entertained the notion of canceling with the guys and stopping by her house.

But business was business. He decided to go forward with the meeting. They were too close to the finish line for him to start acting wishy-washy now. Nicola would have to understand.

But where had she gone in the middle of the night? Why couldn't she have stayed with him and been there in the morning? Where else or who else could have been more important than the two of them being together, even if he was dead sleep? Who was she with? Was she with another man? Was she with someone she cared about more than him? Did she even care about him at all?

The thoughts about Nicola's loyalty made his head throb with pain. It was so intense, he could barely stand it. He called room service and ordered a painkiller. Waiting for the medicine, he felt like his world was spinning around him.

And then the world stopped moving. That's when he heard the voice, a clear voice pleading with him. *She made me do it, Carlos. Your mama. She made me do it. I loved your mama. I never wanted to hurt her. Really, I didn't. Just eat your ice cream, boy. It's your favorite. Eat all of your ice cream.*

The voice was so loud and real that he looked around to see if his father, Hector Salinas, was standing next to him. But Hector was dead. Carlos checked all the rooms in the suite to prove no one was there.

He shook his head and rubbed his eyes. What was happening to him? He hadn't thought about that day since it had happened eighteen years ago. Why could he hear his father's voice as if he was in the room? WHY? It made no sense. No sense at all.

CHAPTER TWENTY-THREE

Ophelia tossed and turned the entire night. She couldn't get her son out of her mind. Tarik had stormed out of her office without a word when she had told him the news. She hadn't seen him that angry and confused since she had first explained to him that Pops was not his biological father. It had taken them both a couple of years to straighten things out after that revelation. Tarik was older now. She was sure his response was pure shock and that he'd calm down.

They had tried to find Eli when the then fifteen years old Tarik had first wanted to meet him. He was naturally curious about him. She'd only told him that he was an artist, and that they were incompatible. So many men abandoned their children that it was unnecessary to fill in details. Most of Tarik's friends were raised by single moms. They usually had very little, if any, contact with their dads. So she fed him the usual dysfunctional couple story. No details. She never told him that Eli was a low down drug addict who had almost killed him because of his negligence.

She also had never told him how she had never loved anyone like she had loved Eli Griffith. Never mentioned that in the first years of their separation, she had prayed he'd clean up his act and rejoin them as a family when he was released from jail. She would have left Pops for him. That was, until Jonathan had come along. When he was born she locked the doors tightly shut on all thoughts of reconciliation.

"I will not think about this shit!" Ophelia shouted out at the night. She pulled herself out of bed, put on her robe and went downstairs to the basement. The stench of beer and wine greeted her nostrils. The party had taken its toll on her usually immaculate space. Surveying the aftermath, she promised, "Tomorrow I will clean this mess, but tonight, I want a little amnesia."

She headed straight for the bar. Not a real drinker, she did sometimes have an occasional glass of sherry whenever her "nerves" got the best of her. This was one of those times. She poured the dark purple fluid into the one clean crystal goblet she could find.

She laughed. Purple. Eli's favorite color. It was that damn purple dress she had worn the night they'd met that had attracted Eli in the first place. She laughed even harder as she remembered how she had battled her roommate over the outfit that night and had won the right to wear it. If she had known all of the crap Eli would eventually bring into her life, she wouldn't have fought as hard.

"Damn the color purple!" she remarked as she drained the glass dry. Still thinking about Eli, she poured more; this time filling it to the brim.

"I need this tonight." As the alcohol took effect, Ophelia slithered onto the plush sectional couch. Slightly inebriated, all she could think about was how it had all began with her and Eli.

She was only a sophomore when they met. Young and beautiful, she had won the homecoming queen title unanimously. Before she knew Eli, her life had been filled with coming-out parties, trips all over the world with her parents, and attendance at a prestigious prep school in her hometown of Nashville, Tennessee.

Eli was a gorgeous, charming, twenty-five-year-old graduate student majoring in art and political science. He'd spent time in Africa running a program for the Peace Corps. Intelligent and articulate, his professors were convinced his art in time would be in the same company as Romare Bearden, Synthia Saint James and Ernie Barnes.

Ophelia was in love with Eli, and he loved and worshipped Ophelia. She was his "Dahomian" queen. They were inseparable after that first meeting. A year into their relationship, she had moved into his small, spartanly furnished apartment off campus. It was a completely different environment from the bourgeois Jack and Jill world her parents, both physicians, had raised her in. Now it was strictly black Bohemian. She was always in the midst of artists, poets, political activists and intellectuals.

When Ophelia's mother, Dr. Victoria Rhodes, visited and discovered how her precious daughter lived, she went on a fierce campaign to destroy Eli and Ophelia's relationship. Her attempts were all in vain. The more she tried to lure her with cars, fancy clothing and trips abroad, the more Ophelia clung to Eli.

At the end of her sophomore year, Ophelia got pregnant with Tarik. Eli begged and pleaded against an abortion. He was convinced it would be a sin to kill God's tribute to their love. Her friends, who thought Eli was a loser with a capital "L," begged her to get rid of both the baby and the baby's daddy. Against Ophelia's better judgment, she sided with Eli, and decided to go ahead with the pregnancy.

Rising up off the couch, feeling toasty and warm, Ophelia raised her empty glass. Tipsy, she spoke to Eli as if he were there. "That's when your fine ass started to drift away, old boy. Couldn't handle the responsibility of being a daddy. And all that…that pot, too. All it did was make you trifling; never finishing shit!"

She found her way to the bar. Emptying the bottle of Harvey's into the glass, she made a toast. "Here's to you, Eli… love of my life…" Carrying the drink with extra care, she went upstairs to her bedroom and sat down in her rocking chair. She rocked herself back down memory lane.

When her parents had discovered that she was pregnant, they'd thought they had leverage. They'd proposed to care for Ophelia during the pregnancy back home in Tennessee until the baby was born. She would then leave the baby behind and finish the last two years at Hampton. When Ophelia tried to integrate Eli into the plan, both parents refused. They thought he was bad news, and felt the time apart would make her see things their way.

Eli, who had finally figured out that he was not the kind of daddy that Ophelia wanted him to be, tried to convince her to take her parents' deal. It was real. He wasn't. He could never give what they could. He wanted to be with Ophelia but since she was with child, he now understood that she needed more than just his loving ways. She needed things. Things a struggling artist couldn't really provide.

She had refused her parents' offer and, instead, she had chosen love.

Ophelia insisted they marry. Eli was not impressed by paper, but since she was his queen, he acquiesced. After a quick no frills ceremony at the courthouse, Mr. and Mrs. Griffith happily moved to Brooklyn, New York, with Eli's favorite relative, Aunt May. Fortunately for them, she had a recently vacated attic apartment. Their plan was that he'd transfer to a New York City school, finish his masters degree and work at nights. She'd work and go to school part-time until the baby came.

Pregnancy changed Ophelia. She became a responsible disciplined woman. Intent on not accepting any help from family, she saved like a miser, knowing that her contribution to the income stream would dry up in the first few months of the baby's life.

Eli maintained his Bohemian ways. He hooked up with the artist community right away. Aunt May was strict, so they couldn't entertain like they had in Virginia. He often partied alone in the city. He never enrolled in school; he didn't see the point. He tried to convince Ophelia that a true artist didn't need paper to confirm his talent. No problem, except Ophelia realized that without the structure of an academic environment, Eli never finished a project. He also didn't like working and couldn't hold down a job. She knew he loved her and the baby that was coming, but just as her mother had predicted, he was useless as a breadwinner.

So, when their beautiful son, Tarik, was born, they agreed to shift roles. He stayed home with the baby while she worked and finished school.

It actually worked well for a whole year. He took better care of the baby than she did and was a better cook and housekeeper as well. Ophelia liked her job and loved coming home to a clean baby and house and whatever new delicious concoction Eli had conjured up in the kitchen. When the baby turned six months,

Eli started painting seriously again. Some of his work was even beginning to sell at the smaller galleries. He was so proud that he could contribute a few coins from the sale of his artwork. He loved his wife and son. Times were happy for both of them then. Their arrangement worked.

The honeymoon ended when her ultra-bourgeois mother took a month away from a busy medical practice to "see the grandbaby." She caused sheer havoc in their household. She criticized everything Eli did or didn't do. She went out of her way to provoke him, hoping to unleash the tyrant she felt lurked deep in his persona. It was futile. There was no ogre hiding within Eli. Just more love. He never showed anger. He always thought it was a waste of creative energy.

This only irritated Ophelia's mother even more, for she interpreted his non-confrontational behavior as additional proof of his weakness. She engaged a vicious campaign to convince Ophelia that there was something very wrong with a wife being the major bread-winner while the husband sat home on his ass doing "nothing but coloring with his crayons," as she referred to Eli's craft.

When the month-long visit was over, Ophelia insisted that Eli go out and get a real job. Reluctantly, he agreed that they needed more money and he had to be the one to bring it in. Aunt May took care of Tarik while Ophelia quit her job and attended nursing school.

Regular work had never agreed with poor, artistic

Eli. He didn't have that kind of discipline. He smoked, drank more, and hung out with his artistic friends. He spent less time with his family and eventually, no time at work. Seeing their paltry savings evaporate, Ophelia had to take on a graveyard shift at nearby Kings County Hospital.

The burden of school, the job, and raising the baby— when she could—grew. Eli was driving her mad. She loved him, but she needed him to be a man; whatever that was. They had awful fights. Or rather she had awful fights. She spent endless hours verbally castrating him, hoping it would shame him into working harder.

He never yelled back. He took it all in and left the house. He wouldn't come back for days. When he did return, he tried to cheer his queen with flowers. Ophelia loved yellow roses. It would soothe the beast within for a bit and she'd forget anger and remember that Eli was the light of her life. They'd make long luxurious passionate love for hours. But somehow, the magic the flowers brought to their relationship always wore off and she'd resume her monologues about his joblessness and worthlessness.

Desperate and frustrated, he could see their love dying. He couldn't pull it together and do what she wanted him to do: conform to the regular world. He wanted it to be like it was before her mother had visited and destroyed their peace. But it wasn't ever to happen like that for them again.

In a desperate attempt to please Ophelia the only way he knew how, he started an abstract painting of a bowl of yellow roses. She fell in love with the piece as he worked on it a little each day. Ophelia was convinced it would be a masterpiece as it represented his best work. She prayed that it would reinvigorate his passion for art and their lives together. She was confident that times would be good again.

At work, she had grown quite attached to an infant whose psychotic mother had brutally abused her at birth. Ophelia was part of the team that had revived the little girl in the emergency room. She immediately bonded with the baby and never missed an opportunity to visit with her during three months of repeated grueling and painful surgeries. The operations repaired the damage caused when the insane mother shoved an object down the infant's throat.

Ophelia even brought Eli around to visit on several occasions. The little girl with the almost hypnotic, sparkling brown eyes, whose life had started in such a tragic twisted way, had captured both of their hearts.

So when Eli started the yellow roses painting, Ophelia was convinced things were turning the corner for them and they could become the little girl's foster family. They had applied and sailed through the interviews with flying colors. On the day she had received word that they had been accepted, she had almost skipped the entire way home. She was happy she had ignored her mother's warning about not marrying Eli. Though they were probably never going to know the kind of wealth she had grown up in, there would always be more than enough love for her, Eli, Tarik, the new baby girl and whoever else joined their brood in the future. The thought of having or adopting more children had made her smile widen. Growing up as an only child, Ophelia had always wanted a big family.

On that same day, as luck would have it, while Ophelia celebrated her good news...Eli was hosting a celebration of his own. While caring for Tarik, some of his artist friends had stopped by to see the new work he was always bragging about. One of his buddies had brought some drugs and the party got started. He was so happy that his friends had agreed that it was his best work, that he had done the one thing that he swore he would never do: get high around Tarik. A little bit of grass had led to a tab of acid, a line of coke and whatever else his friends had in their portable pharmacies. It didn't take long for Eli to totally forget that Tarik was unattended.

Eli and his friends were completely stoned when the toddler woke up from his nap and crawled off the day-bed that Eli, in his negligence, had let him sleep on. Walking freely around without supervision, Tarik sampled the loose drugs that were all within his reach.

Eli, totally out of it, had seen Tarik stumble around the living room. He'd laughed out loud at his son's clumsiness as he kept falling down. He'd picked Tarik up, put him into the crib, and resumed his drug taking. He'd never checked on his son again.

Two hours after the party had been in full swing, Ophelia walked up the stairs to their apartment. The stench of marijuana greeted her so strongly, she almost got a contact high. A cold chill went through her. As she grabbed the knob, she hesitated…because Ophelia knew what was waiting for her on the other side of that door.

Entering, she heard an old scratched-up Isaac Hayes record, "By the Time I Get to Phoenix," skip over and over again. Cocaine, acid and weed were all over the coffee table. Eli and three of his buddies were in a drug-induced slumber. Almost paralyzed, afraid of what she was looking at, she rushed into Tarik's room. Her baby. Her beautiful baby boy. She screamed for what seemed like hours, when she found her beloved son in a coma. Dialing 9-1-1, her fingers moved around the keypad as if they were attached to lead weights.

Disoriented, Eli could not comprehend why police and paramedics were in his house. As far as he was concerned, Tarik was just taking a little nap. It didn't take authorities long to figure out what had happened. There were drugs in full sight when they entered the apartment. The police arrested both Eli and Ophelia for possession of narcotics and child endangerment.

Paramedics rushed Tarik to the hospital where a team of doctors and nurses successfully resuscitated him. After a short stay, he made a complete recovery.

Ophelia's parents took Tarik home when they discharged him from the hospital. They retained a crackerjack attorney that got their daughter out of jail and successfully cleared her of all charges. Eli's confession of guilt made it easy for the lawyer to convince the prosecution that Ophelia was innocent. He and his cronies were sentenced to a maximum of five years in jail.

She never forgave Eli for the hell he put her through, and he never forgave himself. He signed divorce papers, and it was over. Ophelia went on with life—without Eli. All the dreams they shared were flushed down the toilet. The same toilet the drugs should have gone in the first place. They would never be foster parents to the beautiful little infant girl she and Eli had grown so attached to. Fortunately, a family from upstate New York adopted the baby.

When the young, now divorced woman returned from the lawyer's office, the first thing she saw when she rummaged through closets, trying to discard all traces of Eli's existence, was the yellow rose painting. She couldn't throw it away. As much as she wanted to break free of their relationship by eliminating all reminders of him, she didn't have the heart to let go of his artwork. It captured what had been really good about Eli: beautiful-looking; a generous, vulnerable soul, but totally lacking discipline. Hence, it being unfinished.

So she had framed it and had always carried it everywhere she had moved.

Six months after the divorce was final, she met a man twenty years her senior. A good old soul, Richard Singleton. He was an architect who owned a very successful firm. Tarik was crazy about him. Pops, as she always called him, was crazy about the both of them. He intuitively knew she'd never love him as much as he loved her, but he was confident that he had enough love for the both of them. They married and like Pops predicted, they lived happily together.

Pops adopted Tarik. On the day Eli signed the papers surrendering parental rights, he tried to hang himself in jail. A guard found him just in time. His first thought when he was revived was disappointment that he couldn't even handle a simple suicide, let alone something complicated like fatherhood.

Ophelia and her new husband bought a brownstone in the Stuyvesant Heights section of Brooklyn. Pops turned the house into a showcase. It was always the highlight of the annual brownstone tour. He was proud of his handiwork and the supportive wife he'd found in Ophelia.

On Tarik's seventh birthday, Eli had been free and out of jail a few years when Ophelia finally allowed him to see their son. Against her better judgment, she let the ex-con attend the birthday party. Crippling anxiety visited with him the day of the event. He took a little hit of this and a little swig of that to give him the courage to make it through. He arrived disheveled and slightly inebriated.

When he first laid eyes on his son, Eli forced himself to sober up. Big crocodile tears tumbled out of his eyes when he realized how magnificent his boy was and how stupidity had kept him away. He wanted to hug him like he did when he was small. He reached out at him. Tarik could smell the liquor on him and immediately recoiled and yelled out, "Mama, a wino tried to touch me, MAMA!"

Ophelia rushed to his side and saw Eli. She hadn't seen him in five years. Her heart ached when their eyes met. He brought yellow roses for her. She took them. She then could see that he had been drinking.

Tarik, protective as always, stood between Eli and Ophelia. "Mama, keep away from the old smelly wino."

"Tarik, calm down, baby…this is Eli, Eli Griffith… your…your…"

Eli, now completely sober, butted in. "I'm an old… old friend of your mother. She told me about your birthday…thought I'd come. Happy Birthday, Tarik." He extended his hand.

Tarik rejected it. He did not understand how this bum could be one of his mama's friends. He decided to try the polite route. "Nice to meet you, Mr. Griface."

"That's Griffith, Tarik."

Eli interceded by stating, "Ophelia, it's close enough. In fact, he pronounces it better than most."

Tarik looked at the bum and back at his mama. Something was funny about them being together. He thought on it for a second. The kids at the party called out for him to join them. He decided that the bum wouldn't hurt his mama, and, if he tried, well, he wasn't too far away. He could still protect her. He still wished Pops had been there. He would pick this time to be late. Tarik ran off to join the kids.

"He's beautiful, Ophelia; just like you."

Ophelia beamed with pride as they looked after Tarik. Refocusing on Eli, her face registered cold disgust. "He does not know about you. We thought it was easier this way. And now, well, I can tell you've been drinking, or that you're high on something. What is wrong with you? No show for six years and this is how you come? Like a bum!" Shouting now, she added, "Don't... don't come again...don't ever call me...or Tarik again! You are dead to us...you understand...DEAD!"

Ophelia turned and stormed away. That was the last time she had seen Eli.

Revisiting her life with Eli was like watching a gothic ghetto soap opera. But with all the bad thoughts, good memories of Eli and the love they once shared still found an opportunity to resurface. She had realized for a long time that if her mom hadn't interfered and created conflict in their home, they probably would have done all right together.

And wouldn't you know it, Mr. Moms were all very

acceptable these days. But back then a man had to work outside the home and bring in the bacon. She didn't lament too long. Life hadn't turned out too bad for her after all. Pops was gone now, but they had lived a good life together when he was alive. No complaints…no real regrets.

But she had to get something right. It meant seeing Eli one more time. She got off her rocking chair, went down to the kitchen, and boiled up some chicken soup to take to him. And then she remembered how he always liked egg salad sandwiches. She made him those, too.

$\mathcal{C}$HAPTER TWENTY-FOUR

$\mathcal{E}$li woke up that morning happy but much weaker than the day before. Each day he seemed to wake up with less and less energy, like he was melting away. He took a birdbath and changed into clean clothes. He was tired, but still glowing from the concert. He even hummed some of Tarik's tunes. He giggled at his sick self.

A knock on the door brought him off the "concert stage." Who could that be? Meals on Wheels wasn't due until tomorrow. They had left double amounts yesterday. He was still strong enough to use the microwave and make simple meals. But he knew that soon would pass. He figured he'd have to go to the hospice in two months. Probably less. Definitely not more.

He opened the door and almost had a stroke. It was Ophelia. She carried a pot and just ignored him, and pushed her way through the door. "Where's your kitchen, Eli?"

Speechless, Eli pointed to his small kitchen.

They had a good "brunch," as Ophelia called it. She cleaned the pots, pans, dishes, and straightened up. "Ophelia, please you don't have to do that, plus you're not doing a good job!" They both laughed. It was their private joke back in the day. Ophelia didn't have a clue how things worked in a kitchen. Eli outshone her in every way. She didn't have the heart to tell him that she was now considered a domestic goddess.

"So, does he know about me?"

"Tarik? Oh, yes. Pops and I told him when he was thirteen."

"How did he take it?"

"Not well. Called us liars and went on a rampage for two years that found his little butt in a juvenile detention center for six months."

Eli was distressed at this news. He felt responsible. Ophelia added, "But he came out a changed young man. Never had any trouble from him. He even wanted to meet with you. But we couldn't find you..."

"I've wasted so many years; so many." The tone of their meeting had turned too gloomy for Ophelia. Wanting to pep things up, she asked, "Do you have any idea why I came by today?"

"I'd thought you just wanted to show off your chicken soup, maybe?"

She laughed. She got up and looked for her pocketbook.

"You leaving, Ophelia?"

"No. I left something in the car." She rushed out the door and returned a few minutes later, carrying something behind her back. "There's a project you started, and I think it only right that you…" She pulled the yellow rose painting out for Eli to see. "Finish it!"

Seeing the original painting for the first time in years, Eli laughed through tears. He raised his bony body off the leather recliner, and pulled out an updated version of the same painting.

That made Ophelia chuckle. In fact, the two laughed and talked for the remainder of the afternoon.

"What happened to you, Eli? I never heard from you after that scene at Tarik's birthday party."

"That day was a huge turning point in my life; one of the biggest."

"If you don't want to talk about it"

"No, no. I want to go down memory lane with you. You see, that night after Tarik's party, I was in such unbelievable pain. It was the kind of pain substance abusers like me can't handle. I went to a party with my buddies. Begged them to hook me up with some shit that would take a man's mind off everything. And oh boy, did they ever hook me up."

Eli paused as he reflected back to that fateful evening a long time ago. "That night I replaced you with a new mistress; heroin. And she was one demanding, cruel bitch. I stole for her. She pimped me out, Ophelia, stabbed me in the back, and gave me this AIDS. And..." Eli paused to catch his breath.

Thinking he was in trouble, Ophelia rushed to his side. He held up a trembling, bony hand to signal that he was okay. Ophelia hesitantly moved back to her seat. It was obvious to her that revealing his story was taking a toll on him.

She had counseled and held the hands of many AIDS sufferers over the last twenty years. But it was different watching Eli suffer, a man she once loved, and seeing him in such a weakened state. Ophelia couldn't handle her own grief any more and tried to stop him. "Eli, this might be what the kids call *too much information. T-M-I*. We can talk about this some other..."

"NO! I want to tell you NOW! I need to tell you that if I had taken care of my responsibilities the way I took care of that monkey on my back, you and me would be celebrating our thirtieth wedding anniversary. And that ain't no lie; no lie at all. Because, Ophelia, I... I..."

He looked away from her. The pain of the truth was cutting him deep, but he had to tell her. "Ophelia, I never really stopped loving you. Not for one day; not for one hour; not for one second."

CHAPTER TWENTY-FIVE

The voices stopped. As mysteriously as they appeared, they disappeared. Like they never ever happened. Carlos relaxed. He blamed the strange scene in the hotel on the hangover and lack of sleep. He vowed to slow way down on alcohol consumption. In fact, he stopped cold turkey…no beer… no wine…simple tap water did just fine. He never wanted to experience the "voices" again. He never wanted to think about what happened the day his father killed his mother.

All he wanted to do was embrace the good feelings he had about the negotiations with Jeff Moses and the other executives at Mo-Sound records. The meetings moved forward without a hitch. Carlos worked overtime that week with Tarik and their attorney and family friend, Uncle "Link" Powell. They made sure Tarik's debut ran smoothly. Mo-Sound agreed to distribute Infinity's CD, *Introducing: Tarik* and to pick up the bill for the international publicity tour. After that they just had to wait until the entire world fell in love with Tarik's unique sound.

He hadn't seen Nicola since the fiasco in the hotel. The few times he could reach her by phone, they never really discussed their last encounter. She brushed it off as an innocent occurrence and swore up and down it would make their first lovemaking session all the sweeter. His ego and pride couldn't buy that. He wanted to make it up to her.

Waiting for Nicola made him hornier than he'd been all his young life. He masturbated; something he hadn't done since he got out of junior high school. There were always nasty girls around who took care of business for him. The thought of cheating on Nicola never entered his mind. She had changed him. He was a faithful man.

On Friday evening, after they sent the contract back to the company, with all of their amendments, Nicola was the first one that he called.

"Hey, beautiful. Good news! The contract is all but signed!"

"Hi, Carlos. I'm real happy for you. Look, I'm a little busy and…"

"Hey, how's 'bout I slide on up to Harlem and we can finish what we tried to start the other evening. I can be there in…"

Nicola looked down between her legs at Miles, the red-headed midget. His head bobbed up and down as he tongue-whipped her clit. His younger, fraternal twin brothers, Tony and Ernie, also vertically challenged, each held a breast in their mouth as they performed phenomenal sucking maneuvers on her engorged and responsive nipples.

"Uh…uh…ruh…Carlos…I'm a little busy, baby. I'm not even in the city. I'm at my beach house in the Hamptons. Wait a second." She muted the phone to give out "instructions." "Ernie…now, baby…that's too hard…little easier…my left tit is just a wee bit more sensitive than my right…"

The handsome, chocolate-colored, four-foot-five dwarf, who looked divine with his platinum-colored locks, looked at her with brown, twinkling eyes, winked, and said in a deep, Barry White voice, "Sorry, sweetness."

He obeyed her command and resumed suckling her breast; just the way she ordered.

"That's it. Good, Ernie." She looked down on her right side at his mirror image, Tony. At twenty-three years old, and two minutes younger than Ernie…he was the baby of the group. He also had the biggest surprise between his legs…a nine-inch dick! A tool that size on a small man felt much bigger up close. And the little sucker knew how to work it, too!

Wanting to give him all the encouragement that he deserved, she patted his head and said, "Tony, superb job, baby." In response he flitted his tongue back and forth across her nipple. It was the nicest sensation. She growled, "OOOOH...Tony, BABY, that feels good... all of you...OOOOOWOOO!"

Her body writhed in response to the simultaneous action. Who knew a trip to the All-Soul Circus the previous evening would prove so profitable or that three little men could satisfy her so well? They had licked, screwed and taken turns fucking her body all day long.

Oh damn...I forgot about Carlos. "Carlos? Carlos, you still there? Oh good! Look, why don't we hook up tomorrow evening."

Miles, who looked like a light-brown leprechaun with a red mustache and beard to match, lifted his head. The most aggressive member of the trio, he was obviously pissed that she was on the phone and whispered loudly, "Nicola, what's up? Are we gonna do this or what?"

She blew him a kiss. Not liking her inattentiveness one bit, Miles shook his head, but remembering how she had generously sucked his little wee-wee bone dry earlier that afternoon, he gratefully resumed his position between her legs.

"I hear people. Nicola, is someone there with you?"

"Of course, there is, Carlos. I... uh... have a *little* crowd of folks over. We're having a circus of a good time here." All three of the brothers looked up with a big smile on their faces and gave Nicola a thumbs-up sign of agreement.

She smiled back at them and whispered into the phone,

"Look, Carlos. I'm back in the city tomorrow afternoon. Stop by in the evening and we'll stay together as long as you like. Okay? See you then. Bye, baby."

Nicola turned off the phone. She didn't want any more interruptions. "I'm all yours now; let's get this party rolling!"

Lying back on her California King-sized bed and facing a glorious view of the Atlantic Ocean, Nicola primed herself for an explosive orgasm. The Williams Brothers, famous for their juggling act, had worked tirelessly to please her.

She tightly held on to Tony and Ernie. They sucked her breasts as she had advised. Miles spread her legs wide open and put his fingers inside her pleasure vault. Plunging them in and out, like a jackhammer on hot concrete, he stimulated her G-spot.

Just when Nicola thought she couldn't feel any better "down there," his wet muscular tongue returned to duty and whipped her clit backwards and forwards. Miles knew only one speed, the right one, the one that sent her hurling down a path that would surely lead to an enormous release.

Feeling "it" only nano-seconds away, her body tensed up tighter than a drum. Nicola commanded the Williams brothers, "Okay, guys…bring me home…you know the way. OOO-WAH- SHAY! OOO-WAH-SHAY…. THANK GOD FOR THE LITTLE PEOPLE…OH SHIT!!!"

The Hamptons? What the hell was she doing there? Carlos wanted to ride out there and surprise her, but he didn't know where. He had tried to get all of her addresses the other day on the phone, but she had refused to give him the information.

He called back to see if she would let him slide by there tonight. The call went straight to her voicemail. He tried several times that night. No luck.

He felt rejected that she was not willing to make space for him that night. Wasn't she as eager as he was to get things moving in a more intimate direction? Hadn't she dreamt of him every night since they'd met?

The green-eyed monster visited him for the first time in his life. With each postponement or rejection from Nicola, seeds of doubt were planted in his mind. Was she out there with another man? Was she fucking someone else? Was that really the reason he had so much difficulty catching up with her? He could feel an unfamiliar rage boiling in his vessels.

He convinced himself that, of course, she had the same strong feelings for him as he had for her. She was a master at keeping that mystique thing going hot and passionate in a relationship. She wasn't like the young girls he was usually with that were willing to give away all the family jewels in the first twenty-four hours.

Nicola was more about savoring the moment. Tomorrow night would be even better. Just in case, he tried to get all the sleep he could get. No more repeats of their last time together. But more than anything else he did not want those voices to revisit him. And he especially didn't want them popping up when he was at Nicola's.

Carlos was terrified that the memory of Hector Salinas and what he had done to his dear sweet mother would "haunt" him again. Desperate, he turned to the Lord. He got out of bed, got on his knees and prayed: *No more voices. Please, God, NO MORE VOICES…PLEASE!*

CHAPTER TWENTY-SIX

*N*icola waved at the Williams Brothers as they boarded the six a.m. train. Almost missing their connection at Penn Station, the trio planned to hook up with the circus in Philadelphia.

They all had a ball riding in Nicola's salmon-pink Mercedes convertible with the top down. She let Miles, the oldest, drive. He swore he was a demon on wheels… and he proved it by driving all the way from the Hamptons at speeds averaging over ninety miles per hour. How they had managed to dodge the highway patrol, Nicola never knew.

The guys promised to visit her next year. Nicola could sincerely say that she couldn't wait until the circus came back into town.

Walking toward her car, she pulled out a card that Tony and Ernie had given her. The twins, behind Miles' back, moonlighted at very risqué clubs that catered to sexual fetishes. The two were popular on the S&M circuit. They encouraged her to visit Dido's Retreat, the top club in New York City. Never a fan of violence, she almost tossed the card but instead stuffed it in her pocketbook. *Who knows? One day I might get bored and change my mind.*

Smiling all the way to her home in Hamilton Heights, she thought about her schedule for the day. The music mogul, as she had dubbed Carlos, was coming over that evening. She chuckled to herself as she pulled into a parking spot right in front of her house and entered her brownstone. Carlos was so smitten with her that she felt guilty. She had kept him on hold all week long for a reason. She had other prey out there that needed her tender, loving care.

She did a mental count of the men she'd had sex with since she left Harrison three months ago. The math was simple. The Williams Brothers brought the count up to forty-two. She couldn't control her sexual appetite. Nor did she want to.

Like the chick in Spike's movie, *she had to have it*. And she had to have it with numerous people. One man could not satisfy her. Every day since she caught Harrison in the act of betrayal, she'd had sex with as many men as she could find. Her lust was insatiable. The G-shots didn't help.

This morning was one of those rare times when she wanted to stay at home alone. Entering the living room, she walked over to the liquor cabinet, poured herself a glass of Courvoisier, and downed it like water. Still not as toasted as she needed to be, she thought about the thickly rolled marijuana blunts her generous Jamaican Rastafarian lover had left for her the other day. He had tried to coach her on how to smoke and get the maximum effect. All she had done was cough.

Before their love session ended, he had advised her, "Me 'tink it take a woman longer...keep trying...just relax...be happy."

She'd never dabbled in drugs before, but her new hedonistic lifestyle had few rules for behavior. Nicola reached into the hidden drawer of her Egyptian obelisk and pulled three blunts from the generous pile her lover had left behind. Determined to get the "high" she had heard so much about...she smoked all three before she realized that her thinking was different.

A marijuana-inspired wave of peace floated throughout her body relaxing her completely. Collapsing back onto her chaise lounge, she slurred out, "So this is what it's all about..." She felt a mellowness she'd never known before.

And then out of nowhere...like hurricane gale force winds...bad thoughts about her past swept into her conscious mind and blew her high away. The marijuana fooled her with its initial sweetness. It lulled her into letting go of the pathologically tight control she had on her memory. All the crap from her past overwhelmed her mental defenses. She was on a trip down memory lane; a trip the dope and liquor would not let her escape.

What started out as a friendly morning with the three nicest little men she'd ever met had abruptly evolved into an emotional tornado. Nicola flung open the mahogany French doors that led out to her patio. With absolutely no concern of what the neighbors might see or say, she tore off all her clothes, jumped into the Jacuzzi, and prayed the hot, bubbling water would calm her down. She switched on the spa's music system and turned the volume up loud, hoping her preprogrammed array of soft mellow jazz would chill her out.

Twenty minutes later, nothing had changed in her mind. She got out of the Jacuzzi, grabbed one of the thick terrycloth robes that were stored in her cabana and threw it on. Needing to escape, she wished she hadn't left her home out in the Hamptons. Out there she could walk along the endless stretch of beach, and shake off the eight-hundred pounds of memories that were holding her down. Trapped in the city, too high to drive anywhere, she went back into the house.

Pacing back and forth in her living room, she desperately tried to shut out the thoughts about the abuses that she had experienced as a child. As quickly as those images held her captive, visions of Harrison's betrayal would compete for space in her mind.

She could literally see the scene of him and that monster Sebastian screwing in front of the fireplace. She hadn't gone into the den since that day. It was as if it was the scene of a murder. And it was. The victim: her five-year marriage to Harrison.

Nicola was miserable. She could not stop the thoughts. They were coming down on her like a monsoon rain in the tropics. She felt like she was locked in a movie theater…and forced to watch the film about her fucked-up life. Feeling out of control Nicola swore to herself: *It's this damn dope! I'll never touch another joint as long as I live. If it's making me lose control of my mind, I want no part of it.*

A phone call interrupted Nicola's parade of mental horror. It was Carlos,

"Morning, beautiful. Miss me?"

Nicola rolled her glazed over eyes. Carlos was becoming a nuisance. She lied and said, "I was just sitting here thinking of you, baby doll."

"Why don't I come by now, instead of later, and we can think about each other together?" pleaded Carlos.

"As scrumptious as that sounds, I'll have to say no again. Just like I said last night, later this evening is the best time for me." She added, as sarcastically as she could, "Seems like somebody needs to take a hint."

On the other end, Carlos experienced rejection for the first time in his life. It hurt like a knife was cutting through his spine. Trying to re-group, he summoned a smidgen of self-respect and said, "OUCH. Oh, she bites…damn hard, too, baby. Easy. I got an ego to stroke here."

Realizing how fragile Carlos was, and not wanting to dismiss him before sampling his gorgeous super-sized treats, she tenderly purred, "It's more than just your ego that needs stroking, *mon ami*, but, baby, not right now. Let's keep it for this evening. It'll be good and sloppy wet for you then. Okay? Ciao now."

Nicola hung up. *He better be a good screw, for all the trouble he's causing*, she thought. She was happy about one thing. His call did calm her mind down. She was still a little tipsy and insanely tired after drinking and smoking so early in the morning. Nicola dragged her body upstairs to her master bedroom.

For the umpteenth time, she bumped against the pole that she had used on so many occasions to entertain Harrison. Rubbing her head, she remembered her contractor was finally coming by next week to remove it. She kicked the pole anyway and yelled at it, "Shit! What a waste of time; twirling my body up and down a goddamn pole for a motherfuckin' faggot!" Pissed at herself and too high to undress, she fell out on the beautiful satin comforter and collapsed into a deep sleep.

When she awoke three hours later, it was eleven in the morning. She felt normal. The marijuana had worn off. She was herself again. In control. The only thing that concerned her was her healthy drive to have sex with as many men as possible. It was all she cared about. Sex helped her to totally absorb herself in the present moment and block out hateful memories.

Nicola decided Carlos's evening visit would not be enough to quench her thirst. She needed an "appetizer."

She thought about the young basketball player. Nicola had plans for Jonathan. The thought of deflowering a virgin was overwhelming. Thinking about him helped clear her head. She could feel an itch surface that only he could scratch. It was time for the young man to enter the kingdom of lust. Nicola would be his personal escort.

She dialed his cell phone number. The last few days he'd stopped answering her. She was determined that today was his initiation. He would get a full dose of Nicola. She left an obviously seductive message.

Using her raspiest, sexiest voice, she purred, "Listen, Jonathan. I'm throwing Carlos a surprise party, and I want you to help me plan it. I don't know his friends or anything like that. Come by my place, you remember where, at one o'clock. I'll be waiting for you. Ciao, baby."

She never doubted that he'd show. The boy was so hot, horny, and ready for picking, he'd probably come three or four times before he arrived.

But what about Carlos?

Nicola paused for a second. After the Williams Brothers, she was all for family affairs. She was sure the youngster could handle it. Carlos was too love-struck to deal with the "situation." She hesitated and thought about the potential dilemma, the conflict of interest, but also the double delicious, lustful day she'd have fucking both of their brains out. Back to back. And if Carlos discovered her tryst with little Jonathan, well,

Carlos was always telling her that he loved keeping shit in the family.

He might not have meant it quite this way, but that was for them to figure out. As Nicola saw it, her only responsibility was to encourage the young basketball star to leave at a decent hour. If he didn't and Carlos walked in, well, thought Nicola: *As the French always say, Fuck 'em if they can't take a joke.*

With that thought, Nicola laughed out loud, as she prepared her boudoir for a full day of lust.

CHAPTER TWENTY-SEVEN

Sweat poured from Jonathan's temples as he approached the end of his treadmill session. He thought about his mother's jammin', state-of-the-art equipment in her basement, and laughed. He had traveled two hours on the subway to do what he could have done when he first rolled out the bed this morning. But he wanted to be here in Harlem. He wanted to be near Nicola.

A buzzing vibration in his jogging pants pocket signaled that he had a call. He pulled his cell phone out and discovered it was Nicola. What could she possibly want? He didn't answer. Every cell in his eighteen-year-old virgin rod wanted him to pick up the call. He'd successfully dodged her the last few days, and she'd called him at least three times a day. Afraid what the messages might say or rather, lead to, he'd never listened to them.

But today he could not resist temptation. He listened. Sur-prisingly, her message was very innocent. He was almost ashamed of himself for not answering her calls. A surprise party for Carlos. Maybe she wasn't after him sexually after all. She may just be a friendly woman, who performed blow jobs on all her boyfriends' brothers. Anything more than that was strictly forbidden.

That last thought thoroughly depressed him. He wanted more. He'd settle for more of the same if necessary. But he quickly erased those sentiments. No, Nicola was a straight shooter. If she said she just wanted help with the party, that's all she wanted. There would be no repeat of last Saturday's events.

The past week after the concert, Jonathan had felt like a zombie in heat. His performance at practice bordered on horrible. One of the coaches pulled him aside and gave him a serious, "step up your game or step to the curb" speech. Not wanting to screw up his opportunity, he'd immediately snapped out of his "I finally had my first blow job and I want some more of the same" funk.

Every time he pissed, just the sight of his own organ made images of Nicola's mouth around its shaft resurface. He got erections that made his trips to the bathroom last longer than he'd planned. He hid in the stall and had to release himself. It was the only way he could finish basketball practice. At home, he emptied three jars of Vaseline.

It was noon. He had to hurry. Her message said to be there at one o'clock. Lateness was not an option. He threw his phone into his gym bag and in Superman-speed fashion, prepared for his meeting with Nicola. Applying deodorant and cologne almost too generously, Jonathan was extremely thankful that his high school coach had always advised his players to keep a well-stocked gym bag whenever they were on a road trip. Now he understood why. Jonathan could tell it was for those times you might get lucky with a girl.

He changed into a casual, cream-colored outfit he had purchased in one of the small African American-owned boutiques on Fulton Street in the Fort Green section of Brooklyn. Slipping on a pair of leather sandals, a quick glance at a mirror confirmed that he'd put everything on in an appropriate fashion. Jonathan couldn't help but smile. Even he thought he looked good.

He had totally forgotten he had a quarterly meeting with the New York chapter of Teens for Abstinence. As their vice president, it was his job to run the meeting and to stress the importance of their organization's mission statement: It was okay to remain a virgin and wait for marriage.

Confused about his loyalties and responsibilities, Jonathan did not know what to do. He had vowed to stay away from Nicola. The last time with her was supposed to be the last time. Jonathan even had a legitimate reason to ignore her request. His group needed him.

And then it happened. Nicola's face flashed through his mind and he could literally feel her tongue licking his shaft up and down. Never giving the needs of the organization a second thought, Jonathan text messaged the club secretary to let her know he was unable to attend the meeting. Proceed without him. There was no way he could turn down another visit with Nicola. The group was on their own.

Not wanting to carry any extra gear, the basketball star threw his gym bag into a locker. He slammed the door shut, making sure the padlock was secure. He rushed out of the gym, forgetting that his cell phone was inside the bag.

Twenty minutes later, Jonathan's long legs led him through Nicola's front gate. She opened the door on the second ring, wearing an outfit so revealing and seductive that he almost ran all the way back home. He could not handle being alone in the same room with this woman; not when she had chosen to wear a revealing halter top and Daisy Duke shorts that exposed half her ass.

Captured by her erotic spell, Jonathan followed Nicola into her home. He parked any thoughts of resisting her seduction or remaining loyal to Carlos at her front door. He walked in a willing and eager beneficiary of whatever mischief Nicola had planned for him.

CHAPTER TWENTY-EIGHT

Ophelia shot a quick look at the clock. She was late for her visit with Eli. Quickly rummaging through her refrigerator, she pulled out veggies for soup. Even though he only tolerated small sips of the liquid high-calorie shakes his doctors prescribed for him, she was still going to prepare a nice Saturday brunch for them.

Ophelia had visited Eli almost every day that week. She knew there was no fear she'd do something stupid like fall for him again nor did she intend to become his personal nursemaid. After all, he sure didn't take care of Tarik or her when he had his health.

If anything, he'd tried his best to put them through hell and back. Ophelia didn't owe Eli Griffith shit. Thinking about Eli's ugly past made her blood curdle. She almost picked up the phone to cancel the whole day with him.

Instead, she reminded herself that she was a trained nurse; the head of an AIDS nursing program. Every day she and her staff helped countless of clients who were strangers. Regardless of their social history, she made sure they received the best of care. Why should she deny Eli? She was not giving him special attention. She often went into the field to help a patient. It helped break the monotony of the administrative aspect of her job.

As she primped in front of the mirror, preparing to visit Eli, taking more care than usual with her appearance, the truth stared back at her. She had to admit that she'd never been happier. Spending time with Eli had been just what she needed to lift her spirits. She never regretted it. Without the drugs and without a future ahead, the two squeezed the most they could out of the present they now shared. She so enjoyed their visits that she was almost oblivious to the devastating toll his illness was taking on him.

Today she had another reason to visit with Eli. She had had a disturbing dream about Jonathan. She needed to get his advice about what to do. She respected his opinion. For all his years of living at the edge of hell, wisdom had finally rewarded him with a unique perspective about the human condition. Unfortunately, it came too late to save him from the ravages of drug addiction or the AIDS that now drained the life out of him.

It was a gorgeous sunny day to visit the Botanical Gardens in Brooklyn. Ophelia convinced Eli that it would be no trouble to pack his wheelchair in her car and drive out there. Eli was happy that he'd agreed to the plan. There was so much beauty there. The orchids were in full bloom. Each one more beautiful and more exotic than the next. Too weak to walk on his own, Ophelia pushed his wheelchair as they viewed the different themed gardens.

When they stopped under the fragrant magnolia trees to have lunch, Ophelia complained about the ominous feelings she was harboring.

"I don't know what to tell the boy; these are the times I wish Pops was still around." Upset about Jonathan, she got up from the bench and paced back and forth.

"Tell Jonathan the truth. Tell him to stay away from the woman. From what you tell me, he's a bright boy. He'll figure it out."

Eli looked at Ophelia as if he was watching a dream. He could never have hoped to be this near to her. He never thought she would be talking to him; sharing her problems with him. In the last week, she'd met with him every day. She'd brought him soup or whatever little doo-dad she thought would cheer him up.

Eli celebrated the peace they shared. He could tell her anything…and did. In turn, she'd literally dumped every detail of her life since they parted on his shoulders. It was wonderful. It was sheer bliss. Feeling blessed,

Eli knew he would spend an eternity praising the Lord. The only thing he yearned for, but dared not ask for, was a meeting with Tarik.

"Why don't you just calm down, Ofee-poo."

Ophelia stopped pacing and playfully shook her finger in Eli's face. "Nobody has called me Ofee-poo in decades, and don't you go starting that back up. I don't even want Tarik to hear that. He'll never let me live it down." She realized she had gone too far. She had forgotten that Eli was the last person Tarik wanted to see. She did not want him to have false hopes.

But that didn't bother Eli. He just laughed at her. Ophelia looked at him. The disease had literally wasted away all his facial muscles. Every day there seemed to be less and less of him to see. He was evaporating right in front of her. It depressed her so much that she stopped looking at his bony frame and just stared into his warm eyes. They still had so much life in them.

"Anyway, Ofee-poo, call him up and speak to him. Call him right now, if you feel it's that urgent, or wait 'til this evening. Whatever you do, don't worry yourself to death."

Ophelia had to agree with him. Anxiety was eating her inside out. But she couldn't help it. She had awakened that morning with a maternal sick-feeling-in-the-gut sensation, and she knew it had to do with Jonathan and that Nicola person. It was so hard for her to talk to him. Since he had joined that abstinence group, she felt there was no need to counsel him about safe sex. He had already figured it all out, as far as she was concerned.

But around Nicola? That she-witch? A woman with a twisted sense of values? She could still see how Nicola had shamelessly poured herself all over Jonathan's private parts at the concert. Originally, she thought it was her eyes playing tricks on her. But when she caught Nicola on the bed with Tarik at the after-party, she knew what the bitch was capable of.

Nicola was indeed a beautiful temptress. Of that, there was no doubt. Her baby's morals and ethics were undergoing a challenge and temptation that few young men could resist.

Eli was right. She was going to talk to him now, or at least schedule a time when they both could calmly discuss, "the birds, the bees and nasty women like Nicola." She pulled her cell phone out of her bag and called. There was no response. It disturbed her, that she couldn't reach him. She left a message. That sick feeling in the bottom of her stomach got just a little stronger.

"Eli, I can't reach him. What am I going to do?"

"Ophelia, baby, he's okay. Don't worry; the vice president of Teens for… What were they advocating again?"

"Abstinence; my boy believes in it."

"Like I said, Jonathan's a pretty strong cat and he can handle himself. Now, let's go see those begonias."

Pushing his wheelchair through the gardens, she

thought about his advice and realized that old shriveled-up Eli had a damn good point. Jonathan was a good kid. He had a pure heart. In a month, her baby was going away to college. He had turned eighteen a few months ago. He was a man now. She didn't have to worry about him and women.

Regardless of all his shining qualities, or the fact that he was no longer her little boy, Ophelia knew she would have the talk with him that evening; even if she had to track him down all over New York City.

CHAPTER TWENTY-NINE

"Come on in, Jonathan." As if sensing his disapproval, she added, "Excuse this outfit, but central air-conditioning is not quite up to par today, and well, I get easily overheated."

She shot a sultry glance in Jonathan's direction, to see if the effect of her outfit and attitude had any impact. The beads of sweat beginning to form over his brow were all the confirmation she needed.

Jonathan also felt the heat. But, it wasn't because of a faulty cooling system. Nicola escorted him upstairs. "Hope you don't mind, but the only room where the AC is working, is in the guest bedroom."

Jonathan's mind was moving fast and going nowhere at the same instant. Would he mind being in the same bedroom with Nicola? Of course not.

"Nicola, whatever you think is best. It is kind of warm in here."

Nervous, he wiped the perspiration off his forehead. He silently prayed that his antiperspirant worked. Unsure, he wondered if he had even remembered to put any on. Poor Jonathan. He was a bag of worry. A whole bag of worry and hopefulness that Nicola would repeat her performance and suck his dick as dry as a bone.

He tried his best to ignore the queen-sized, four-poster bed, lusciously decorated with a red satin comforter and matching pillows. He instead focused on the walls and window treatments. Nicola had decorated the guest room to pay homage to Black Hollywood, past and present.

Adorning her stylishly painted walls were giant, framed posters promoting classic movies like *Sounder*, *Shaft* and Spike Lee's phenomenal *She's Gotta Have It*. Still nervous with hopeful expectation, Jonathan fidgeted with the cute cinema knick-knacks displayed on the night table and the armoire. "Nicola, this room is great."

"It's my favorite room, Jonathan. Sometimes I jump on this bed and imagine that I'm one of the great divas of the screen."

With that, Nicola slithered on the bed in almost serpentine fashion, locking eyes with the young basketball star all the way. She lay on her stomach, supported by her elbows. Her breasts, barely covered by the skimpy halter, swung in a mesmerizing, pendulous fashion.

Jonathan's eyes followed the swing of the arc her breasts made. He was totally under her spell. There were no thoughts of Carlos, the teen group, or anything else on the planet. He knew he was not leaving the room the same way he came in.

Nicola motioned for him to join her on the bed. "Come on over. You look so hot over there, and it's so much cooler here."

She pulled back the spread, revealing matching satin sheets. Nervous, he swallowed hard and sat on the edge of the bed. Feeling quite uncomfortable, and not knowing what to do next, he thought it best to proceed with their intended agenda. "Well, uh…uh…Nicola, it's awfully nice that you want to give Carlos a party. I mean, he would really like it."

Nicola interrupted him. "You mean, like you would like this?" She peeled off her shorts, revealing a bare bottom. She spread her legs wide eagle and stroked the inside of her thighs.

Jonathan gasped. He had never seen a woman nude in the flesh. It was so much better than in the videos. Ashamed of his response, he jumped up from the bed and turned his back to her.

"I'm sorry…sorry, Nicola…I don't know if I should see you like this, I mean. I'm sure Carlos wouldn't want this."

"Tell me, how many people are in this room right now?"

"Just, uh…me and you?"

"I want you to imagine that it's the end of the world

and we're the last two survivors." In her sultriest, sexiest voice, she beckoned, "That could be the case right this second. We *are* the last people on Earth right now. Uh-huh. And what if we only had a few moments left? What do you think we should do, Jonathan, with only a few minutes left on Earth? Hmmm?"

Like a child accepts a nursery tale as gospel truth, Jonathan suspended all other beliefs. He and Nicola were *indeed* the last ones on the planet.

Nicola pulled him back onto the bed. "That's right, sweetheart. It's just you and me."

"Yeah, you and me, Nicola."

She rolled him over onto his back, and removed his clothes in a gentle but hurried fashion. When she peeled off his drawers, his cock sprang to attention.

"The last hard dick I'll ever see." She licked it, and closed her eyes as if in prayer. "Jonathan, thank you. Thank you for spending these last moments with me."

She pulled off her halter, freeing 38 double-D breasts. Like a child in a toy store, Jonathan reached out to fondle them. Nicola guided his hands to her nipples. Not knowing any better, he squeezed them hard. She winced. "OH…baby, just roll them back and forth, with your fingers; it gives me such pleasure."

Jonathan, an eager student, did as she instructed. She exhaled with pleasure. "Ooooh, that's good, Jonathan. Now, just lick them with your tongue. Remember it's the last time for us."

As he'd seen in videos, Jonathan tried to give her tits the best licking she'd ever had. He wanted her to feel good, on this, their last night together on the planet. He licked one nipple, while twirling the other one with his fingers.

"Jonathan, I'm getting so wet inside."

Confused, Jonathan pulled back. "I'm sorry...I thought."

She pulled his hands close to her breasts. "No... no...I'm getting sticky wet inside 'cause I like what you're doing. See..." She lay back on the bed, never letting him go. She led his hands between her legs, and guided his fingers gently inside her treasure vault.

Jonathan's eyes bulged. It was wet...creamy and warm, just like all the books had described it. He wished he could get a job where all he did was probe Nicola's wet insides all the rest of his life, but somehow he knew, with his luck, there'd be too many better-qualified applicants for the position.

Nicola guided his hand to her clitoris. "The world will end any second, and I don't want to leave without you massaging my master spot. It gives you all the power, all the power." Jonathan rubbed the area with his fingers. "Oh, baby, not too hard...softer...softer... in circles...make circles. Ah...you got it. Oooh...Ooooh! Feels so good.I'm...I'm...You make me so good and wet, baby."

He checked, and indeed, she was super lubricated.

"Will you…will you lick it for me, Jonathan…just a little tongue."

His body stiffened. He'd seen men give women head in the films, but the way his buddies always talked about eating pussy, it sounded like about as much fun as eating a cinnamon bun smeared with shit.

He quickly erased that image and, instead, remembered that this was his last time on Earth with a woman. If that woman wanted him to eat her, then by-golly, that's just what he was going to do. He lowered his head and imagined that eating was equivalent to skating. He made his tongue travel across her stiffly engorged clitoris in a microscopic figure-eight motion. Excited by Nicola's response, he rather enjoyed the whole process.

Nicola moaned. "My last moments will not be in vain, SWEET LORD SWEET JESUS!" Encouraged by how eagerly her young student responded, she gave him new instructions. "Now, Jonathan…take the tip of your tongue, baby…and whip it back and forth…real fast… just like that…a little faster now…okay, baby…right there…don't stop…keep doing it." Her muscles tightened as she felt an orgasm sliding into her realm. "Oh GOD ALMIGHTY, BABY…THIS SHIT IS GOOD… JONATHAN, YOU'RE GOOD, BABY!"

Pleased that he was making her feel so nice, the young basketball star obeyed his muse and increased the rate of his tongue's motion over her clitoris. He could feel its texture stiffening. Remembering what he had seen in a movie, he used his free hand to fondle her nipples.

Nicola's body writhed in pleasurable response. "I'm coming, Jonathan, Oh God, I'm coming! OOO-WAH-SHAY....OOO-WAH-SHAY...OOO-WAH-SHAY!!!" The powerful orgasm ripped through her entire body. If it had been an earthquake, the entire East Coast would have fallen into the sea. Lasting for what seemed like hours, Nicola's legs clamped tightly around Jonathan's head, forcing him to stop eating her. He thought she'd never release him, but she did.

In total awe of what had just occurred, he said, "Nicola...Nicola..." She was unresponsive. He yelled at her, thinking she was seriously in a coma. "NICOLA!"

Slowly becoming aware of her surroundings, she weakly responded, "Yes, baby?"

"Did you have...did I give you...uh...an orgasm?"

"Oh, yes, you did...oh my God." She hugged him tightly. "You did, and I've got to reward you for that." She kissed Jonathan, and then whispered in his ears, "What do you want me to do for you?" His dick was as hard as a tank and he wanted only one thing from Nicola. But he was still afraid to ask.

"Jonathan, talk to me, baby. What do you want me to do for you?"

He avoided her eyes and looked away. As if reading his mind, she stroked him with her hand. "Oh, you've got a nice dick. If this will be the last one I see, I could not complain."

"Nicola, I... I don't have a condom."

"I'm taking birth control pills." Jonathan frowned,

but Nicola reassured him, "You don't have to worry about having a little Jonathan running around."

He relaxed. He was in good hands with Nicola. Jonathan trusted her. Surely, she wouldn't do anything stupid to jeopardize either of their futures.

"Now, I'm going to take you where you've never been before. Is that okay with you, Jonathan?"

As she inquired, her hand freely stroked his pleasure rod up and down, squeezing all the blood from his brain straight down into his dick. This excited him beyond all he could imagine. The moment was finally going to happen.

For a fleeting second, as Nicola guided him inside her, he thought about his vow to remain chaste and pure until marriage. But who knew that he and Nicola would be the last survivors on Earth?

At that second of revelation, Jonathan's dick landed in new territory. It was land that was wet, warm and greeted his eager rod with a cobra-tight grip. In and out, he screwed inside of Nicola. In and out. Slow at first, he was just trying to feel every inch of her warm sweetness.

Digging repeatedly into her wet vastness, he knew how the miners must've felt when they'd first discovered gold. He yelled out loud. The pleasure was unquantifiably good. He plunged in and out, deeper and deeper, faster and faster. Nicola responded in kind. Matching his rhythm. "That's it, Jonathan. Let it out. Feel all of it. Oh, you make me so wet. So good and wet and juicy."

He could feel her wetness as he entered and exited. His pace, controllable at first, was now out of control. Like a wild bull let out of the gate, his body bucked back and forth; repeatedly ramming his hot shaft into Nicola. And then, it started. He could feel his first real non-masturbating orgasm coming. There was no turning back. He kept slamming his concrete-hard rod into Nicola. His balls made sharp, slapping noises as they banged against the cheeks of her ass.

"Nicola…Nicola…this is it…this is…AHHHHH-AHHH!" It happened. He erupted inside her. *It will never feel that good again*, he thought, *but I'll spend my life chasing that feeling*. Still inside, he rocked their bodies together as tiny aftershocks of pleasure caused creamy, sticky fluid to seep out of Nicola. *And now*, thought Jonathan, *the world can end and go to hell, because I finally got myself "some."*

They repeated their performance again. This time they both came together. At the moment of their shared exaltation, they yelled out in unison. Anyone passing under her window would swear they were rehearsing a song from a gothic opera. Exhausted from the activity, they collapsed back into the bed, laughing as they tried to avoid wet spots. Lying in Jonathan's long, muscular arms, Nicola caressed his balls as he gently stroked her nipples. They were in paradise. Population: two.

The phone rang and interrupted their peace. Jonathan warned her, "Don't answer. There might be one more survivor. Someone we won't like."

Nicola laughed. "Hello, Carlos. Oh, baby."

Jonathan sat up. He had forgotten that they were really on an inhabited planet, one where Nicola was actually his brother's old lady. Still experiencing post-first-screw syndrome effects, try as he may, he could not remember the name of his organization. He held his head down in shame. Tomorrow, he planned to mail in his resignation.

"Carlos, of course, I'm looking forward to tonight. I've made special plans for us."

Jonathan was amazed. After all they had done in bed that afternoon, she still had energy to do it all over again with Carlos. Nicola was some kind of woman. Always a pragmatist, he decided to follow her lead. As long as it led him back to her bed, screwing both their brains out, it was okay with him.

"See you in thirty minutes, Carlos. Hurry, baby. Ciao." She hung up the phone and gave Jonathan a sad but knowing look. A look that said, *"It's time for you to go now."*

He kissed Nicola on the cheek and gave her one long last hug. She whispered in his ear, "I'll see you after practice on Monday. I've got some new things to show you."

Jonathan was happy. He still felt guilty about their meetings—but like the immortal classic suggested, if fucking Nicola was wrong, he didn't want to do right.

CHAPTER THIRTY

Nicola jumped out of the bed and started tidying up, removing their "love-soaked" sheets and tossing them into the laundry hamper. "Got to hide the evidence." She looked over at Jonathan. He was quickly throwing on his clothing.

"I've got to get out of here."

Remembering how well he'd performed, she planted a kiss on his cheek. "Yes, my dear, you must, and I must take a good long soak in the tub. So you'll have to let yourself out." Jonathan tried to pull her close to him. She pulled away, blew him a kiss, and walked out the room. She yelled back, "You'd better go now. Carlos should be ringing that doorbell any second."

Jonathan slid on his sandals and, taking her hint, rushed down the stairwell and out of the door. Just as he turned the corner and descended down the stairs of the local C train stop, Carlos pulled up in front of Nicola's house.

Carlos rang the bell several times. Wondering if Nicola had forgotten their date, he got back into his car. He figured she probably went to the store to get something for the evening. Trying to be patient, he sat in the car for ten minutes before calling her on the cell. "Nicola, where are you?"

"I'm right here, baby, waiting for you."

Carlos, his back facing Nicola's entrance, immediately swung around and discovered her standing outside the door, wearing the skimpiest pink lace negligee he'd ever seen. He hopped out of his SUV, swept Nicola into his arms and carried her into the house. They locked lips for what seemed like hours.

"Oh, Nicola, I missed you so."

"Me too, baby. Take me upstairs to my bedroom. Let's finish what we couldn't start the other night." She licked the inside of his earlobe, a particularly sensitive spot for him. His body ached to be closer to her. He carried her up the stairs and entered the master bedroom.

"Welcome to my boudoir, Carlos," she whispered.

His eyes quickly swept around the huge room. "Nice spot."

He laid Nicola down on the bed.

Proud of her room, she wanted Carlos to notice the decor. "All of my bedrooms have themes. As you can see, this is reminiscent of the Caribbean."

Not wanting to take his mind off of Nicola, he did recognize that she had re-created a bit of the islands. The canopy bed with rich mahogany postings, a huge ceiling fan and wooden shutters on the windows did create an island ambience. All the furnishings represented a different island she'd visited. Haitian, Cuban and Jamaican art covered the sand-colored walls.

Of all she had in the room, the pole piqued his curiosity. "Check this out. Hey, I bet you can work it, girl. Why don't you give me a little show? Huh?" He kissed her deeply, intrigued by the prospect of his love performing a pole dance. She pulled away when he playfully insisted on a show. "Come on, just a little sample, please?"

Nicola cursed herself for not removing the damn thing right after Harrison left. She had vowed never to perform the sultry dance again for any man…for any reason. She made a mental note to remind her contractor to get rid of it as soon as possible.

"Baby, I'm sorry. Why don't we forget about the little pole and concentrate…" She grabbed for his pleasure rod and stroked it. "On the only pole that really matters in this room."

He moaned in response.

In no time at all, Carlos forgot all about the pole and completely removed their clothing. He didn't want to waste a single moment not being inside of Nicola. It was all happening so fast. Carried away by the rapture of the moment, they were two lovers who had waited far too long to be together. "Nicola, if you knew how bad I wanted to be with you." He sucked on her breasts and fondled the valley between her legs. She responded by stroking the longest pole she'd ever encountered. She could not wait to experience all of Carlos.

Carlos had never approached a sexual encounter with such reckless abandon. He usually took his time, controlling the pace. But not with Nicola. Nicola attacked his dick with her mouth, licking it up and down and forcing it down her throat almost to the point of gagging. She was highly turned on by the massiveness of his organ. He plunged it down her throat, ramming it as far as it would go. Carlos was ecstatic. He'd never met a woman who could handle his tool so effectively. Most women tried to eat the whole thing, but none before Nicola had succeeded.

The deeper he pumped into her mouth, the more she could accept. It was blowing his mind to a point where he could feel his orgasm mounting. He wanted to be inside of Nicola when that happened. Deep inside. But Nicola was sucking the hell out of his dick. He never knew it could be so good. He was too close to coming and he didn't want it to be that quick. He had to slow it down. After falling asleep on her in the hotel, he didn't want her to think he couldn't control himself.

Carlos sent up a prayer for help and immediately felt like a heathen. He rarely prayed, and the one time he did he was asking the good Lord to delay his orgasm. But he was desperate and his orgasm was surely coming. It would take divine intervention to stop it. He shouted, "Oh Lord, Jesus, help me…HELP ME, JESUS!"

Nicola looked up at Carlos. His passionate response excited her and she was encouraged to allow his entire twelve-and-one half-inch dick slide down her throat. She wanted all of him. "Jesus…save me NOW!" Carlos was seconds away from exploding.

His cell phone rang and instantaneously broke his connection with his penis. Grateful for the distraction, Carlos promised faithfully to go to church and make a big donation. His intense sexual response faded as habit forced him to pull out of Nicola's hungry mouth. Nicola gently yanked it back. "But I have to answer that," he pleaded.

She looked at him and demanded as sweetly as she could, "The only thing you have to do is fuck my brains out."

Torn between Nicola's demands and a habit he'd long established, he ignored the phone. Nicola won. He resumed his activity and once again forcefully pumped his anxious dick into Nicola's mouth, gradually refocusing all of his attention towards her. The phone rang again. This time he had to answer it. He pulled away from Nicola.

Nicola sat up in the bed, pissed that he disobeyed her orders. She promised, "I'll make you pay for this."

Carlos blew a kiss at her.

She smiled, knowing full well that she would make good on her threat. She thought about how interesting it would be when he discovered how she was administering sexual therapy to his brother. But Nicola was a patient woman. There was no use rushing to an obvious end. Especially when both Jonathan and Carlos were promising to be such excellent lovers.

Carlos pulled his cell phone out of his leather bag. "Hello?"

Sitting in her kitchen, Ophelia nervously spoke into the phone, glad she had finally reached a real live person. "Carlos? Carlos, it's your mom."

"Mama Ophelia...Ma? What's up? Is there anything wrong?"

What does she want? he thought.

"No, everything's fine. I wanted to say hello and..."

Carlos hated himself for answering the phone. He loved her dearly but she had picked the wrong time for chitchat.

"Mama, I'm a little busy, so I'm sorry, I have to..."

"Have you seen Jonathan, baby? I'm looking for him. I'm worried about him."

"Jonathan? He's probably hanging out with the guys in the camp. He's always back before dark. He's fine."

"Yes. I guess he is." He could hear the concern and fear in her voice. He immediately felt sorry for her. "Don't worry about him. He's a big boy."

Eavesdropping on the conversation, Nicola fully agreed with Carlos, but for a different reason. She smiled privately to herself.

"Carlos, you're right, I'm overdoing the mama role this time. I just have this feeling that something is not right. But I'm sorry to bother you. Thanks. And baby…"

"Yes?"

"You take good care of yourself, and like I always tell you young boys, be careful now. There's a lot of stuff out there that you have to watch out for, if you know what I mean."

"Yes, I know what you mean." He knew exactly what she meant. Ever since he started dating, she always ended every conversation with a safe sex warning.

"Love you, baby. And if you see my baby, you tell him to call his mother."

"Okay…bye, Mama."

Carlos put his cell phone back in his bag. Knowing that Nicola would not tolerate any additional interruptions, he turned it off. Though it saved him from coming too soon, his mother's call had broken the mood a little more than he had bargained for. He was also now conscious of the fact that he'd entirely forgotten to wear a condom.

On the top ten list of Carlos's supreme laws, always answering a call followed the number one commandment: Thou shall never swim with fish without a lifejacket. Though he was certain that Nicola, his love, was squeaky clean, and he really didn't think having a baby with her was the worst thing that could happen, he always wrapped up before sex. Looking over at Nicola, impatiently waiting for his quick return, she looked like a perfect angel. On Earth only for him.

But still, his mother's advice reverberated through

his soul. He reached into his wallet and pulled out his supply of condoms.

"Oooh! Let me put those on." Nicola yanked them out of his hand. She read the label: *Super triple X mega-sized condom*! "Did you have to special order these?" Nicola chuckled.

Carlos blushed as he allowed Nicola to slip the rubber onto his hot rod. He rolled Nicola onto the bed into a supine position, crawled on top of her and in one motion entered her. "Oooh shit, that feels good! Nicola, I've waited too long for this."

They consummated their relationship several times that night.

CHAPTER THIRTY-ONE

Ophelia paced back and forth in her kitchen. Speaking to Carlos did not soothe her one little bit. Since she left Eli's that afternoon, she had tried to reach Jonathan. She left several messages on his phone. Not being able to contact him only made her premonitions seem like prophesy. She had to speak to her baby. She left several messages on his cell.

Images of Jonathan trapped in a car wreck or worse, some urban violent scenario, danced through her brain. Every week she saw flowers posted in front of apartment buildings as the community paid its respect for yet another young Black man or woman who'd been gunned down by bullets. But as real as that threat was… Ophelia was primarily concerned about Nicola and what havoc she could cause for her baby.

Ophelia got a glimpse of herself in the kitchen mirror that hung over her sink. Her reflection wasn't pretty at all. She was acting like a raging lunatic. Her son had done nothing to deserve the lack of faith she had in him. Jonathan was, after all, a responsible eighteen-year-old high school graduate who had earned the right to have a curfew that was at least a little past four o'clock in the afternoon.

She made herself a cup of chamomile tea and sat in the living room. When she finished the last drop, Jonathan burst through the door. Breathing a sigh of relief, she yelled, "Jonathan, do you have a moment?"

Jonathan felt sorry for his mom. Her lecture was three hours too late. Out of respect and pure love, he listened attentively as Mama Ophelia laid down the laws of forbidden liaisons; meaning stay away from Carlos's girl. She held back nothing in her complete condemnation of Nicola.

Jonathan saw her mouth moving about safe sex practices, but he did not, or rather could not, listen to the message. All he could think about was how wonderful Nicola felt. It was as if he was three years old again, and his mother had caught him with his first piece of candy. There was no way she could get the chocolate out of his hands then, just like there wasn't a thing she could say now to make him to stay away from Nicola. Her two-hour lecture fell on deaf, albeit respectful, ears.

After his mother released him from "class," he replayed the afternoon session with Nicola over and over. He stayed in his bed all Sunday, imagining he had never left her side. The thought that she was now sharing herself with his brother, did not upset him one bit. He felt no jealousy. Only relief that Nicola had included him on her very elite list of those she screwed.

After speaking with his mom, he realized that he did not have his cell phone. After a quick search, he put two and two together and figured he'd left it in his gym bag. It was in his locker. In his haste to meet with Nicola the previous day, he must have left it at the gym.

The next day at the gym, he found his cell phone. Checking his messages from the previous day, he had several from his mother. Jonathan tried to remember what he was doing when he got all those calls from his mom. A slow, mischievous grin filled his face when he remembered that while his mother desperately tried to reach him to warn him about "dangerous liaisons" he was having one of his own with Nicola.

His smile broadened as he listened to the latest message from Nicola: "I enjoyed our meeting yesterday. Unfortunately, we did not get a chance to complete all items on the agenda. Please stop by and we can continue our business. Call to confirm. Ciao."

Jonathan jumped ten feet in the air with joy. He had feared he might be just a one-night stand for Nicola. That message told him otherwise. There were more delightful sessions in his future. He frowned when he realized that, at some point, their little affair would have to end. Until then, he was going to savor every moment of Nicola's company.

When he returned home and checked his computer, the Teens for Abstinence Committee had posted several messages. Newly deflowered and feeling the power that it inspired, he thought, *to hell with the Teens for Abstinence group*. He sent an e-mail informing the group that he was no longer a member in good standing. He resigned. The very next thing he did was call Nicola. He left a message confirming that he indeed wanted to continue their "meetings."

For the next two weeks, Nicola and Jonathan met every day after basketball practice. During those hours, she introduced him to several different sexual practices. They assumed Karma Sutra positions that weren't well known to most folks. Tantric love methods where Nicola convinced him that her orgasm lasted long after he went back home to Brooklyn.

In the short time they were together, Nicola turned Jonathan into a skilled love machine, one any woman would pay good money for. She was proud of her student. He learned quickly and, much to her surprise and extreme pleasure, he even added a few of his own innovative methods.

Jonathan rarely considered how their affair would affect

Carlos. He knew that when he left Nicola's place at six, Carlos would take his place later that evening. He no longer winced when Carlos declared how deeply he loved Nicola. He felt nothing when he bragged about how blessed he was to have a woman like her. Jonathan only silently agreed with Carlos, that yes, they were both blessed to have Nicola.

During the late afternoon, it was he and Nicola in the guest room. Carlos had the master bedroom in the evening. Everybody was happy. Everything was going to be all right for everybody.

CHAPTER THIRTY-TWO

"*P*ut that thing away." Tarik walked into Carlos's bedroom, shocked to find him cleaning a .22-caliber gun. Carlos didn't blink.

"I know how to use this. Remember Pops showed me how on those hunting trips?" Carlos held the gun up, marveling at how shiny it looked. He pointed it toward the window as if aiming it at an unfortunate victim. "Anybody comes up to one of us at a concert or an event, *KAPOW*, right between the eyes."

"I never liked those trips with Pops; only went that one time."

"Yeah, you cried like a pussy when they shot the deer."

"I'm a lover, not a killer."

"Don't let Sherry hear you say that."

"She feels the same way I do about guns—they're dangerous and you only wind up usually hurting your own damn self...so get rid of it, Carlos."

"Check this out…a gun in the right hands protects. Look, you're getting up in the world. What if one of those wannabe gangster rappers trying to make a name for themselves by getting cheap publicity wants to pull up on you?"

"I'm not a gun man. Put it away, Carlos. It makes me nervous, knowing you have it."

"Since I've been with Nicola, I feel a lot better with this at my side."

Tarik looked at his brother and shook his head. So, the real reason for the piece of steel was the new girl in his life. With the memory of her "attack" still fresh on his mind, Tarik knew Nicola, Carlos and the gun were a lethal combination. There would be trouble.

"Oh, so the gun's not really for me; it's for Nicola. Carlos, I tried to warn you 'bout her. She's the most beautiful woman I've ever seen, I'll give you that, but…"

Carlos threw up his hands. "Hey, I get enough of this 'Nicola's a big bad witch' advice from Mother. Don't need it from you, too. I know who she really is. She's a woman who really loves me, and only me. Get it?"

"Whatever you say. If you like her, that's your problem. Your big problem! But remember, ain't no good ever gonna come from a gun. But you grown; over twenty-one."

"And this gun and me is all legal and shit. Don't worry 'bout the gun and don't worry 'bout my woman. I can handle both." Carlos slipped the gun into a shoulder holster and looked at his reflection in the mirror. He struck several Hollywood-style poses, pulling his gun out swiftly for effect.

"I'll probably never use it, but I got to have it near me."

Frustrated and unable to fight Carlos's twisted logic, Tarik turned and walked out the room. Carlos slammed the door behind him.

Returning to the mirror, he kept posing with the gun. Carlos's thoughts raced back to Nicola's side. There was rarely a moment he didn't have her on his mind. He wanted to be with her every free moment he got. Much to his disappointment, she resisted his attempts to get closer.

When he suggested that he move in to her home, without explanation, she blurted out, "Hell no!" He thought it was about money. She laughed in his face when he volunteered to pay all the expenses. He couldn't figure her out.

She never said the words, but he knew that she loved him. He could feel it.

Or did he need to feel it? For the past few weeks, Old Satan played with his mind. All night long, whenever she brushed him off refusing to see him, explicit scenes of her fucking some other man would taunt him. He couldn't sleep. He couldn't concentrate during the day. He snapped at everyone around him.

And the dreams he had. Dreams of his father beating

his mother. Accusing her of cheating on him. Hector Salinas tortured his poor mother. Afterward, he would always take little Carlos to the ice cream parlor. He could order any flavor he wanted.

And as he ate his favorite strawberry cone with multi-colored sprinkles, his father would try to explain why he'd beat his mother. She was bad, he would tell him. She had other men. He would always declare how much he loved her. All Carlos would do as he listened to his crazy father was lick his ice cream as it dripped all over his clothes.

Later that night, the dreams of his childhood revisited him. This time, Hector beat his mother with his police baton. She pleaded with him to stop. Little Carlos stood in his bedroom, petrified. Only six years old at that time, he went into his parents' master bathroom. He looked up at his father, tugged at his pants leg, and begged, "Poppi, please, don't hit Mommy. Take me to get ice cream."

It was that pleading child's voice that reverberated in his mind. It made the adult Carlos scream, as if screaming could change the past. Make everything right. Ophelia, who was downstairs reading in the living room, heard his scream. Jumping up from her chair, she flew up the stairs, taking two steps at a time. Banging on his door, she yelled, "Carlos, baby, are you all right? Open this door!"

Carlos woke up, drenched in sweat. He opened the

door and saw Mama Ophelia staring at him with a concerned look. "What's wrong, Mama?"

"Boy, you were in there yelling like somebody was killing you."

Carlos got back in bed. The memory of the nightmare still clung to him.

"I just...had...I just had a bad dream...that's all." Ophelia sat down on the bed next to him and pulled him close to her like she had done when he was younger. Carlos needed her comfort and did not resist. Never telling her what was on his mind, he let Mama Ophelia rock him back to sleep.

CHAPTER THIRTY-THREE

*N*icola took a long, luxurious bubble bath. The weekend had been particularly entertaining. Carlos and Jonathan were just what the doctor ordered. The therapist she visited immediately after the break-up with Harrison had advised long-term counseling and pills for depression to help her deal with her wicked childhood and the shock of Harrison's betrayal.

After one visit, she never returned. She intuitively knew following their advice meant she'd never wean herself off their "couches." No, she had chosen a different "couch." One of her own design. Sex was the best medicine. And the more the better. Throw in a couple of vodka martinis and hot bubble baths, and she could feel real psychological progress.

First off, she no longer felt like a victim. After dealing with all the men she had had in the past three or four months, she now knew how the world worked. There are the users and the used. Unfortunately, when she was young and couldn't protect herself, she was used. Though he denied it, and swore that he truly loved her, she was convinced Harrison used her to cover his alternative lifestyle.

Nicola now knew that by living a life driven by lustful needs, where she chose her mates and discarded them at will, she was in the coveted role of the user. Somehow, she didn't think a goal of traditional therapy would lead her to that conclusion. The therapists wanted her to spend years and years in self-analysis where one day she could claim to be a whole person who had no guilt about what had happened to her.

Well, she took a speedier course through the therapeutic melée. Very shortly, after her past revealed itself to her, she figured out that she didn't commit the crime of abusing a child— her adopted parents preyed on her. *She* was the victim. There was no need for her to take a guilt trip. Burning those bastards was justifiable.

She looked at the time. Nicola jumped out of the tub and prepared for her trip out of town. If she was going to make her evening flight, she had to speed it up. The Williams Brothers had called her earlier that day to let her know they were doing shows in the Miami area. Nicola missed the three diminutive men who had brought her so much joy and pleasure.

Driving in the backseat of a limousine, en route to JFK International Airport, she remembered that she was supposed to spend time with Carlos. He wanted to do something "special" with her. She hadn't even paid attention when he told her about his plans. She cancelled her date with Carlos. Sent him a text message. She never even considered his feelings when she invited three of the naughtiest, sexiest little men in the world to spend three days with her at her South Beach home.

CHAPTER THIRTY-FOUR

*L*incoln Powell was a successful, fifty-five-year-old corporate attorney, who stepped in after Pops had died and had helped guide Tarik's career. Carlos and Tarik were grateful for his counsel. Thanks to his expertise, Tarik had received more than the usual percentage of profits. This was highly unusual for a new artist. Fortunately, they had planned very cleverly from the beginning, and were presenting the record company a complete package. All they really needed a label for was distribution and a broader promotional campaign.

To celebrate closing the deal, Uncle Link, as the young men called the man that had been Pops' best friend, took them all out for lunch at Ava's Place, the famous soul food restaurant in Harlem. A favorite haunt of celebrities and political power-brokers, Link usually took his high-profile clients there after he won their cases.

Waiting for their meal, Tarik sat at one end of the table, doodling abstract stick figures on a pad. His mind was a gazillion miles away. The irony of discovering that his absentee father was "lurking around" and dying was just a bit much on his plate.

He'd wished him dead so many times and now that it was a real possibility, he didn't know what to make of things. Here he sat at the top of the world. His career was slammin', he had found his soul mate in Sherry, but still, just hearing about Eli Griffith made everything null and void. Instead of extreme joy, he was experiencing painful anxiety.

Carlos, sitting on the opposite end of the table, was just as cheerless as Tarik. Nicola had left for an out-of-town business trip. She sent him a text message. Not even a phone call. When he tried to call her back to suggest that he tag along…he could only reach her voicemail. It killed him to realize that he had done the very same heartless thing to the women he had dated.

Uncle Link was at a loss. He thought the two young men would be in a great mood after their successful business negotiations. "Tarik…Carlos…is everything okay? You both look like someone died. This is supposed to be a celebration. You two have worked so hard for this moment. Why the gloomy faces? Is everything okay at home? Is…is Ophelia alright?" asked Link with sincere concern in his voice.

"It's okay. I got a little something nagging me on the

brain, that's all." Tarik stared at both Carlos and Link. Realizing how his mood was freaking them out, he switched back into his usual jovial self to reduce the growing tension. "But, it's alright, everybody. It's all good. I'm here listening. You know I'm down with whatever you guys say. "

Tarik changed his mood, but not Carlos. He kept calling on his phone…trying to reach Nicola. Link, disturbed by the young man's behavior, asked, "Carlos, who on God's earth are you trying to reach on that phone?"

"His girlfriend, Nicola. Good luck with that one." Tarik's eyes widened as the waitress placed huge plates of smothered chicken, macaroni and cheese, and collard greens with corn bread on their table.

"Nicola? I met her at the party at your mom's. Beautiful girl. How is your mother doing, by the way? I heard she had met with, what's his name, Eli Griffith, her first husband?" He was obviously trying to get into Ophelia's business. He had waited so long to make his move on her that he was pissed at the thought that some other man had beat him to it.

Carlos smiled for the first time that day. Since Pops' death, his mother had never looked at another man… that is until Eli came back on the scene…and with his diagnosis, he knew nothing was happening there. Mama Ophelia needed the company of a good man, and Uncle Link fit that description.

Trying to encourage the six-foot, ruggedly handsome man from Pops' hometown in Florida, he said, "Don't worry, Uncle Link. The dude's dyin'. You still have a chance with our mother."

Upset that he'd been caught, the lawyer who was never at a loss for words, started babbling like an idiot and slipped back into a thick Southern dialect that only surfaced when he was upset. He blurted, "But…but…I…I…I wasn't trying to…you know…get with your mother…that was…uh…never my intention. Um…um…help me out here, boys, please!"

Both Tarik and Carlos started laughing. Everybody liked Uncle Link. Having him for a stepfather would not be the worst thing to happen to the family.

"Chill out, Uncle Link. By the way, the dude, Eli Griffith? He's my father. Pass me the hot sauce, Carlos. Would you, please?"

CHAPTER THIRTY-FIVE

The thin, curvaceous model wore a G-string, diamond-studded pasties, and a pair of "fuck me so hard I go into a coma" pearl-lined stiletto pumps. She lured Tarik into a tiny room where there was only a bed inside. A long-stemmed rose lay on top of a white satin comforter.

Looking at her with wanton lust and desire, he held her tightly in his arms and kissed her red, plump, juicy lips. He then lifted her up, threw her down on the bed, and crawled on top of her writhing body. His song, "Don't Say No to Me Tonight," the first single from his debut album, played loudly in the background.

"Cut...cut...cut...Tarik...baby...I ain't buying it!" Kevin Rivers, the director, got out of his chair and stormed on the stage. He headed straight for Tarik. "You're holding the girl like she was a head of cabbage! You threw her down on the bed like she was a sack of fuckin' potatoes! LOOK AT HER…SHE'S GOR-GEOUS! You don't treat a woman who looks like that that way!" Frustrated, he threw his hands up in the air. This was the thirtieth take for a scene that should've been finished two hours ago.

Tarik rolled off of the girl, happy to be away from her. It wasn't natural, being with a woman other than Sherry. He hated making the music video. Why couldn't he just perform on stage? That's what he loved doing. Not this Hollywood fake stuff.

The video director was frustrated. He could not make Tarik relax. At his wit's end, he finally turned to Sherry for help. She had tried her best to run the shoot all day with her suggestions. Just to get some peace on the shoot, he made an ultimatum that either she zip it up or get off the set. She chose to be quiet. For the past two hours, she had not made a single comment.

Begging her now for help was a tad ego deflating for the award-winning film director. He was pissed that he had to do the shoot at all. Unfortunately, his nasty little cocaine addiction had gotten him tossed off the coveted "A" list and on to the "I better do music videos if I want to pay the mortgage" roster.

"Okay…okay…Ms. Sherry…what do you think I should do? Your man is eating up precious money. I can't shoot this shit and make it look right. I ain't that good."

Sherry triumphantly rolled her eyes at the director

and jumped off of her seat. She grabbed Tarik's hand and pulled him over to a private corner of the set.

In a quiet but serious voice, Sherry looked at her husband and begged him, "Honey, these kind of videos are part of the process of making you a star."

Tarik interrupted, "But, baby, I can't wrap my mind around it, and I've been distracted with the Eli thing. My mama is hanging out with him and…"

"Sweetie, we'll deal with that Eli issue after the video. For now, this is the *only* thing we need to think about. You need to know that I want you…*no*…skip that. I *need you* to be sexy as hell with that woman in that video, just as if it were me."

"Huh?" Tarik couldn't believe what she was saying.

"Baby, the girl is gorgeous. And she's nice, too. I had a lovely little conversation with her earlier." Sherry embellished the "nice" and the "lovely" part. What she actually did was to inform the little video-hussy with the perfectly chiseled face, that if she messed with her husband, the next person she would need to see would be a plastic surgeon.

"And, Tarik, just in case I'm making you nervous, I'm leaving right now. I trust you, baby. This is just a video. Ain't nothing real about it." She pulled Tarik closer to her and kissed him on the cheek. "See you later tonight."

As she walked out the stage door, he could not help but admire how good she looked from behind. He loved big asses and Sherry was well endowed. He wanted to tear it up right then and there. He couldn't wait to get home and make love. He looked for the director and told him he was ready to continue. Completely relaxed, he gave Kevin Rivers exactly what he asked for. It turned out to be an excellent video.

Riding home alone that night, Tarik thought about the song choice for the video: "Don't Say No to Me Tonight." He had written it the night he'd begged Sherry to make love to him. His mind drifted back to that moment.

"You mean you want us to do *what*?" Sherry stopped preparing their lunch, and came out from behind the counter in what Tarik thought was a threatening manner. He loved the girl for her fiercely strong personality, but he hated to admit that sometimes the five-foot-two little giant intimidated him. Sherry flopped down next to him on the couch and stared up at him in a defiant gaze.

"Well, we've been together for almost a year now, and I was just wondering when—"

Sherry cut him off. "Six months ain't a year. I told you before, Tarik, ain't no punk in me. Don't play me for stupid, baby!"

"Goodness, woman. Okay, six months. Look... I...I love you and I want to make love to you. Why won't you let me make love to you, baby?" Tarik tried to pull Sherry closer to him, but she jerked away and started laughing at him.

"Who does that crap work on? You sound like a broke-down old blues record. I hope you're not putting stuff like that on your CD."

"But...but, baby—"

"Don't baby me. I'm not blind. I see all those little groupies at the clubs with their tongues hanging out. Why don't you go get yourself some from one of them?"

"Now you're insulting me. You know you the only one. Hell, I'd even go on *Maury* and take a lie detector test for you, girl."

"You don't have to do all that. Look, I do feel... special when I'm with you. Since my Benny died overseas, you're the first man I've let get this close to me and Javon. But I'm not a one-night stand, and I'm not ever gonna be just a notch in a rapper's..."

"I'm not a rapper; I'm a neo-soul stylist. I keep telling you that."

"Whatever. When my son's father died, I wanted to crawl up under a rock. But I didn't. I had to take care of Javon. I didn't chase after the first man I saw to give him a daddy either. No, I finished college and became the best mother and woman I know how."

"And baby...you 'da best."

"I'm not running a hotel up in here. If and when we decide to do that thing you want so badly, it'll be because we're committed to each other and if we pass the test."

A questioning grimace quickly replaced Tarik's easy smile. "What test you talking about?"

"You know...HIV...syphilis...herpes. You've seen those ads. When you have sex with a person, you're sleeping with everybody they've been with. And honey, as fine as you are…and between just you and me, you are a very fine and good Black man." Tarik blushed, but it was only temporary because she added, "But you sure ain't worth dying for."

Tarik laughed at the memory. Queen Sherry. His lady. She didn't take no shit. But she always gave a whole lot of love. It was an entire year before she gave the green light for "the test." By then he was so smitten with the woman, he proposed the day the doctor revealed their results. They were both squeaky clean.

They married at the Brooklyn courthouse a few months later. Their wedding night was their first time together. Tarik realized he had only had sex with other women. It was very different when you loved the person. It was the best loving he ever had.

Loving and living with Sherry proved profitable in that she had an extremely healthy work ethic, a trait he knew he lacked. With Sherry as his muse, he changed his ways. He now wrote prolifically and practiced his music faithfully on a daily basis. The discipline he developed led to the success he was now enjoying in his career.

Now, with the video behind him, he could focus on Eli Griffith. He knew his mother was spending a lot of time with him. Last time he spoke with her, she had even casually suggested that he visit him. But he didn't want any part of him.

Later that evening, at home with Sherry, Tarik sought answers to the growing confusion in his soul. Seeking to run away from his problems, he grabbed Sherry in bed and aggressively, almost savagely engaged in love-making. He had entirely skipped any foreplay. This one was for him.

Confused by his aggressiveness, Sherry begged, "Baby, slow down. What's wrong?"

"I need you real bad. Just this once, okay?"

Sherry felt like she was with a stranger. Before that night, Tarik was always a considerate lover. Always making sure she was ready. Though he was not a well-endowed man, he made up for it by his generous ways of petting and holding her tenderly.

But this time was different. He kissed her mouth once or twice and then tore her panties off. He grabbed his stiff penis and shoved it into her, roughly, and with-out explanation. He could have been with a stranger. He thought, it would have been better if he had been. Soon as he entered Sherry, the pressure of his growing problems totally deflated his erection. Tarik rolled off Sherry and turned his back to her.

Sherry lay on her side of the bed, unsure of what to make of it all. Insecure feelings surfaced and she won-dered if that witch Nicola, the one Carlos brought to the party, had anything to do with Tarik's performance problems. Or did the video chick ignore her threat and try something behind her back?

Sherry found her core center of strength and discarded all doubts about Tarik's fidelity. The only truth that mattered was that he was in bed with her now… and she knew he loved her with all his heart and soul.

No, it wasn't another woman; it was something else. And she was going to find out. She turned over and lovingly stroked and caressed Tarik's back.

"Baby, what's wrong? Is it something I did, or said? What just happened? This, this ain't like you."

He turned over, grabbed her and held her close. "Baby, I'm sorry. I don't know what got into me. All I know is that it's you and me…and ain't nobody ever gonna get a chance to get between us."

"'Cause you do know what I'd do if somebody tried, right, Tarik?"

"Baby, you ain't ever got to go there. Not with me, you don't."

Sherry relaxed in his arms. A little reassurance always worked. It helped him to regain and keep his erection. This time they made love passionately.

Later that night, as they lay in bed cuddled up with each other, Tarik told Sherry the entire story. He explained that his dark side, the "hell hath no fury like an abandoned child" side, wanted to have that knockdown, drag-out, shout-out talk with Eli. The one where he gets the opportunity to tell his father what a miserable low-down excuse for a human being he was. He wanted to rub it in his face; how successful he'd become. He hadn't needed him after all. He wanted that conversation. No, Tarik explained to Sherry, he *needed* it.

The confusion entered when the "live and let live," mellow, mystical, spiritual side of Tarik just wanted to let his father die alone in whatever peace he could create in his final days. He knew that dying from AIDS was no picnic. It was a hell he'd never wish on anyone. Even Eli didn't deserve quite that much.

After all, he hadn't walked away from a welfare momma without any means of support. His mother's family was financially well off and according to the history, Pops was on the spot soon after they divorced. Tarik had never known a day of material want or need in his life. But should he go see this man? Now? After all this time? What was the point? Or was that the point after all? Did he really need a reason to see him?

Sherry listened to Tarik. Never interrupting him. She massaged his slumped shoulders. She knew what her husband needed to do. "I'll go with you, Tarik. You don't have to do it, but you do need to go see him. You'll regret it, baby, if you don't."

He pulled away from her and jumped up out of the bed. He paced up and down the bedroom floor.

"No. NO! Oh crap. Yes. Who am I fooling? Mama was right. You're right. I do need to see him."

"That's the right decision, baby. The only one."

He got back in the bed and pulled Sherry close to him. Her warm body melted away all of his doubt.

A week later, he called his mother on the phone.

"Hello."

"Mama, it's Tarik."

"What's going on, hon'?"

"Well, actually, Sherry and I think it would be a good idea if I met with this guy before he croaks and all of that. Think you could hook it all up? I mean, do you have a way of reaching him?"

"I have some connections that might make it possible for the two of you to meet. Just let me arrange everything. And Tarik?"

"Yes, Mama?"

"You've made the right decision, son."

"Uh, I have to go. Talk with you later. Love you."

Tarik pulled his car out of the Mo-Sound record company's parking lot. He had just finished re-recording one of the tracks on the CD. If everything went their way, this time next year, he'd be on the stage accepting a Grammy or at the very least, presenting. Joy was erupting in all places within him. But it was not lost on him, that he was also excited about the possibility of meeting his father.

On the other side of town, in Eli's tiny little abode, Ophelia put her cell phone back in her bag. "Guess who that was?"

Eli looked at her puzzled. "Who?"

"Your son. He wants to meet with you. How do you like that?"

Eli could not contain his smile. "I think I like that a whole lot."

CHAPTER THIRTY-SIX

"Tarik, I'm with you. Baby, I'm here for you. You can do this." Tarik looked up at the clean, modestly designed building, where on the second floor, his mother and Eli waited for him to arrive. At first, he regretted bringing Sherry along, but now that he was actually there, he was glad to have her there to lean on.

"How do I look?" Eli looked in the mirror at himself. A bony, emaciated face stared back at him. "Like shit."

Eli frowned.

Ophelia shook her head and patted Eli on the shoulders for support. "Don't worry about your looks. Believe me, Tarik is not the least bit concerned with outward appearances. Remember what you always said on campus?"

"Yeah, beauty's only skin deep. But you know I was a bigger hypocrite then, Ofee."

"What do you mean?"

"Though I always preached that skin-deep crap, I

made sure my old lady was the finest girl on campus."

Ophelia blushed liked a young coed. "Oh, Eli, stop flirting!"

He laughed. He always laughed when she came to visit. Today the laughter helped to calm his nerves. He was so anxious about finally meeting his son. A knock at the front door promised to end his stress.

"Come in; the door's open."

Tarik and Sherry entered the tiny apartment.

"Tarik, how, how…are you?"

"Fine, oh…this is Sherry, my wife."

"Pleased to meet you, Mr. Griffith. Hello, Mama Ophelia."

"Sit down, young people, sit down." Eli was in heaven. He couldn't believe that he was in the same room as his son. He had so much love in his heart for him. He could never express it all. He knew he would take it with him to his grave. How proud he was of this young man. Sherry and Ophelia served as mediators to help the conversation between the two strangers flow easily.

"Tarik, your concert was, how do the young folks say these days? *The bomb*!"

"It was alright."

"Don't be modest; I was there. Right, Ophelia?"

"Yes, we were all there. It was some concert."

Tarik smiled. There were awkward silences at first, but gradually Eli's natural personality surfaced and he became an entertaining host. By the end of the visit, he was telling them stories about the art world and making them all laugh. Tarik was surprised by how relaxed he felt around this man. He could never relate to him as a father because that honor would always be held by Pops. But he couldn't help but like Eli. He didn't even feel sorry for him and his illness. Though Eli was obviously a very sick man, living his last days, he never insisted that folks throw pity parties for him.

Tarik visited his father two days later. He came without Sherry or his mother as chaperones. He wanted to have a man-to-man talk with him. He asked Eli to tell him about his life. What he heard made him glad that this man did not raise him.

"Son, I was one of those men who just had the bad habit of making the wrong choice. Unfortunately, I got stuck with the consequences of those decisions." Eli paused to catch his breath. He looked at Tarik, and thanked God that his son would never live the kind of life he had chosen. "Before I knew it, my life was littered and poisoned by the consequences of my bad decisions, bad behaviors and now my life."

Unable to complete the thought, he rolled his wheelchair over to the window, and looked out. On the tree branch, a mama sparrow fed her hungry babies. Eli shook his head. If he had even had the sense of a bird, maybe he would have taken better care of Tarik. Angry with himself, he looked back at the son he never fathered.

"Tarik, I always wanted to come and meet with you and your mama. But I wanted to do it with style. No drug habit. Successful. Money in my pocket. I kept thinking… next month, I'll clean myself up. Start painting again. But, next month would come and go, and I still was no closer to getting my act together. Then I ran out of next months. You're all grown now, and I got no more next months."

Tears fell down Eli's face. He rarely traveled down memory lane these days. It was far too draining. He preferred to conserve his energy and celebrate what life he had left. But today, he had to take the trip back with his son.

"When you almost died because of my stupidity."

"What are you talking about?"

Eli looked at his son, and realized Ophelia and her people had never told Tarik the story surrounding his first incarceration. How on the worst day of his life, he had made a decision to get high in his home with so-called friends. The decision that almost cost him Tarik's life. They probably didn't want him to know what kind of monster had sired him.

"Eli?" Tarik knew he was about to hear something that was more painful than a man should have to bear.

"They never told you, did they?"

Tarik sat motionless, afraid that movement would convince Eli to keep quiet. "Eli, I need to know all the truth. I deserve that much, I think."

His son was right. He owed his son the entire story

of what happened. Telling him the tale, the unedited version, was as painful as he thought it would be. But he had to do it. The truth of his life was the only thing he could leave his son. Maybe he'd avoid some of the pitfalls that had tragically tripped him up.

He cried like a baby when he described how it was pure torture, wondering if he'd ever come out of that coma. How he begged and bargained with God to take him instead. Judging by the life he eventually led, God had definitely made him keep his side of the bargain.

Hearing how he had accidentally got into Eli's drug stash and almost died made Tarik look at his biological father. His mother's version always made it seem like he just had a little drug habit and they couldn't make it. He'd left because he could never come back after the incident. There is no coming back after you have relinquished parental responsibility.

He thought about his adopted son, Javon. He vowed to protect him from harm. Something his own biological father didn't have the strength or clarity of mind to do. Still, Tarik did not—could not—hate this man. A man who self-admittedly was incapable of making a right decision.

All he said to him was, "Guess you've done some pretty dumb things."

Eli was relieved when he finished the story and Tarik didn't spit in his face as he felt he deserved. "Yes, I guess I have."

He saw that his son did share some similar characteristics with him. They both loved beauty, poetry, and art. They were kind men who wouldn't hurt a soul, at least not intentionally. He was also glad that they were different. Tarik was extremely disciplined. He must have gotten that from the man they called Pops, because he sure didn't get it from Eli. Lack of discipline and courage and a never-ending supply of stupidity were his tragic character flaws. Thank God, they weren't inheritable traits.

What they had most in common was precious. They both would only love one woman in their lives. He told Tarik that Sherry was a good woman for him. "That one, she don't take no shit from you. I can tell."

Tarik laughed. "No, she does not."

"Always treat her like a queen. That's where I really blew it. Not treating your mother as she deserved was the dumbest thing I ever did."

Later that day, Tarik stopped by his mother's house and shot some pool with Carlos.

"What did he look like?" Carlos watched as Tarik expertly hit striped balls into pockets.

"Huh?" With only one of his balls remaining on the table, he missed putting it away.

"Do you look like him?" Carlos grabbed his stick.

"I don't know. Maybe. Yeah. I might have looked like him back in the day."

"Might? Seven ball in the side pocket." Carlos slammed

the yellow striped ball just seven centimeters short of its intended goal. "Shit!"

"It's hard to tell." Tarik positioned his stick and aligned the cue ball directly on the path of the twelve ball. "This baby's going into the corner pocket." As he promised, it rolled right into its target. Carlos, obviously more interested in what was being said, barely noticed.

"Why?"

Tarik set up his next shot. "He's thin. Wasted looking. What can I say? The dude's dying. He looks like shit. Eight ball, right there, corner pocket, for the game." The eight ball followed Tarik's command and disappeared down the hole. "Want to try and beat me one more time?"

"No, I've had enough." Tarik and Carlos put the pool sticks away and cleaned off the table, just like Pops always taught them to. Carlos went to the bar, and pulled out a soda from the refrigerator. He opened the bottle, took a long swig, and wiped his wet lips off with the back of his hand. "You glad you went?" Tarik collapsed on the leather sofa and let out a long sigh. Carlos stared over at his brother, waiting for a reply.

"Now that I've seen him, spoken with him, and even understand him a little, I can honestly say that I'm really glad we had a chance to hook up."

"Maybe. If it's all right with you, I'd like to go with you and meet him."

"Sure, but we better go soon. I don't think he'll be

around much longer. Hey! No beer, Carlos? When did you start drinking sodas?"

Not wanting to reveal the trouble he was having with dreams and voices and Nicola's disappearances, all Carlos said was, "Man, I'm watching my waistline. Just like you should. You got to look good in those videos, man. The young girls like to see a six-pack. Know what I mean?" They both laughed.

But for Carlos the laughter was empty. It had been a week and he still hadn't heard from Nicola. Where was she? He couldn't stand not knowing. She was driving him mad. If she loved him, she had a funny way of showing it.

CHAPTER THIRTY-SEVEN

After Tarik's visit, Eli's condition deteriorated. He was so weak, Ophelia had to hand-feed him the soup she made. He refused to go to the hospital. He did not want to die there. A week later, Tarik brought Carlos, Jonathan and little Javon to meet with him. He brought his guitar and spent the entire afternoon singing songs. It was a party.

Eli was delighted by the visit. Little Javon, who remembered Pops, could not understand how Tarik had two fathers and exclaimed, "Are you my daddy's daddy? Really? He has two daddies?"

They tried to explain it to Javon, but it would not stick. He finally threw his hands up in the air and said in an exasperated, high-pitched, little boy voice, "Okay... okay he has two daddies. I have two daddies, too."

Eli laughed. "He's a delightful child, Tarik. I'm so glad you brought him today."

When it was time for everyone to leave, Eli's strength had just about disappeared. He could barely raise his hand to wave. "Good-bye, everybody. If you only knew how much joy you've all brought me today."

"Don't talk, Dad. Save your strength. See you next week."

With that, everyone left except for Ophelia. She closed the door after them.

"Did you hear what he called me, Ophelia?"

"I heard it, Eli."

"Funny. It's only one word and I so don't deserve it, but I sure loved the sound of it."

Ophelia returned the next day. She had only planned to stay a few hours. Later that afternoon was Jonathan's final basketball game and she did not want to miss it.

She knocked on the door several times, calling out his name. Eli did not answer. Ophelia then knew something was very different about this visit. He always yelled back at her with some cute comment. Ophelia's heart pounded rapidly in her chest. She instinctively knew that doom would greet her on the other side of the entrance.

She used her key, pushed the door open, and discovered why he had not answered. There lying on the bed was Eli, gasping for air. She ran to him and cradled him in her arms. He breathed a little easier. "Eli, let me call the paramedics," she begged.

"No...Let me go. I'm ready. I've seen my son. I've seen you, the love of my life, and now I'm ready."

He had signed a paper refusing treatment. She couldn't force him. Tears flowed down Ophelia's cheeks. She knew he was right. "Ophelia, play his music for me." She popped one of Tarik's tapes into a cassette player. "Ophelia...I...I...love you, baby."

"I always loved you, too." Ophelia rocked him in her arms for what seemed like an eternity. They sat in silence listening to their son's music. By nightfall, Eli had stopped breathing.

CHAPTER THIRTY-EIGHT

*N*icola felt guilty about the way she had been treating Carlos. She threw him a bone and dragged him out to her beach house in the Hamptons for the weekend. Except for the nightmare he'd had the previous evening, he was delightful company. Carlos and she were driving back into the city later that evening to catch Jonathan's final basketball game at Madison Square Garden. Nicola, surprised by how much she was actually looking forward to it, was eager to see her young pupil "shoot the hoops."

Carlos was downstairs preparing breakfast for them. He had bragged so about his prowess in the kitchen, she had given him the opportunity to prove it.

Sitting on her chaise lounge in her bedroom, she oiled her new micro-locks hairdo, marveling at how simple it was to care for short hair. She thought about all the time she wasted sitting in beauty parlors with stylists, caring for her thick usually unmanageable waist-length hair.

"What the hell!" The sound of metal crashing against cement startled her. Dropping the bottle of Clara's Grandbabies scalp oil, Nicola rushed to the window and peered through the luxurious silk bedroom curtains made from material she and Harrison purchased on a business trip to Lagos, Nigeria about two years ago. What she witnessed brought a smile to her lips.

"The boy has finally lost his mind," she whispered to herself. In the midst of her Asian-themed beachfront patio, amongst bamboo trees, rare exotic plants and a Jacuzzi, Carlos rummaged through her garbage cans like a homeless man looking for his next meal.

It's got to be here. I know someone's been with her. I know it...I just know it. Carlos looked up at Nicola's bedroom window. He thought he saw the curtains move. He couldn't let her catch him spying. Shame pushed aside the insane waves of jealousy that fueled his search. He looked at the nasty piles of garbage scattered around the trashcans and wondered how he, a man that never gave a woman a second thought after he fucked her, had sunk so low.

None of Carlos's thoughts resided in sane territory. Try as he may, for the past few weeks, he could not shake the feeling that someone else was in the bed they shared. He felt for the gun in his shoulder holster. The moral caution that prevented him from fully stating to himself, or to others, what he would do if his suspicions were accurate, was quickly evaporating.

The comfort he derived from the cold steel assured him, on a deeply visceral level that, if challenged, he would use the gun to protect his property. Nicola was his and only his. He would teach whoever violated their relationship a lesson they'd never forget. He clutched the gun tightly, affirming that nothing in this world could keep him from crossing the line if he discovered someone with Nicola.

Continuing his search, he quickly learned that Nicola was a meticulous shredder. If there were proof of another lover, he'd never find it amongst the tethered strips of paper neatly arranged in bundles.

"Looking for something?" Nicola's seductive voice broke Carlos's train of violent thought. Busted, without a single word he could create to defend himself, he spun around and faced the most beautiful woman in his world. Nicola wore a fuchsia-colored, Ophelia Reed outfit that hugged the dangerous sexy curves of her body. Completing her designed-to-kill look were purple-beaded, five-inch spiked pumps that perfectly matched a beach bag Carlos had purchased for her in Southampton.

She was a vision. All thoughts of her infidelity temporarily fled out the door. She was his. All his. He greeted her with a deep tongue down her throat, and held her so close she gasped for air. Pulling away, trying to catch her breath, she could barely whisper, "Take it easy, baby. You trying to kill me? I don't want to miss little Jonathan's last basketball game...okay?"

Following her back into the house, Carlos was taken by the rear view of her perfect body. He knew other men, as he was now doing, lusted after her. He wished he could turn her into a Muslim woman and have every body part covered, except for her eyes. But he knew that outfit would not hide her beauty, especially since it was those very eyes that vexed his soul at night.

Before she could enter the house, he grabbed her again, pulling her close, and whispered, "You stay next to me during the game, you hear?"

Amused by his attempts to possess her, Nicola chuckled to herself. Playing along, she looked up at him, and in her most sincere voice replied, "Whatever you say, baby."

CHAPTER THIRTY-NINE

Sweat poured from every orifice of Jonathan's hot, muscular body. With only fifteen seconds left on the clock, there were no timeouts remaining for either side. Though he was the highest scorer, his team was still behind by two points. The visiting team possessed the ball. The forward that Jonathan guarded, dribbled the ball toward the net, positioning himself for a lay-up. If successful, the team's dream of a win would end. Never ready to call it quits, Jonathan took advantage of the three inches that separated him and his opponent by smacking the ball out of his hands and throwing it down court into the waiting hands of one of his teammates.

With ten seconds left, Jonathan ran to join his teammates. The player who caught the ball missed the hoop. Another teammate retrieved the loose ball and tossed it to the only man who had a three-point court advantage...Jonathan. Of all his skills, the coveted three-point shot was his weakest.

Heart pounding in his chest, Jonathan caught the ball, leaped into the air and threw it, praying it would make the net. As the ball sailed toward the hoop, he dropped his head, afraid of the outcome. A thunderous burst of applause confirmed he had made the shot. The bell rang. The game was over. His team was victorious.

His teammates lifted him up and carried him off of the court, cheering. As he traveled past the stands, he shot a look over to see Tarik, Sherry, Carlos, Javon, and especially Nicola. As were most folks in the gym, she was standing and cheering as loud as she could. Jonathan smiled. It made him feel good to see her get excited about something other than the sex they shared. The only sad moment of the entire evening for Jonathan was realizing he and Nicola would never "know" each other again. He was leaving for college in the next few days.

The locker room quickly filled with coaches, the press, and family members. All were gathered to cheer the winning team. Jonathan was so happy about his achievement, that for a moment he totally dismissed the guilty feelings he nursed whenever he was around Carlos.

"You were phenomenal out there!" Carlos hugged him tightly.

Tarik joined in the bear hug, too. "I knew you could play, man, but what you did out there tonight wasn't just playing...you were like...like...Jordan, man."

Not to be left out, little Javon mimicked his dad and yelled as loud as his little voice would allow. "Yeah, Jordan...just like Jordan, man!" He then added, "Uncle Jonathan, Uncle Jonathan...lift me up to sky...all 'da way up!"

Jonathan lifted up his little nephew and put him on his shoulder. Javon squealed, "Ooh, I'm the tallest boy in the world!" They all looked up at Javon and laughed.

"No, Javon...tonight *I'm* the tallest guy...and the happiest!" Jonathan meant it. He had never felt as much joy as he did at that very moment, surrounded by family, friends and an adoring crowd.

Taking a shower in the gym after the game, Jonathan replayed the night. His body was wet and sticky from all the Gatorade and champagne fans and teammates had poured over his head. It was the best time of his life. The only other moment that could compete was his first love session with Nicola. Scenes of her licking his extended manhood up and down flooded his mind's eye as he lathered his private parts.

He smiled to himself. They had said their good-byes Friday afternoon, right before she and Carlos left for her place in the Hamptons. She had given him a blow job that she promised would last the rest of his life. She had delivered the goods indeed. He'd shot so much hot bubbly juice into Nicola's mouth, he had to perform a Heimlich maneuver just to keep her from choking to death.

Dressed and ready to meet with his family, Jonathan burst into the lobby only to discover Tarik and Carlos wearing grim faces.

"Hey, guys, you act like you just lost your best friend."

Carlos was the first to speak up. "Uh…Eli passed. Tarik just got the call."

CHAPTER FORTY

"Nicola, girl, you got to slow down." Carlos, exhausted from her insatiable demands, collapsed on the bed. "I need a little recoup time. We been doing it all morning long. I am not a machine!"

"Oh, the big bad Carlos can't handle little old Nicola. Oh, poor baby." She licked his earlobes ever so softly. Distracted and concerned about their future as a couple, he squirmed in response. "It's not just that. It's..."

"We'll make it in time for the funeral, don't worry. I'll just lick your entire body clean; you'll be very presentable." She continued to lick every muscle on his body.

"Nicola, baby, I love the loving, but well, we never talk."

"What you want to talk about, sweet thing?"

"I want to talk about us; our future; relationship stuff. I thought you ladies liked that kind of talk?"

"Us is good. Us is *real* good." Nicola gently stroked the entire length of Carlos's manhood. She never stopped marveling at the glorious nature of his dick. Whoever said size didn't matter, had never met Carlos Singleton. Responding to Nicola was the only thing Carlos could do, "Oh, baby, you do have a touch. But, I'm serious about you. I mean, us."

Stroking him even more, Nicola suggested in a raspy voice, "And I seriously want to go for round two."

"It's more like round five, but who's counting." He sat up on the bed and looked at Nicola. "I enjoy our lovemaking, but I just want to know. I want to hear it from you. How do you really feel about me? About us?" Carlos pulled himself away from Nicola's touch. He rummaged through his bag and pulled out a velvet-covered jewelry box. He returned to the bed and presented the box to Nicola.

"I wasn't going to give you this until dinner tonight, but… well, I hope you like it."

Nicola opened the box and pulled out a pair of beautiful diamond earrings. They were identical to the one he wore in his ear. She put them on and rushed over to sit at her vanity. She admired the exquisite jewels in her mirror. "Jonathan…I mean… I mean, Carlos, they're…"

"Jonathan? Damn. You keep calling me Jonathan. That's the third time this morning. Why you got him on the brain? What's really going on here, Nicola?"

Never missing a beat, and never taking her eye off her reflection in the mirror, Nicola concocted a flimsy excuse. "You know I went to see his game the other day, and well, I got caught up with the crowd. Everybody cheering his name. Everybody shouting 'Go, Jonathan… Go, Jonathan.' You were there. You know how it was."

Nicola paused and looked at Carlos's reflection in the mirror. He was so whipped with jealousy she almost laughed out loud and spilled the beans just to see how low his spirit would drop. Instead of going in for the "kill," she simply added, "Guess I still feel that 'winning' spirit."

She stood up, and performed a sexy little cheerleader chant. "Go, Jonathan. Go, Jonathan." She turned around to face Carlos to see if her explanation bore any weight. Did he swallow it or would he challenge it?

"You're right. It was a damn good game. Hell, even I keep saying his name in my brain once or twice. My brother is one bad-ass motherfucker."

"And so are you, my big man. These earrings are gorgeous." She slipped back into the vanity chair.

Carlos kissed her on her neck. "I'm glad you like the earrings, Ms. Nicola." Nicola smiled up at him. He was cute and a darling in the bed. It would be difficult to replace a man with Carlos's equipment. With that thought, she slithered back into the bed and taunted him. "Come here, baby, so Momma can thank you the right way."

Carlos looked at her. Seeing her nude, chocolate body wearing nothing but the jewels he'd given her, made his limp pole morph into a marble statue of wanton lust. He had to fuck her, but he was out of condoms.

"Nicola, oh, I do want you, baby, but I'm all out of rubbers. Maybe later."

Nicola rubbed the inside of her pleasure vault and pulled out a sopping wet finger. She rubbed the thick moistness along the tightness of his shaft. "Mmmm, this is good stuff, baby." She kept re-lubricating her fingers with her natural juices, then massaged the love lotion up and down his massive rod. "I won't get pregnant on you, baby. I promise."

Carlos's intellect whispered loudly that he should postpone his visit to Nicolaville till he was properly suited with a rubber. But Carlos couldn't hear it. Several times that afternoon, before they'd left for the funeral, the young man had plunged every inch of his raging passion inside Nicola, pumping what seemed to be gallons of hot, bubbly potion. He had never enjoyed sex as much.

He loved, cherished, and needed this woman and he would never let anyone or anything come between the two of them. Not even a rubber condom. He trusted her. No matter what his momma or brother said about her, she was a good, clean and virtuous woman. Most importantly, he was convinced that he was her one and only.

Carlos paced downstairs in Nicola's living room. He looked at the antique grandfather clock and knew they'd be late, if they didn't leave right then. Taking advantage of a media opportunity, he shared Eli and Tarik's story with the press. The nature of the father-son relationship, the HIV/drug connection and his brother's blossoming fame, proved to be a journalist's gold mine.

Carlos's phone had rung off the hook from reporters wanting to know the full story. He expected more than a few media folks at the funeral. He wanted to be there to intercede and make sure Tarik got the right kind of press. Looking at the time again, he yelled upstairs, "Nicola, baby, we gotta leave now."

She responded, "In a minute, dear."

Primping in front of her vanity, reluctantly preparing for a funeral she did not want to attend, Nicola seriously considered dumping Carlos. His possessiveness, although cute in the beginning, was starting to bore her. Though he performed masterfully in bed that day, his attempts at making their relationship deeper than it was would only mean less fucking and more talking.

She was done with conversations. She had had plenty of them with her husband. She had even enjoyed talking with him. A lot of good that did.

Harrison James. She hadn't spoken with him in weeks. There were financial forms from her ex-husband that she needed to sign. She made a mental note to get a courier to deliver them to him after the funeral.

She was pissed at Harrison. He had only generated the recent glitch in their divorce settlement to force a meeting with her. Thank God, her lawyer negotiated a deal where all she needed to do was sign on the dotted line. He still sent letters of apology begging for her forgiveness. Lines and lines of trying to remind her how good they used to be together. She shredded all of them. After all these months without him in her life, she still had no desire to look him in the eye.

CHAPTER FORTY-ONE

Thompson Funeral Home had served the Bedford-Stuyvesant community for thirty years. They started as a small storefront business. Casualties of heroin and crack addiction, the gang wars and the AIDS epidemic created a bumper crop of business for the Thompson clan. They reinvested earnings and purchased a cluster of five brownstones that they renovated into one contiguous building. The restoration was so extravagant that the demand for their services increased exponentially.

Big Daddy Thompson, the founder, loved fine art and devoted an entire floor to display his prized possessions. Wanting to share his collection with the community that had supported his business so faithfully over the years, he opened it up to the public.

To entice Nicola into coming to the funeral, Carlos "mentioned" that Thompson had just acquired originals by Romare Bearden and abstract artist James Little. Her love of art made her change her mind.

Carlos drove his mother's blue Cadillac to the funeral. Ophelia was in the back of the car, quietly suffering. She already missed Eli.

Nicola sat next to Carlos in silence. She hated funerals just like she was beginning to hate her relationship with the "music mogul." With Jonathan in the picture, the thrill of possible exposure brought with it an excitement that had helped fuel their tryst. Now that that was over...the only thing left to entertain her was Mr. Big Dick and his clinging ways.

She had stopped prowling restaurants, bars, and the internet for partners. Focusing on and nurturing her relationship with the two young men had helped quench her insatiable sexual appetite. Visits with the infamous Williams family served her purposes as well. All of her affairs had helped her in some wonderful way to heal. The despair that took up residence in the pit of her soul after she discovered Harrison's secret, was now vanishing.

Nicola had reached a turning point in her quest to purge the misery of her tortured childhood, as well as Harrison's affair. She pulled out her compact mirror to powder her nose. Ophelia's bitchy reflection glared at her. Nicola smiled. *You won't have to worry about me much longer*, she thought. After the funeral today, both Carlos and Jonathan would be history. Mama Ophelia could have both of her boys back.

Ophelia sat in the backseat of the car fidgeting, wishing that the funeral was behind her. As they passed by Tompkins Square Park, a view of the basketball court reminded her of her son. "I hope Jonathan makes it in time for the services."

"Don't worry, he'll be here. One thing about him, he's a man of his word. Very reliable. And you shoulda seen him at that game, Mother. He was magnificent. I'll sure miss him when he goes away to school."

"Me, too. He's a great kid," Nicola added.

Ophelia ignored Nicola, as memories of her making sexual advances at poor little innocent Jonathan at the concert flooded her conscience. Dismissing these disturbing thoughts and visions, Ophelia commented, "I'm so sorry I didn't make it to his last game…I was… with Eli…I hope…I hope he'll forgive me."

"Don't worry, he understands. Plus, there'll be other games for you to attend. Did he tell you that the new expansion team in North Carolina, the one owned by Bob Johnson, offered him a spot after his high school graduation?"

"My boy is going straight to college. I don't care what Bob Johnson offers him."

"He'd be a fool to turn a professional team down that offered him mad money in the millions now, versus possibly getting injured within the next four years on a non-paying college team and missing his chance at the pros."

"Maybe you have a point, Carlos. I don't know."

"'Course I do. After basketball, if he still wants to do the doctor thing...he could get a degree then." Carlos laughed as he added, "Hell, he could buy himself a hospital with all the stupid money he's 'bout to make."

Ophelia's thoughts drifted back to Eli. "I don't know what I'm going to do with his ashes."

Nicola suggested, "Well, he was an artist, a native New Yorker. Spread his ashes at the beach, Coney Island."

Proud that Nicola had made such a logical suggestion, or rather happy she was finally breaking her sulky mood, he overly supported her suggestion. "Isn't that a good idea, Mama? A great idea, don't you..."

Still not settled with the fact that her son was dating such a low-class vixen, she snapped back, "Eli hated the damn beach, and hated Coney Island most of all; said it was too 'common.'" She smiled to herself, feeling she had struck a target. Carlos was too stupid to see this woman for the piece of work she really was.

She was going to miss her time with Eli, but now she could devote more attention to her boys. Make sure they all get back on the straight and narrow. Especially Carlos. He was not himself since he fell for the tramp. His confidence level had slipped into the toilet. He was more agitated than usual; even snapped at her for the littlest things.

And the biggest tip of all was the nightmare. After that evening when she rocked her grown son to sleep, she knew he needed her help and support. After the funeral was over, she was going to insist he visit a counselor to talk about his problems. She was not going to take "no" for an answer.

Her boy Carlos. Who would think he would fall so hard and so stupid for a woman? Ophelia shamefully hung her head down low. Who was she to judge? She had loved Eli, a poster pin-up for the wrong man, all her adult life. But right or wrong…it was still the sweetest feeling she had ever experienced.

In the deep place she only visited on romantic moon-lit nights she reflected back on the good times she had spent loving and being loved by Eli. She felt blessed by the time she shared with him in the end. No regrets. But Ophelia was determined to give Ms. Nicola a regret or two.

The quiet in the car was almost deafening. They passed St. John's Hospital. Carlos took a cheap stab at making conversation. "Ms. Nicola, we are now passing by my birthplace. The famous St. John's Hospital." Realizing how very little he knew about Nicola, he inquired, "By the way, where were you born?"

Nicola looked away. She was going to avoid the answer, but something deep inside her wanted to tell the truth. It probably had something to do with her making this her last time with Carlos. "I wasn't born in a hospital. They found me in the Nicola factory, a few blocks away from Kings County Hospital. My adopted parents named me after the building."

Ophelia perked up. "What did you say?"

"My mother escaped from a mental institution, gave birth to me in the building, tried to kill me and then jumped out of the window."

She turned around to smile at Carlos's mother... hoping the story would horrify her. Seeing those sparkling eyes reconnected Ophelia to the past. This couldn't be the same infant she'd help nurse back to health all those years ago; the beautiful baby girl she and Eli were planning to adopt?

Carlos held his breath. Though he tried, he could not utter a single word. He never had any idea about Nicola's past.

Ophelia was in shock. She needed more information. "Your parents? Where are they?"

"Never knew my father and my mother. Like I said, they died when I was born. I was adopted by the Martins."

"And your adopted family. Where are they now?"

Nicola, surprisingly calm during Ophelia's inquisition, decided against full disclosure, smiled broadly, and said, "When I was twelve...they...they, uh...died in a fire. After that, I lived in a group home until I left at eighteen for college. End of story."

Ophelia sat still, staring straight ahead. This was the baby girl she and Eli had fallen in love with. This piece of shit sitting next to her son, if fate had been different, could have been her daughter. Knowing and feeling the evil in the girl, she shuddered when she considered that maybe life had been less than kind to her.

If Eli hadn't messed up that day, so long ago, they could have spared Nicola the horror she must have witnessed. Ophelia now knew that those beautiful brown eyes that had captured her and her husband so many years ago, held secrets...secrets that made this girl act out pages scripted by Satan himself. For the umpteenth time since she'd first met Eli, she cursed his soul. His weakness had once again brought grief to the people he loved.

Feeling genuine compassion for her, she admitted, "Nicola... I...I knew you when you were in the hospital. In fact, as crazy as it may sound now, Eli and I came very close to adopting you."

"Now, wouldn't that have been special."

"Yes, wouldn't it have?"

Ophelia shared the entire story with them. How Tarik almost died thanks to Eli's drug use. Trying to repress tears, Nicola maintained a cool, indifferent composure. She didn't want to tip her hand that the tale of how she had missed being adopted by Eli and Ophelia had set off an emotional explosion deep down in her soul.

All things considered, Nicola knew Ophelia was a good woman. And as far as she could tell, had been a great mom. Ophelia rightfully didn't like her because she knew she was screwing her son and nephew. There was no reason to expect a warm welcome from her. She respected Ophelia for protecting her family.

Nicola fought back a tear. Nobody ever protected her. It was only until she met Harrison, that she felt safe with another human being. Oh, yes. If Ophelia had raised Nicola, her life would be different.

But life was what it was and somebody, somewhere, was going to have to pay for her pain.

CHAPTER FORTY-TWO

"I look like a grown man, don't I, Daddy?'

"Yep…like a man, Javon." Tarik readjusted his tie.

Javon looked so cute in his suit. They had decided to bring him along at the last minute when the babysitter fell through.

Tarik looked at the clock on the wall. They would arrive so late, it didn't make any sense to leave. "Sherry, I'm sure it's over by now. Maybe let's just skip…"

"Now you know you have to go. These things never start on time. Just call up someone and tell them we're on our way." Tarik looked at Sherry and Javon. His family. He thought about how Eli had given up his family so easily. He still couldn't fathom how a man walks away from the people you love most in the world. He could never abandon Sherry or Javon or the new baby Sherry and he were bringing into the world. He went over to Javon, picked him up, and gave him a big hug.

"Why you hug me, Daddy?"

"It's 'cause I just love you. That's all. I just love you."

Sherry looked at her husband and thanked God for blessing her with such a good man.

The ceremony was at five. It was almost six o'clock. Javon had fallen asleep in the backseat. Deep in thought, Tarik drove slowly. Sherry had to nudge him once or twice to drive off after the traffic lights turned green.

"Are you giving the eulogy?"

"Who me? I didn't know him that well. Mr. Thompson's going to say a few words Mama prepared."

"He wanted to be cremated?"

"Eli wasn't fancy. He wanted no frills. He even told us not to claim the body so that he wouldn't be a financial burden."

"What?"

"Well, if no one claims the body, the corpse is sent to Potter's Field."

"But your mother wouldn't have that, I guess."

"You know, I finally figured it out about those two. I always kind of wondered why Mother was so committed to caring for Eli."

"Well, she is a nurse, and she's genuinely a compassionate person."

"No. It went way beyond that for those two. He wasn't just another patient. I saw them together and how they were with each other. I'd never tell Carlos or Jonathan this, but I'm certain that for my mother, Eli was the one."

"The one what…he was a damn dope addict!" Immediately regretting what she said, she softened and added, "I'm sorry. I didn't mean to talk about your father like that."

"Let's get this straight for once and for all. Pops was my father. Eli was a tragic person who figured out life too late and I'm cool with that, too. And you're right; he was a junkie who didn't give a shit for nobody but the next high. But I think…I mean…I know there was a time that he wasn't a junkie. And that was the time he was the one for my mother. They were soul mates."

Javon's eyes opened, only to discover he was still trapped in a car seat. Impatient with the journey, he whined, "Daddy, we 'dere? We at the sleepytime place?" Sherry and Tarik stole shocked glances at each other. Evidently, he still remembered the explanation about death they'd shared with him a few months ago when he'd asked about his first daddy. The response that comforted him best was that death was a very long sleep; a sleep so good that you never wake up.

Sherry smiled and leaned back to readjust his belt. She patted his head. "We're almost there, sugar pie." Tarik looked at his son through the rearview mirror, marveling at how precious he was. "Baby, give my brother a call. Tell him we're almost at the sleepytime place."

Happy that he would finally see where his first daddy had fallen asleep, Javon clapped his hands joyfully.

CHAPTER FORTY-THREE

They held the service in a small intimate chapel on the second floor of the Thompson Funeral Home. Ophelia placed the copper urn containing Eli's ashes on a prominent pedestal located in the front of the room. She looked at it for a few moments. Discovering Nicola's identity had the unfortunate effect of reminding her of what an asshole Eli had been. The intense sadness she originally felt about his passing had mellowed considerably.

She shook her head and turned around to find the woman who should have been her daughter staring out of a window. The faintest trace of maternal urges compelled her to go to her. Comfort her in some way. At the very least try to understand and treat her like a human being who'd been shortchanged so early in life. Ophelia, not knowing Nicola's full story, intuitively knew losing two parents at such a young early age and growing up in a group home had to be a hellish existence.

Instead of reaching out to her, she made a mental note to try to be civil with her when Carlos brought her around. Regardless of her history, Nicola was still a hoochie mama playing her son.

Nicola stared out of the window. She was numb. When Ophelia first explained how Eli's negligence had stopped her from becoming their foster child and ultimately their adopted daughter, a rage penetrated through her that she hadn't felt since she burnt down the Martins' house with them in it. She wanted to reconstruct Eli's ashes to throw him in the very same flames; only after first cursing him out for being so worthless.

Rather than dwell on the past, she immediately fell into her old pattern of burying her feelings and locking them away as soon as possible. Since Nicola made a habit of not crying over the things that did or didn't happen, she forced herself to stop lamenting over past circumstances she could not change.

"A penny for your thoughts, beautiful." Carlos grabbed her around the waist. Instantaneously, Nicola summoned her thoughts back into the present. A time she could do something with.

"Isn't it wild? We could be brother and sister. I'm... I'm really glad old Eli messed up...the way he did," Nicola lied to herself and Carlos.

Never questioning her lack of remorse, he kissed Nicola on the cheek. "I'd much rather have this kind of relationship with you," he added, "...besides, from what you told me, life didn't turn out too bad for you... now did it."

Nicola smiled politely. He didn't know about the hell she went through in her childhood. She hadn't even told him the full story about why she and Harrison divorced. She looked at him as he stared at her with loving eyes. He was in love with a woman he knew nothing about. What a fool.

Carlos grabbed her hand and led her out of the chapel. "Follow me." Jumping at an opportunity to abandon her gloomy thoughts, she obediently followed Carlos down a long hallway.

Waiting at the end of the hall next to the bathroom was Carlos's destination, the gallery entrance. A sign hanging from a brass doorknob warned patrons not to enter. Construction of a new office was underway. Carlos eagerly proceeded through. "Don't worry about the sign. I pulled a few strings," he said, trying to impress a very unimpressed Nicola. "I know the owner. They're just about finished with the work. He said it was okay to come in and check out the art."

He held the small of her back as he escorted her into the gallery. From the entrance, Nicola and Carlos could see directly into a partially constructed room that was located at the rear of the 1,000-square-foot space. The only furniture inside the owner's new office was a beautiful chaise longue lined with genuine leather.

The "what-coulda-been" blues kept trying to bring Nicola down. She needed something to help pep her up. Help her stop thinking how Eli had blown her chance for happiness. When she saw the chaise longue, she immediately knew the biggest blues chaser in the world was hanging not on the wall but right between Carlos's legs. She dragged him into the office, happy to discover the chaise longue was big enough for the both of them.

Nicola stood in front of Carlos and grabbed his crotch. With deliberate intent, she ripped down his zipper, reached into his pants and forced his instantly responsive rod into her well-lubricated mouth.

Shocked, Carlos pulled back and stuffed his semi-hard tool back into the safe haven of his underpants. "Nicola, please, baby, please, not here. Not with my mama down the hall. Not at a funeral. Didn't I give you enough this morning?"

"I'm too nasty for you, baby?"

"Yes, Nicola, I think you've hit my limit. We cannot fool around in the funeral parlor."

Like a spoiled child, Nicola pushed out her bottom lip and turned her back on Carlos.

He zipped up his trousers and pulled Nicola out of the office. "Baby, I brought you here because of the art, okay? Let's look at the nice pictures on the wall. I'll take care of other things; later."

Nicola looked at Carlos. He didn't know it, but later would never happen for him. This would have been their last time together. After finding out about his mother, she wanted nothing more to do with him or his family.

But she did like the pictures that graced the walls of the modest gallery. Nicola was in her element. Next to sex, art was her biggest passion. Thompson's collection was indeed impressive. Nicola stopped in front of an original painting by Annie Lee. It was called "Blue Monday." A lithographed copy of the same picture hung in her dining room.

"I know how she feels."

Carlos looked at the painting depicting a black woman sitting on the side of the bed with her head hanging down, obviously dreading the day ahead and contrasted her with the vivacious woman he had fallen hopelessly in love with.

"Nicola, I don't see you like that at all...not one bit."

She turned around and kissed his cheek. "I don't think you see me at all."

Confused, he looked at her with a puzzled look. "What you talking about? Of course, I see you; all of you."

"You go on back to your family. I'll be along shortly."

"But, baby, I wanted to spend this time with you..."

"Go deal with all those media people. Go on; don't worry about me."

"Nicola, please..."

Nicola looked at him. Begging like a punk. Reminded her of Harrison. They were both pathetic. She decided right on the spot she'd had enough and yelled, "And... I'm not attending the service. I'll stay here. Just come get me afterward and take me home!" She turned away from him to look at the picture hanging before her.

Carlos was crushed. He wanted her by his side. "But... Nicola...you...you promised..."

"I said I'd go to the funeral parlor to see the art. Never said anything about the service. I told you, I hate funerals."

Desperately trying to convince her otherwise, he put his arms around her waist and pleaded, "But you'll get bored back here all by yourself, baby."

"A service for a burnt-out junkie won't be long, and besides," she looked back at him and winked mischievously, "Nicola knows how to entertain Nicola."

Laughing, she pulled away from him and paid full interest to the art, ignoring him totally. He wanted to protest, but she had told the truth. He did need to take care of business and the complete service wouldn't take more than fifteen minutes. And she had said repeatedly how she hated funerals.

Still, he thought she could make this one sacrifice. He'd do it for her. He'd do anything for her. He loved her. He knew then, it was clear as a Windex-cleaned window, that she'd never make the same claim because she didn't love him the way he loved her.

Dragging his poor, rejected body out of the gallery, he wondered why this woman, whom he had given his all to, couldn't return his love. Could the answer simply be that he was in love with someone who didn't exist? Was Nicola right? Did he not see her for who she really was? A chill went down his spine.

Or had his mama read her right the first time they met? She called her a tramp and a whore. Maybe she was screwing other men. The same green-eyed monster that forced him to rummage through Nicola's trashcans now possessed Carlos's mind, body and soul.

Shaking his head, as if trying to erase all doubt, Carlos tried to compose himself before entering the funeral parlor. He could see that quite a few music industry people had arrived. He didn't have time for the jealous band that was beginning to play in his head.

Instead, he went into the bathroom and forced himself to calm down. He had to totally reject his mother's notions about Nicola and embrace the soothing thought that the woman he loved was really a fine lady who had a healthier than normal sexual appetite; an appetite that she allowed only him to satisfy.

Carlos relieved himself at the urinal. He looked at the mirror but it was his father, Hector Salinas's face that stared back at him. Carlos's mind snapped. He was no longer a confident young man on the verge of owning a successful record company. He was a seven-year-old boy watching his daddy rip a diamond earring out of his mother's ear.

Hector, is you crazy! I just bought those earrings. There's nobody else but you... You're a slut and I'm sending you to heaven to purify yourself. I warned you to stop sleeping around... Hector. No, don't do it. Don't pull the trigger... Poppi, don't shoot Mommy. We just bought those earrings at the store... Don't lie for this slut. A man bought those earrings. Your mother's bad, boy. Real bad. I'm sending her to heaven to make her good... BAM! BAM! BAM!... Poppi! Mommy's bleeding. Mommy's bleeding. She's not moving... Poppi bought you strawberry ice cream. It's your favorite... Poppi, why you pointing the gun at my head. Please, Poppi, don't point the gun at my head... Don't worry, son. Just eat your ice cream. When you finish, you and me are going to heaven to be with your mama and everything's going to be perfect for us. We'll be happy in heaven because Mama will be a good woman in heaven. No other men. Just me and you. Hurry up and eat your ice cream... HECTOR SALINAS! THIS IS THE POLICE! WE'RE COMING IN... Poppi, it's the police...Poppi... don't pull the trigger...BAM!

Lying on the bathroom floor in a fetal position, Carlos trembled. He heard the voices and he could see the scene as if it was taking place right in front of him. He saw his father putting the gun in his mouth and pulling the trigger. He heard it go off as his head exploded into a million pieces. He could see his father's body collapse into a pool of blood next to his mother.

Someone kept banging on the bathroom door and yelling, "Hey, is anybody in there? Hello? Is anybody there?"

The noise revived Carlos and helped him grab hold of a thin thread of sanity that brought him back to the present. He yelled back, "I'll be out! I'll be out in a few!"

The powerful flashback had drained him. His mind was in complete chaos. He needed to rearrange his attitude if he was going to make it through the funeral.

As if attempting a baptism…he splashed several handfuls of cold water on his face…hoping the shocking temperature would return his unstable mind back to normal. He continued this for what seemed like hours, but still the man in the mirror confirmed that nothing had changed but time. Carlos could feel he was easily slipping down a mental path that led to nowhere good.

CHAPTER FORTY-FOUR

*J*onathan ran up the stairs four steps at a time. An overwhelming urge to relieve his bladder that he'd ignored during his entire trip to the funeral home was now demanding immediate attention. He burst through the door and ran into Carlos in the foyer.

"Carlos…"

"Glad you made it."

"Am I too late?"

"No, Tarik's not even here yet. We're waiting for him to start."

"Hey, where's the bathroom?"

Still weak from his experience in the bathroom, Carlos absent-mindedly pointed down the long hall.

Jonathan quickly followed his directions. He found the bathroom. Upon exiting, he saw that the door to the gallery was partially open. Though the sign said, "Do

Not Enter," he could hear a woman humming. The voice was very familiar.

Nicola stood in a far-off corner with her back to the door, in deep thought. She was examining a Nigerian statue. She was still trying to shake thoughts of how different life would've been if Ophelia had adopted her.

Sneaking up on her, breaking her concentration, Jonathan covered both of her eyes. "Guess who?"

Nicola twirled around to face him. "It could only be you!" They hugged each other tightly and warmly. Nicola was glad to see him. She needed to think about something other than a missed opportunity that she really had had no control over. Sex as always, would be just what she needed to preoccupy her mind and put her back in a happy space. She had not expected an opportunity to spend time alone with Jonathan again. One more chance to feel his young, muscular arms frantically search her body like a poisoned man hunting for an antidote.

Jonathan, though not as talented a lover or as well-equipped as Carlos, beat him out in the eagerness department. Nothing was sexier to her than a man who had to have it. He was always horny. Always ready to go several times on the love treadmill. Carlos, phenomenal tools notwithstanding, occasionally was blasé about screwing. She thought of how he had rejected her earlier.

Her mind quickly drifted back to an afternoon she'd spent with Jonathan. Their lovemaking session had absolutely drained her. She'd fallen asleep in his arms, only to be reawakened by his attempt to sneak his steel-hard shaft inside of her without disturbing her. She remembered how innocent he looked when she opened her eyes and caught him in the act. He'd said apologetically, "I'm sorry, I didn't want to wake you. But I...I had to get some...more. Is it okay?"

She only smiled and whispered, "Hell, yes!" He continued to shove himself deep into her opening. Aroused, she had responded in kind, her walls lubricating, giving Jonathan's manhood a full VIP reception. He pumped into her with such gusto one would think he received an e-mail warning that this would be his last visit to Nicolaville.

He kept striking her hot spot with a perfect level of pressure, catapulting her passion to a volcanic erupting zone. They rocked together like two ships caught in a perfect storm; their bodies swaying together. Coming together, thick hot fluid leaked out, heralding the consummation of their passion.

Nicola smiled as she remembered that passionate afternoon and got horny all over again. The memory was so powerful she ground her hips against Jonathan's body. He responded in kind. Like two virgins trying to get an orgasm without the actual deed, they dipped and grooved their limbs hard against each other's organs, hoping that the friction, even through clothing, would bring them the excitement their bodies desired.

Rock hard, Jonathan whispered, "For Christ's sake, Nicola...the funeral—"

"What about the funeral?" Nicola was so excited, he couldn't reason with her.

"You can't...I can't...we just can't do this."

Nicola pulled herself from him. "Oh, but we can... and we will."

She headed for the entrance door and slammed it shut, locking out all thoughts of the life she could have had with Ophelia. Pleased that soon she would be so immersed in erotic ecstasy...she'd never think about her childhood...never think about how she might have never been tortured by the Martins. *In just a few seconds,* thought Nicola, *it'll just be our two bodies rocking together...erasing all the negatives in my past.*

CHAPTER FORTY-FIVE

Pull yourself together, Carlos whispered to himself. He needed to focus to work the funeral the way he planned. Drawing on all the energy he could muster, he eventually calmed down and morphed into the image of a confident young man who was more than capable of taking care of business.

Scanning the room to see who had attended, he discovered Uncle Link huddled in a corner with his mother. A smile crept into his face. He knew the shy, but extremely successful, attorney had a crush on his mom. Carlos did not disapprove. He knew Pops would have given his best friend his approval as well.

Slowly regaining control of his mind, Carlos was pleased that the little funeral they had planned was turning into an event. As he had hoped, members of the press did attend. With a little help from some of his friends, the word had obviously spread that Tarik's dad had passed. Even a few artists, who saw the announcement in the paper and remembered Eli, came to pay their respects. In total, there were almost seventy-five people present.

He saw a young rapper who he and Tarik had considered producing in the near future. He quickly greeted him and engaged in a conversation, hoping that keeping busy would help extinguish the insane inferno blazing in his mind.

Ophelia had Tarik pull together a CD with Eli's favorite tunes. Jazz from old timers Ike Quebec, the Duke, Queen Ella and Lady Day. The music played softly in the background as she and Link updated each other on their lives.

Tarik finally arrived with Sherry and Javon. Ophelia held out her arms for her young grandson. He ran into them and greeted her with a big, sloppy kiss.

"How's my favorite grandbaby doing?"

"Good, Grandma Ophelia. You gonna show me where they go to sleep?"

"Sleep? Sherry...?" Ophelia looked at Sherry and Tarik, not understanding what Javon was talking about.

"It's a long story; we'll tell you later." Sherry kissed Javon on the cheek. "Mommy and Daddy will show you the sleep place... later."

"Mama, I'm sorry for being so late." He asked hopefully, "Did we miss it?"

Tarik looked around and realized that the chapel was

packed. He had expected only the immediate family. "Who are all these people?"

"Sweetheart, there was no way I was going to start this without you. As for this crowd, most of these folks are Carlos's friends and a few of Eli's old artist cronies. Now let me go tell Arnold we can start with the ceremony."

Arnold Thompson was pouring it on hard. It was only his second time presiding over a funeral. Though he'd been groomed to take over the family business, a spiritual calling too powerful to ignore had dragged him to divinity school. He had finished his first year and he was eager to lead a flock to glory and welcomed any chance to deliver a service. He poured out a powerful message for Eli and his passing. There wasn't a dry eye in the house as he dramatically testified about the complexities of life.

Bored as most children were at events like funerals, Javon fidgeted and kept getting in and out of his chair. He was getting on Sherry's last nerve. "Keep still, baby, please." She leaned over to Tarik. "I knew we should have gotten a babysitter."

"We tried, remember?"

Sherry sighed. She was really going to have to expand her babysitter file. Now that Tarik's career was catapulting, she often had to attend functions at the drop of a hat. She had sworn she'd never get a nanny, but it was becoming an unavoidable choice.

As Javon squirmed out of his seat for the fifth time, and Tarik lifted him up and made him sit on his lap, she made her decision. Monday they would start interviewing nannies. Especially now that there were twins on the way, she would need the extra help. She smiled. Tarik didn't know. She had discovered the news at her first prenatal visit. The doctor had scheduled another appointment in two weeks. Tarik was coming. That's when she would surprise him.

Sherry was happy. She looked over at her talented handsome husband. He was bouncing their son on his knee, trying to quiet him down. She smiled. Even with his busy schedule, he always made sure that family was his number one priority. She no longer harbored doubts about Tarik's fidelity. After he had been so candid about what Nicola had done to him at the after-party, she knew he was an honest man.

During the service, Ophelia sobbed like an abandoned baby found on the steps of a church. Pissed at Eli for the loser he was, she still cried. She hadn't dropped a single tear at Pops' funeral. Everyone then had thought her a brave woman.

But now she knew why she didn't cry for Pops. It had nothing to do with courage. It was all about that silly, makes no damn sense at all, crazy thing called love. It made a difference. Eli had been her one and only. Worthless as he had been, she mourned that she'd never share time with him again. He had finally kicked his habit and cleaned up. So sad they would find themselves only to be separated again. This time for good. The irony of it all wasn't lost on her.

And what about Nicola and how she was the little baby they were going to adopt? They never had a chance to raise Tarik together. If their love had triumphed, she wouldn't now have to decide how to tear Carlos away from the evil vixen she knew Nicola had become.

Carlos could not listen to the sermon. What was Nicola doing? There wasn't that much artwork in that room. He tried to relax and get a grip on himself and sanity, but he was losing the battle. He wanted to go back and drag her to the service, but he knew it would piss her off. He didn't want her to think he was spying.

But curiosity was bugging him out. His thoughts made no sense. Of course, she was still examining the artwork; appreciating the nuances of the statues. He remembered how she literally spent an hour studying one bowl at the Egyptian exhibit at the Metropolitan Museum of Art. It was then that he fully realized how much she loved art. He made a mental note to take her to Egypt to tour their museums and visit the pyramids on her next birthday.

He cringed inside. He didn't even know her birth date. If he thought hard about it...he really didn't have much information about her life. He only knew two things about Nicola for sure... she liked to fuck and she liked to fuck a lot.

She was just looking at the pictures. He knew that. But it still did not plug up the mental hole that leaked out all of his better judgment. His mind had taken an unexpected turn into jump-to-conclusion land and he was two seconds from exploding. The doubt he had about Nicola's character was consuming all his good sense. The thoughts in his mind were like demons partying hard at a sinner's convention.

What if she's not just looking at pictures? Could she have slipped out and decided to be with someone else? The thought sent icicles through his veins. Visions of another man caressing his woman's body made his blood boil. Like a knee reflex, he felt for his pistol.

He shook his head. He had to stop the crazy thinking before it was too late. Before Nicola, he'd seen guys go off the deep end over a woman. He'd always laughed at them. He wasn't laughing now.

*C*HAPTER FORTY-SIX

*N*icola was not satisfied with heavy petting. She turned off the lights in the gallery, grabbed Jonathan, dragged him into the office and pushed him down on the chaise lounge. Knowing what was going to happen next, Jonathan liberated his sledge-hammer-hard rod from his pants. He pulled Nicola to him, parted her legs and shoved his fingers past a silk beaded thong. She was wet and she was ready. In a deep guttural voice, he claimed, "We don't need these." He ripped off the thong and threw it on the floor.

"Oh, Jonathan, baby." Excited by his assertiveness, she impaled herself on Jonathan's glistening pole. She glided up and down its full length. "Ooh, it feels too good."

Jonathan was losing it. The thought of fucking in a funeral home was as absurd to him as it was erotic. Hard, cold dead bodies contrasted with his granite dick. Nicola grinded on him with skill. He reached into her open blouse and fondled her breasts.

"Jonathan, lick my nipples. Lick them like I taught you, baby." He obeyed. "You so good to mama; so good." She slid up and down his shaft. With each landing against his body, her pleasure knob was stroked. "Touch my spot, Jonathan. Rub it good; rub it real good."

Like a robot, he massaged her joy button just like she liked it. First slowly, and then speeding it up, applying just the right amount of pleasure. Feeling an orgasm coming, Nicola rode his dick stallion-style, like she was racing competitively. The prize...ecstasy.

Carlos couldn't help himself. He had to see Nicola. He got out of his seat in the middle of Thompson's sermon. With every step down the long dark corridor, fate accompanied him. He was never going to walk down a hall the same way again.

Hector's voice kept whispering: *Eat your ice cream, boy...that Nicola's a slut.* The voice was driving Carlos insane.

Before turning the knob on the door, he hesitated for what seemed an eternity. Hector commanded him: *Turn the doorknob, boy...she's in there fucking somebody... you know it. Open the door...eat your ice cream.*

Growing madder by the minute, Carlos heard voices from behind the door. A man and a woman. He couldn't make out the words, but even he knew that the couple beyond the door were engaged in an intimate moment.

Jonathan was going to explode any second. He couldn't hold back...not anymore. "I'm gonna come, Nicola. I'm gonna come, baby!"

It was a race to see who would be first. Nicola rode him, all the while her love-button kept smashing against his body, sending a thousand watts of creamy electrical current up her spine. Reaching the finish line...the gates of pleasure opened. She was there. She screamed out loud in celebration, "Ahh... Ahhh...oh Jonathan... JONATHAN!'"

Carlos's heart was racing. Mad adrenaline pumped through his veins. The conversation he heard was now fully audible. He could hear what the couple were saying. Nasty talk. Nasty, I'm-enjoying-this-fuck kind of talk. And he knew it was definitely Nicola's voice. He had heard it too many times before.

He entered the gallery. It was dark, but he could still make out shadows. He saw Nicola's thong on the floor and the two bodies on the chaise longue, both engaged in a furious sexual dance. He knew it was Nicola. She was coming and she was letting everybody know about it. She wasn't even the least bit ashamed or worried that someone might discover her.

"Daddy, I got to go make pee-pee." Tarik looked at the little boy who had mischief painted all over his face. He figured it was just a ploy to leave the ceremony, but he took him to the bathroom anyway. Soon as he set the little bugger down, he ran away from him, heading straight down the hall.

Tarik chased after him. "Stop running, boy." Glad to be free and out of the room and all the solemnity, the little boy wanted to play with his daddy.

Tarik repeated his warning. "I said stop now, Javon!"

"Daddy can't catch me!" Laughing, Javon stopped in front of the gallery door.

"Boy, if you go in there, I'm gonna take..." He reluctantly added, "I'm gonna take my belt off!"

Javon laughed. His daddy, who had threatened him so many times before, and had never laid a hand on him, hadn't even worn a belt today.

The precocious child reminded him. "Daddy don't have no belt."

Pissed at himself and his smart-alecky son, he tried to rush ahead of him to stop him. "If you go in there, boy, your butt is mine!"

Javon pushed the gallery door wide open and turned to face his father. Javon just laughed and squealed, "I'm going to see the sleepytime place." As far as he was concerned...he was playing a game with his daddy. Tarik grabbed for him and missed.

He smiled back at him and ran into the room.

Carlos never heard Javon enter the gallery. He never heard his brother yell after the boy. It never registered. Before he knew what he was doing, the gun was in his hand and he was pulling the trigger. Bullets pumped out that ricocheted all over the room. He finally stopped when a sharp, intense, explosive wave of pain traveled from his scrotum to his penis. "Oh shit…I blew up…I blew up my dick!" He turned and saw that little Javon had collapsed in a puddle of blood.

Everything was in slow motion. He barely heard Tarik yelling at him and screaming out for help. He never saw Jonathan holding what was left of his knee. The last thing his mind allowed him to contemplate before a curtain of unconsciousness completely engulfed him… was Nicola. How was she? Where was she? Where was Nicola?

Sherry and Ophelia burst through the door.

"OH MY BABY! OH MY GOD! WHO DID THIS?" Sherry looked at her son and knelt down next to him. Tarik cradled the young boy in his arms. Blood bubbled out the corners of his mouth.

"Mommy…Daddy…am I…am I at the…the sleepy-time place?"

"Yes, baby…yes, Javon!" comforted Tarik.

"Good, Daddy." And then his eyes closed; never to open again. His body grew limp in Tarik's arms.

"Javon…JAVON…BABY!!!!" Sherry screamed out. Tarik cried.

Sherry looked around. She knew it was somebody's fault. The only one standing without a scratch on them was Nicola. Without any explanation…she knew the bitch was behind it all.

Sherry got up from where her dead child lay and jumped on Nicola. Nicola tried to defend herself, but she was no match for a mother who had just lost her child. Sherry forgot all she had learned about anger management and beat the snot out of Nicola.

CHAPTER FORTY-SEVEN

Nicola felt like a human being for the first time after the funeral. For the first time in three weeks, she was sobering up after doing nothing but drinking alcohol and watching the wounds that Sherry had inflicted upon her heal.

Nicola dragged herself into the bathroom. She looked at her reflection in the mirror. The swelling around her eyes had finally gone down. Marveling at the purplish discoloration from the black eye Sherry had given her, she thought, *That little woman packed one hell of a punch. But I deserved it. She shoulda killed me.*

The plastic surgeon who stitched the cuts over the rest of her face, reassured her the scars would be almost undetectable and, if they were noticeable, he could use his magic on them and make them disappear entirely.

But it wasn't her face that troubled Nicola. It was a

dead little boy. A senseless death that she felt responsible for.

Every time her mind cleared, she could still see Tarik cradling Javon in his arms. She could still hear him screaming for someone to help. And Lord, the tears. The tears he shed on that dying child's face and the way it mixed with the bright red blood that pumped out from that fatal gunshot wound. That's what tortured Nicola the most.

Every time she read the newspaper delivered to her door, or turned on the TV and saw a news report about the incident, it brought the image back. The pain of the memory made Nicola head to her well-stocked liquor cabinet and guzzle down whatever she could, trying desperately to dull the memory. All it did was prolong the inevitable. She would have to face reality one day soon.

Today was evidently the day. Nicola took a long hot bath. Still feeling unclean, she took an even longer shower. She threw on a sweat suit, thinking she could forget by running on the treadmill and building up a good sweat. The more she ran, the vision and memory of what happened at the funeral wiped away all other thoughts and concerns.

She turned off the treadmill and ran out of her home gym. Fueled by an idea she was sure would help, Nicola stormed into her ex-husband's office and rampaged through his desk. She let out a sigh of relief. *Thank God.*

It's still here. This will help me...it always did before. She picked up what she hoped would help soothe her soul... a strand of rosary beads...beads blessed by the Pope himself.

Looking for the most tranquil spot in her home, Nicola ran up to her rooftop patio. Sitting on a bench, for two hours straight, she dutifully caressed each individual bead, silently praying and confessing her sins in mantra-like fashion.

At the end of two hours, feeling no spiritual solace from performing the ritual, she ripped and tore the beads off the strand. They flew off in every direction, creating chaos as they landed on the wood planks of the patio floor. Frustrated, seeking comfort and relief, she yelled out to God:

Punish me, please!!! Punish me...not that boy...not that boy...But I'm a victim, too.

Eli...That damn dope addict...He's lucky his ass got away... lucky he's dead...'cuz I'd kill him all over again...if he hadn't messed up my chance of being adopted by a normal family... his normal family... hose evil demon bastards who did adopt me would've never had a chance to fuck me.

Maybe things would've been different...maybe I would have seen that my husband was a faggot back in the beginning... I wouldn't have married him...and then I wouldn't have been at that funeral parlor screwing that young boy...trying to...soothe my pain...MY PAIN. My pain hurt Carlos... made him jealous...made him blind with jealousy...that's why he pulled the trigger...and hurt Jonathan and then killed little Javon...that precious child...that beautiful baby boy. He'd still be alive!

Staring at her image in the mirror, and caressing the scar on her neck, she derived some soothing pleasure as a new idea began to gestate in her tortured mind. A smile, her first one since the tragedy, slowly climbed into the chiseled features on her face.

Someone must be punished! Somebody has to pay. I need to know that other folks feel the pain, too. I need to make someone feel that hurt. I need to hurt somebody...so I won't feel this pain...I need to punish these motherfuckers. All those folks who hurt children...women...the innocents...all of them. Hurt them bad. Hurt them like I was hurt.

Damn you, Eli...Damn the Martins...glad I burned both your perverted souls to hell...fucking with kids like that... and damn you, too, Harrison...for not loving me like a man... like I needed you to...DAMN EVERY LAST ONE OF YOU!!

I will hurt them.

I will make them feel pain.

All of them. Every last one.

Insane with frustration, insane with the idea of rendering punishment, Nicola went outside of her house and found her car. She opened up the glove compartment and dumped everything out, frantically searching for information. And then she found it. The business card the Williams twins had left behind. It was an advertisement for the S&M club in Greenwich Village. That's where she needed to go. That's where she was headed.

But the good Lord was running Nicola's show that day for sure. As she turned around to rush back into her home to prepare for an evening of carnal-inspired violence, He sent her a spirit of wisdom and good old common sense. It grabbed hold of Nicola, held her tight, and never let go.

It finally dawned on Nicola…that she needed to stop the madness in her life…not intensify it. Beating strangers with whips, chains or whatever device she could put her hands on, was not the solution. It was time to stop punishing the world, herself, or anybody else for the events that had taken place in her life or Javon's.

It was time to ask for help; time to figure out how she could become a complete person for the first time in her life. Nicola took the card advertising Dido's Retreat, crumpled it up and threw it in the trashcan. She walked back into her Harlem brownstone a newly born woman; ready to change her life.

On her long laundry list of things to fix in her life. she prayed she got the opportunity to mend bridges with Carlos. Her heart leaped out to him when she read about his hellish childhood in the newspaper. It made her re-think about who he was. In her angry fuck-everybody-in-sight whirlwind, she had never given the man a chance. All he ever wanted to do was love her.

She and Carlos were, in some respects, soul mates. When other kids were jumping Double Dutch, playing stoopball and feeling safe in the arms of loved ones, they were fending off sick, out-of-control adults. How did they find the strength and courage to survive their early years?

She didn't know the answer, but she knew who did. Nicola dropped her head in a humble, respectful pose and prayed to the heavenly Father one more time that day…and this time she didn't scream or yell:

Good Lord…please show me and Carlos and all of Your children who never had a chance…show us the way to that same well of strength…let us tap into it, just one more time… just one more time, would You, Lord? Could You please… could You please let the healing begin?

CHAPTER FORTY-EIGHT

From his window seat on the Boeing 747, Jonathan blankly stared out at the thick dense clouds. Angry, jagged streaks of lightning lit up the sky. Caught in a massive storm system, the plane jerked passengers and crew back and forth. *Getting back home to New York*, thought Jonathan, *would not be easy. But then again, I don't deserve easy.*

A toddler cried in the aisle next to him. The crying reminded him of Javon. Poor little innocent Javon.

It was almost nine months ago. Jonathan was still in the hospital recovering from knee replacement surgery when they held Javon's funeral. He could still see his mom sitting at his bedside, describing the event, telling him how tragic it was to see the little brass coffin with everyone's beloved Javon inside.

"When I went to console Tarik and Sherry," his mother had told him, an occasional tear staining her cheeks, "...all they would say...and not to me, mind you...

they acted like I wasn't even standing there. All they would say to each other was how cute Javon looked in his grown man suit. And when they viewed the body, they just fooled around with his little black satin bow tie, the one I had bought for him."

Jonathan had tried to stop his mother. The details of the funeral were too painful for him. He begged, "Ma, it's okay. It's over now."

But she ignored him and continued with her story. "Jonathan, it was really emotional in that church. To see Tarik and Sherry up at that little casket fidgeting with that tie. And they were laughing and giggling and having a good time by themselves. They even started clapping when they adjusted the tie the way they wanted it."

And then she paused, like she was seeing the scene right in front of her. "Then they stood there for what seemed like hours staring at him...kissed him on his cheek...and smiling a smile that was...unnatural...not a tear shed between them!"

Jonathan remembered his mom then getting out of her chair. She stared out of the hospital window to look at the East River. He knew she was trying to pull it together, so she could finish the story with some dignity. But she couldn't. The nurse in her had held it back for as long as she could.

Close to a complete tearful breakdown, she reminisced, "Jonathan, baby, they treated that little boy like, like he was taking a nap. Only this time, this time, that sweet, sweet baby wasn't ever waking up."

A middle-aged flight attendant gently shook him and made Jonathan momentarily stop thinking about the past. "Sir, we're landing, please buckle up."

Jonathan pulled the seat belt around him and snapped it in place.

Getting off the plane, Jonathan felt some discomfort in his knee. It reminded him of the physical therapy sessions he endured after the surgery. Jonathan loved therapy because of the pain. He knew he was crazy, but he always felt emotional relief whenever his knee sent waves of excruciating pain through his body. He even refused the pills the doctors offered him. Physical discomfort helped dull the memory of the tragedy.

In the beginning, he even tried to deny himself sleep. He hated falling asleep because his dreams betrayed him. They were always about him, Nicola, and their sexual escapades. He'd awaken with a hard-on or have intense wet dreams. He was ashamed of his penis and his sexuality. It had betrayed him. He wanted to blame Nicola, but he couldn't. No matter how his family tried to console him. He knew better. Sex during a funeral. What kind of pervert was he?

If he had known his affair would upset Carlos to the point that he wanted to kill, he would have never spent the first moment with Nicola. For all the erotic pleasure that she offered him, it wasn't worth the outcome of that afternoon.

It was all his fault. He should have been stronger. He should have tried to resist Nicola. He was weak. That he would never play basketball again seemed like a small price to pay for his crime, considering that an innocent child was now dead because he couldn't control the animal between his legs.

As for Carlos, surgeons could only reattach half of his penis. Jonathan thought about how he was always so macho about his organ. Now he was so out of it mentally, he didn't have a clue to his own identity. After surgery, when they told Carlos about the consequences of his actions, he totally shut down mentally. He was in a complete catatonic state. They had to put him in the psychiatric ward. Deemed unfit to stand trial...he was sentenced to prison for the criminally insane.

And Nicola...

After the scene in the funeral home, she had vanished. He didn't know where she was, nor did he care.

Skimming through a biology book while waiting for his mother to pick him up, Jonathan thought about his future. He had started college at California Tech a semester late. He had a lot of catching up to do, but since Jonathan had no time for the usual college socializing and fraternizing, he focused entirely on his pre-medical studies. His diligence paid off well, too. A near-perfect grade-point average for his first completed semester proved that he was on his way to becoming a fine doctor.

After the fiasco during the summer, his mother had insisted that he attend sessions with a therapist to help sort out any post-traumatic emotional issues. It was a wise choice. The counseling, which he'd continued at school, had helped him to negotiate the truckload of guilt he carried around after Javon's death. He had made some progress, but he still had a ways to go before he was able to look himself in the mirror.

Coming home for a visit before he started summer school was what he needed. He wanted to see his mom, and Tarik and Sherry's new babies. But, most of all, he needed to see Carlos.

CHAPTER FORTY-NINE

"That's right, Link, dip her, hold her lovingly, and Ophelia, be coquettish. Play with his affection." The dance instructor encouraged Ophelia and Link as their bodies swayed to the demanding rhythms of the tango. Couples stood on the side watching as Link dipped Ophelia's body in tune with the music. Their eyes locked in a romantic gaze. They were one with the music. As the music from Ravel's "Bolero" ended, Link spun Ophelia out and then snapped her body back close to him with the skill and grace of a professional. Both he and Ophelia collapsed together on the floor, laughing as their classmates applauded.

Link pulled Ophelia up and hugged her tightly. They were both intensely proud that they had finally mastered the intricacies of the tango.

They'd been working on it since they first started coming to the school three months sago. Since Javon's and Eli's funerals, he had made it his mission to be by her side. He loved this woman, and she truly needed him. It didn't take long for him to figure out that Ophelia needed to get involved in an activity that would take her mind off of her problems. He had ulterior motives in that he wanted her to spend time with him. An advertisement for ballroom dancing caught his eye. He remembered how much he had enjoyed dancing back in his college days. Because of his legal practice, he hadn't danced in years.

Link persuaded Ophelia to join the class with him. She hesitated at first; other than African dancing with its free-flowing nature, she'd always had problems with other styles. It was as if she were born with two left feet. Link insisted, and finally wore her resistance down. He had to drag her there the first few weeks. As she slowly discovered that she did have skills and that Link was an amazing partner, she found herself looking forward to the class.

With each time on the dance floor, their relationship matured. Link changed his entire schedule to accommodate the classes. They went from one to three times a week. Accustomed to working over eighty hours a week, it was the first time in his adult life that he made his personal life a priority. He never regretted his decision to spend more time with Ophelia. His life was now full with joy and laughter as it had never been before.

The dance class helped take her mind off of Carlos,

Javon, Jonathan, and the terrible events of last summer. She was so grateful for Link's friendship. Friendship that evolved into a full-fledged romance.

When the noon class was over, Link drove Ophelia to JFK airport to pick up Jonathan. Driving in his car, she glanced over at the lean, muscular, ruggedly handsome attorney and wondered why she had never considered him while Pops was alive. Since the dance class started, she realized the raw sexuality that oozed out of every pore of the man's body. Had it always been there? All those years?

She'd always thought that Eli would be the only passionate love in her life. She thought it only happened once in a lifetime. Ophelia was delightfully surprised to discover that after all the years since Eli, she was still a vital, hot-blooded woman…and Link was her mean, lean sex machine.

With Link at her side, there were no more thoughts of bad times. No images of funerals, a dying child or mentally ill sons. There were no ghosts of Pops or Eli standing between them frowning down on their new-found love and romantic intimacy.

She looked at her left hand at the big diamond engagement ring Link slipped on her finger a week ago when he proposed marriage. Without hesitation, Ophelia accepted. Link had business in Europe to take care of in July, so they decided to get married in Paris after the merger he was working on was completed.

For their honeymoon, they both rearranged their schedules so that they could spend an entire month on the island of Oahu in Hawaii. Link had purchased a sprawling four-thousand-square-foot home with a private beach ten years ago. The busy attorney so rarely had free time to stay there that he rented it out to tourists. Wanting the villa to be in good condition when he and his new bride arrived, he hired an interior decorator to make sure everything was perfect for them.

The traffic coming from JFK airport was not bad. It was a beautiful spring afternoon in late May. Summer was definitely in the air. Link had slept over the previous evening. Thinking about how they had made passionate love all night long, caused a stirring between Ophelia's legs.

She looked over at him. When Pops was alive, they all socialized together. Link would bring his girlfriends by the house, Ophelia always thought, for their approval. He dated very desirable, accomplished women. No matter how she or Pops tried to persuade him to settle down with one of them, he always eventually found something wrong with the women. He never kept a relationship longer than a year. Looking down at her ring again, she wondered if she was the reason for his bachelor- hood all these years.

Listening to him humming and watching him smiling as he drove his beloved jet-black Cadillac to the airport, she massaged his leg. His smile deepened as he quickly glanced his approval in her direction.

"Link, I really enjoyed last night with you." She caressed the growing firmness in his crotch. Link moaned out in pleasure.

"You know what, Nurse Ophelia?"

She leaned closer to him and replied in a sexy voice, "No, what?"

"You are making one Southern boy very, very happy."

Jonathan enjoyed the ride back home from the airport with Uncle Link and his mom.

"So you guys do all that old-fashioned fancy dancing?" Jonathan was curious about his mom and Uncle Link's extracurricular activity.

Link, proud about his and Ophelia's shared love of the tango, yelled back at Jonathan, "You should see your mother on the dance floor."

"When I started, I had two left feet. Didn't I, Link?"

"Two left feet, for sure. And she kept stepping on both of mine!"

"I did not!"

"Yes, you did. I got the podiatry bills to prove it."

"You're horrible, Link!"

Link laughed out loud. He enjoyed teasing Ophelia.

"Mama, you can't dance. We always laughed at you when you tried, remember?"

"You should see her now, Jonathan. She floats on the floor just like Ginger Rogers."

"And he's definitely my dark-chocolate Fred Astaire." They all shared a good laugh together.

Later that evening, at the dinner table, with just him and his mom, Jonathan decided it was time to talk about serious things. While he was away at college, his mother had shared very little information about Carlos's progress.

"Mama, tomorrow I'm visiting with Tarik and Sherry."

"Wait 'til you see your new nephews…they are beautiful!"

"I'm real eager for that. But, I want to see Carlos before I leave for school next week. I really didn't want to go without seeing him. That is, if he'll let me."

Tears welled up in Ophelia's eyes. She only wished her boy was sane enough to refuse his visit. Carlos had been in and out of a catatonic stupor ever since he was committed to the psychiatric prison. She did not think Jonathan needed to see him like that. She knew he was still wrestling with his own demons. In his current state, seeing Carlos might reopen wounds for Jonathan. She didn't know if it was worth the chance.

"Hon, I don't know if I can arrange that for you on such short notice." Never a good liar, she turned her eyes away from Jonathan and said, "Visits have to be approved weeks in advance, and I don't think…"

"Mama Ophelia, I can always tell when you're not being straight with me."

"But, but, Jonathan. Look, baby, Carlos is bad off; real bad. It's not a pretty sight. Maybe, maybe next visit, when you come home for the summer. Then we'll…"

"Mama, I'm going to summer school. I'm not coming back for quite a while. Look, I *need* to see him. Please try and arrange it. Would you, please? For me?"

Ophelia looked at her youngest son. She could tell from his pleading eyes that he needed this visit. It wouldn't help Carlos, but maybe Jonathan needed to see him to help heal.

"I'll see what I can do. Maybe, maybe you and I will go and visit him on Monday."

CHAPTER FIFTY

Sherry hung the phone back into its cradle. So Jonathan was back in town for a short visit. Her feelings were so mixed she didn't quite understand what her feelings were. Having him around made her think back to that horrible day. She never really blamed Jonathan, but he was part of the reason that Carlos snapped that day and ended her baby's life.

Nicola; that bitch. I shoulda killed her for all the trouble she caused in my family. Sherry still had nightmares about whipping her ass. Unresolved anger, left over from that day, seeped back into her veins. Trying to practice what her co-counselor at the job had suggested, she quickly re-focused on what was happening in her life now. Sherry's "now" was all about Tarik and her new babies. *There ain't no space in my world for Nicola or her shit!*

Pleased that she had successfully neutralized her anger, Sherry looked up at the wall clock. Tarik should burst through that door within the hour. He was always punctual. One o'clock in the morning. The twins were still asleep, but they'd wake up just before Tarik put his key in the door. They were on their daddy's schedule.

It was so hard to get the boys back to sleep. But since he'd started on the second CD three months ago, he'd missed seeing the boys during the day, and despite her protests, he still snuck in the room and woke the boys up. She gave up when she accepted the fact that she was married to a musician who kept crazy hours. Sherry rearranged the family's schedule so that they could all spend that golden hour together when Tarik returned home from the studio.

After Javon died, Tarik was almost obsessive about spending time with her and the boys when they were born. She knew he took responsibility for his death. He'd even said one night soon after he passed, that if he'd never met her, Javon would still be alive. She cursed his ass out the night he told her that. For even thinking something that stupid. It was such idiocy to her. But in the quiet of the morning hour, even she knew that what he had said did have an absurd ring of truth.

But she never dwelt on those issues. Tarik's guilt haunted them like demons. It took them months to tackle them together. But they were eager to get back to normal. The twins were on their way and they needed a healthy mommy and daddy to survive. She focused on Tarik, rather than her own demons. She had them, too. It was easier wrestling with his.

Sipping on a glass of cranberry juice, Sherry plopped down on a recliner. Having Jonathan in town stirred up old feelings about the incident. She admitted to herself, that she'd never really grieved for her beloved baby. She knew why, too. He had never left. She still felt him. She sensed his presence especially strong when the babies were two months old. She'd catch the twins laughing and giggling in the room. The laughter was always too loud to be made by just two babies. She definitely heard a third, older giggle.

She'd run in sometimes, expecting to see Javon, the sound was so convincingly his. She shared her thoughts with Tarik. He had also sensed the same presence in the house. They spied on the kids with the baby cam. They were both convinced the two infants were literally staring out as if there was someone with them. They agreed that Javon was watching over his brothers. It gave them comfort. It made Tarik's thoughts about his responsibility in the matter, vanish. Sherry smiled to herself as she thought, *In place of all that ugly guilt is our family's love for each other…including Javon.*

Tarik looked at the car's digital clock. It was two in the morning. He'd been coming home at this time for the past two months. Sherry was so understanding. He'd thought he had to do a lot of explaining. But no. She took it all in stride, and even stopped yelling at him when he snuck in and woke up the babies.

After winning the Grammy for Best New Artist of the

year and the MTV video award, he was busier than he wanted to be. He had to admit keeping his mind on the work did help him to avoid thinking about Javon so much. For that, he was grateful.

He walked into the front door of the home he shared with his wife and two kids. He heard Sherry telling their five-month-old sons that it sounded like Daddy. The two, Nehemiah and Isaac, squealed with delight when he entered the nursery. Sherry greeted him with a warm kiss.

"How the session go tonight, baby?"

"Making real progress. Should be finished very soon. And then the tour."

"I can't wait. These hours are so grueling. I know you want to spend more time with me and the kids."

He hugged Sherry tightly. "Soon; we'll be together soon."

"Baby, don't you know when we ain't together, we together."

Tarik pulled back and looked at his woman. She was not only physically beautiful but inside she was the queen he worshipped. Looking at Sherry this way, as if seeing her for the first time, he made an important decision.

"You know, woman, I absolutely love you."

"You'd better!" She playfully threw a punch at him.

This loving feeling he had now with Sherry was real. It was good, rich, and special. Suddenly free from the weight of his guilt, he picked her up and playfully swung her around. The boys squealed with laughter.

"We'll take a trip. Just you and me."

"What about the boys?"

"That's what nannies and grandmas are for. It'll be like a second honeymoon." The trip would be a reaffirmation for him. A cleansing after all the grief that was in their life. Later that night in bed, after making passionate love to each other, Sherry basked in the glow of their love.

She remembered how she was in the beginning of the marriage. She never let her guard down. Didn't even let him make love to her without a condom. But everything changed after the incident. After losing Javon, the closeness they'd always shared just deepened. She knew her man as she knew herself. They were one. The trust was pure. It was their blessing after losing their son.

"Oh, forgot to tell you. Jonathan called."

"Haven't spoken to him since he left for school."

"I invited him to Sunday brunch. You'll be there, right?"

When he'd last seen his brother before he'd left for school. he was still partially blaming him for what had happened to Javon. But now, in the light of the love he shared with Sherry, his new babies and the wonderful memories of a sweet four-year-old boy, he had no mixed emotions about Jonathan.

"Not see my baby brother? Hell, I wouldn't even think about missing it."

CHAPTER FIFTY-ONE

*J*onathan felt extremely uncomfortable waiting in the visitor's reception area. There were guards and orderlies posted everywhere overseeing the visits. He watched a female inmate bang her head against a table repeatedly as she shouted out profanities. Three orderlies pulled her away from the old couple who'd come to visit their granddaughter. They dragged her out of the room kicking and screaming. Jonathan turned to his mother.

"How's Carlos's condition usually?"

"When he's on meds, he's a…he's a mess! Worse than the woman we just saw."

And it was true. Every time they found a combination of medications that brought him "back," Carlos could not handle reality. It was always the same scene. He'd look at what remained of his penis and scream. Then he would rant and rave about Javon, and scream out for mercy, begging God to put him to death. He would try to mutilate himself with whatever objects he could find.

The medical staff would discontinue the meds and he'd slip back into a walking coma. He was like a zombie. Most times when she visited Carlos, all he would do was stare out in to space. Unresponsive. He didn't even blink when she would call out to him. It was torture for her to see him like that. Ophelia faithfully visited him every other week without fail. She never gave up hope that one day he would come back.

Jonathan shuddered to think that Carlos acted out like the woman he had just seen. Quickly wanting to reassure him, Ophelia added, "But he's off meds now, and here of late, he's usually just quiet. Very quiet."

"Is that good or bad?"

"Well, it depends. Here he is now."

Jonathan turned around. Two guards and a doctor led Carlos into the area. Both his hands and feet were in chains and he wore drab prison attire. Jonathan called out to him.

"Carlos. Hey, man…it's me…Jonathan."

But as soon as Jonathan saw him up close, he realized that he was talking to a zombie. There were no signs of life or brain activity in his face. Carlos never looked his way. Never even looked at his mother. Jonathan could not believe it. His once gregarious, cocky brother was now a card-carrying member of the walking dead society.

Tears flooded his eyes when the enormity of Carlos's condition and how sick he really was finally smacked Jonathan upside his head. The guard led Carlos to a chair across from where Jonathan and Ophelia were sitting. They pushed him down, not hard but deliberately into a chair. Carlos never acknowledged anyone's presence in the room. He just stared out into space. He was there but he really was not.

Jonathan desperately tried to connect with him again. "Carlos. How you doing? It's me, Jonathan…talk to me…yell at me…something, man…anything!"

Ophelia put her hand over Jonathan's and shook her head, signaling for him to calm down. Jonathan sat back in the chair. Nothing could have prepared him for this. Jonathan broke down and cried out to himself: *Is this what Nicola and I did to him? We should both rot in hell.*

"Hello, Carlos. It's Mama Ophelia. I've brought Jonathan to visit. You know Jonathan." Carlos never looked at them. He just rocked in his chair and stared out into space. He was in another time zone.

Not giving up, Ophelia continued, "Carlos, baby, how are you today?" She spoke to him as if he understood her. She talked with him as if he was listening. He never even grunted in response. This non-person who greeted her on visits. Sometimes she got angry with him, thinking that maybe he wasn't trying hard enough.

Angry or not, she still visited and spoke to him just like folks did to comatose victims, hoping that somewhere there was a sane part of Carlos listening. She kept faith that one day that part would strengthen and regain control.

Jonathan couldn't stand to see Carlos in his present condition. He'd expected his visit might agitate Carlos. He anticipated that Carlos might still be angry with him. He could handle that. But he could not deal with the vegetable who sat rocking in the chair as if he was trapped in a dense mental fog.

He'd give anything if Carlos snapped out of it and confronted him. Throw a punch or two at him. Whip his ass. That would be wonderful. Jonathan rose out of the chair and walked over to the window, wishing that the visit would end. Wishing that he had never come in the first place. He knew he could never erase the vision of whom and what Carlos had become.

Drained from the visit, Jonathan and his mother rode back to Brooklyn in silence. While negotiating heavy rush-hour traffic, Ophelia tried to put Carlos's visit behind her by immersing herself in thoughts of her upcoming nuptials. Calling it a pre-honeymoon vacation, Link had dropped by the house early that morning before she left with Jonathan, to tell her that he had booked a cruise to the Caribbean. In three days, they would fly down to Miami and then hop on a ship for an eight-day trip visiting Puerto Rico, Martinique and the Cayman Islands.

She needed the trip and looked forward to the special time with Link. Anything to take her mind away from Carlos and the scene that greeted her every other week when she visited him at the institution.

The entire trip home, Jonathan's mind played vicious guilt games with him. He thought seeing his family would help him find peace in some way. When he spent time with Sherry, Tarik and their beautiful twins, he was pleased to see how happy they were. How they appeared to have moved on since the tragedy.

Seeing how his mother was engaged in a new relationship with Link encouraged him that progress was possible. But the trip to see Carlos shattered any hopes he had that peace or closure would ever be possible for him. He couldn't wait to get back to school to see his counselor. He needed help.

Before she went to bed later that night, Ophelia opened a manila envelope. It had arrived earlier that day in the mail. Inside were several pages of documents. A note on top read:

Dear Mrs. Singleton,

By writing this letter to you, I am probably breaking every law of client privacy on the books. I did surveillance work for Nicola James almost a year ago. After seeing you interviewed on television about the tragedy that took place at your ex-husband's funeral…I realized that you were the nurse who held baby Nicola in a photo taken when she was an infant in the hospital.

My investigation revealed horrible things about her past. When I heard that you would have adopted her if not for your husband's drug issues, I wondered if you had known her full story…would you have been kinder to her in that interview. The press, media and you so viciously attacked her, that it upset me. I always felt that she, too, was a victim in the tragedy. In defense of Mrs. James…I felt compelled to share the contents of this package with you.

Thank you for your patience.

Sincerely,

Max Whitlow

Private Investigator

After reading the documents, Ophelia cried like a baby. Upset, a call to Link was the only thing that would calm her down. After their conversation, she knew what she had to do.

The next morning, Ophelia contacted the private investigator. "I got your package, Mr. Whitlow. Now tell me, how can I reach Nicola James?"

CHAPTER FIFTY-TWO

*N*icola rushed home. It was their anniversary. They'd been married one year. She was expecting their first child, and she'd never been happier. But it wasn't easy. Four years ago, when she'd received an unexpected call from Mama Ophelia, she would have never guessed it would have led to the pure joy she now experienced in her life.

After that call, she'd started visiting Carlos. At first, he didn't even know she was in the room. Slowly but surely, he began to "notice" her. When the psychiatrists saw the way he'd responded to her, they'd added "visits with Nicola" to Carlos's therapeutic regimen. That and electroshock therapy seemed to do the trick. After four years in the institution, the parole board released Carlos in perfectly healthy mental condition.

When he left, Nicola was by his side. The first thing

they did when he got out a year ago was to go to Atlantic City and tie the knot.

Their life wasn't perfect. Though they had good relations with Mama Ophelia and her husband, Link, nothing in the world could change Sherry's and Tarik's mind. They refused all attempts at reconciliation. Carlos was disappointed, but he understood why they refused.

Carlos was still proud of his brother's career. Tarik was now a bona fide star. He had added acting to his list of accomplishments. His crowd-pleasing performance in a box-office hit had movie critics predicting he was a shoo-in for an Oscar for Best Supporting Actor.

Jonathan, now a second-year medical student, initially had trouble with their relationship. He changed his mind when he saw how normal Carlos was and that Nicola was no longer the vixen he once knew. Seeing them together helped Jonathan resolve the guilt he had carried around with him for years.

When Nicola pulled into their driveway, a young woman was waiting for her outside her home. She looked like a professor. Young, she wore bifocals, carried a worn briefcase and had a seriously intelligent look on her face.

"Hello, are you Mrs. Nicola Singleton?"

"Yes, I am. May I help you?"

"My name is Winsome Collins. I'm a journalist with the Associated Press. I have news that might be of interest to you." She looked at Nicola's pregnant belly and added, "And your family."

The press had treated Nicola so badly in the past, she didn't want anything to do with Winsome or her news. But something about the young woman made her reconsider. After checking her credentials, Nicola led her into her home.

"Mrs. Singleton, for the past year, I've been writing a book about Tarik's father, Eli Griffith."

"About Eli? Not Tarik? Strange choice."

"I started off with Tarik, but Eli's story was far more appealing." Not interested in anything about Eli, Nicola looked at her watch. Carlos was due back any moment. Ms. Collins would have to speed up this interview.

Winsome could tell Nicola was about to throw her out. "I can tell you're busy, so I'll get right to the point. Did you ever work at Riker's Island, Mrs. Singleton?"

"Why, why yes, I did. Many, many years ago. Why is that important?"

"My research revealed that when you were employed there, you were the technician responsible for an error that put Eli in a very unfortunate situation. It was why a gang led by a notorious male prostitute raped him. His name was..." Winsome looked through her papers, searching for the rapist's identity, but Nicola knew who she was talking about.

"His name wouldn't be Sebastian, would it? A big, old, ugly yellow devil?"

"As a matter of fact, it is."

"That damn bastard has followed me." Scenes of Sebastian and Harrison screwing popped up in her mind for the first time in years.

"My investigation also revealed, and I know this might be painful, that your first husband…"

"Sweetie, I know Harrison's gay. Sebastian was his lover; that's all ancient history."

"So, you did know. I wondered about that. Anyway, Sebastian is now dying in a hospice from complications of AIDS.

"That I didn't know."

"I wanted to interview you for the book. But I also strongly suggest that you get tested for HIV. I've already contacted your first husband, Harrison James."

"How is he?"

"Not too good. He tested positive for HIV."

Nicola was in shock. The baby was also upset; she was kicking more than usual. Nicola held her head down low. If what the journalist suggested was true…she could possibly be carrying the disease. She thought back at the year she screwed anything in sight. If she was positive, she'd have a hell of a time contacting folks.

Then she thought about the people she loved and cared about who might be affected: Carlos, Jonathan, and her baby. The baby was due in three months. Nicola ran out of the house to go to the hospital. She had to know. There were too many people she needed to protect with the information.

CHAPTER FIFTY-THREE

*N*icola felt warm. A thermometer's reading proved she was running a fever. She had been feeling weak all day long. Getting ready for her four-year-old daughter's first day at pre-school and preparing dinner for Carlos and his business partners later that evening, even with a full staff to boss around, had drained her tank. A cough that would not respond to the antibiotics her doctor had given her three weeks ago was really wearing her down.

Out of breath, she barely made it up the stairs to her bedroom. Coughing all the way, she checked on Cisely. She and the nanny were having a good time together. She looked at her precious child. The excellent prenatal care provided by her obstetrician and the anti-viral medications she prescribed for Nicola during the pregnancy protected her baby. After her last lab test at eighteen months, Cisely was officially HIV free. She was a healthy, smart little girl that her daddy Carlos spoiled absolutely rotten.

"Hi, Mommy. Did you buy me the new toy I told you about?"

"No, you have to ask your daddy for that."

"But you promised, Mommy!"

"Me and your daddy will talk about it later." Her beautiful little girl, with two long plaits, pushed out her bottom lip and turned into a little ogre. If she didn't love her so much, she would have pushed that lip right back in. Elsa, the nanny, had a concerned look on her face.

"Mrs. Singleton, you don't look good."

"I don't feel good, either. I'm going to lie down and take a nap."

Nicola barely made it to her room. She lay down on the bed hoping that sleep would revive her. It usually did. When she opened her eyes two hours later, paramedics were shoving an oxygen mask over her face. They were preparing her for transport to the hospital. Carlos was screaming for them to help his wife.

A week later Nicola was still in the intensive care unit, barely hanging on to life. The doctors explained that Nicola was no longer just HIV positive. She now had AIDS.

Carlos was upset. After four years of taking the pills and hoping that they could keep the disease at bay, the worst had finally happened. Watching the love of his life fighting to stay alive was too much for him to bear.

Nicola's condition slowly improved. They all thought she wouldn't make it, but she proved everyone wrong. After a month in the hospital, Nicola came home. She was frail and had lost weight. But she was determined to live as long as she could. With Carlos by her side and her little girl to love, maybe she could beat the odds.

Two years later, Nicola was still fighting for her life. On her first day back home from her most recent stay in the hospital, Nicola sat propped up in bed watching Carlos count out his supply of pills for the day. Still only HIV-positive, he enjoyed normal health. From the beginning, he decided not to skip doses. Counselors explained that non-compliance would only encourage the development of full-blown AIDS.

"Carlos, you're one lucky bastard." Nicola stretched out and yawned.

"I'm lucky you and I and Cisely are together, I know that." He bent over and kissed her on the cheeks. Though he fought hard to keep away from death, he never once thought about abandoning her. For better or worse. In sickness or in health. Those vows meant everything to him.

"Bring the mirror over to me, baby." Carlos hesitated. She looked like hell, but he brought it to her anyway. "I look better today than yesterday, I guess. What day is it?"

"Tuesday, baby. It's Tuesday."

Nicola's mental functions would come and go. Her memory was like Swiss cheese. The private duty nurse brought Nicola her afternoon dosage of pills.

"I wonder what these things are gonna do to me?" She swallowed them all in one long gulp and washed them down with water.

Nicola's problem from the beginning of treatment was that doctors had had a hard time finding the right balance of medications. She did not tolerate the varying combinations of drugs. It didn't help that behind Carlos's back, she would miss dosages, thinking she could avoid the nausea, diarrhea, and bleeding abnormalities that made her life miserable. Her persistently low CD4 count, a measure of how sick her immune system was, made her vulnerable for opportunistic infections. Folks with normal levels rarely contracted these devastating illnesses.

In eighteen months, since she'd had her first AIDS-related illness, she'd had three episodes of pneumonia, the last time requiring ventilator assistance. Three months ago, blurred vision and altered mental status, brought with it a diagnosis of toxoplasmosis, a rare parasitic infection. Dark scarring lesions of Kaposi's sarcoma covered her once beautiful face.

Carlos looked at his wife, still lovely in his mind, as she primped in front of the hand mirror. She was literally wasting away. Without an appetite, pounds melted off the body that men had once worshipped. She was ninety-two pounds when he brought her home from the hospital. Looking at her deep sunken eyes, he felt it in his bones that he was bringing her home to die.

Today was a good day for Nicola. She was lucid for the first time in a week. Often the dementia would cause her to hallucinate. Always patient, Carlos would hold her in his arms while she had long conversations with invisible people.

But as luck would have it, Nicola did respond to a new treatment protocol that doctors suggested she take. This time around, Nicola followed the doctor's orders. Her appetite improved and she gained good solid weight. The hallucinations went away.

Carlos, inspired by Nicola's health, felt their lives normalize again. Not knowing how long she'd be in what appeared to be remission or whether he might develop AIDS himself, he planned a year-long trip for the entire family.

He took Nicola, their daughter, Cisely, and suitcases filled with medications on a cruise around the world. Carlos was determined that for whatever time they had left together, they would spend it in happiness and joy.

$\mathcal{E}$PILOGUE

$\mathcal{T}$hrough teary eyes, sitting next to her daughter, Cisely, Nicola watched the young soprano's angelic face effortlessly sing "His Eye is on the Sparrow." "Sing it till there isn't a dry eye in the house," were Nicola's only instructions to the vocalist. She often hummed its melody to Carlos while cradling and rocking him to sleep. It seemed to comfort both of them. Now that was no longer a concern. Nicola's man, the one she loved so deeply, had left her forever.

The vocalist continued to sing. Her five-octave voice made every word come alive. Nicola could feel the Eternal's presence with her. It comforted her so. She thought back over the last two years.

Nicola's faith had wavered so many times since Carlos had developed AIDS after they'd returned from their cruise. It had reached rock bottom when, on a bone-chilling February morning, Carlos had lapsed into a coma. Doctors had put him on a respirator and he was fighting for his life. That was the day she'd wandered into the small corner church and first heard the song about the Lord and his sparrows.

She'd heard it many times before, but somehow on that day it took on an especially deep meaning. She understood finally and completely of how the Creator watches over even the smallest of his creations. Surely, just surely, he would watch over her family. With that promise of support, she could face Carlos's inevitable end as well as her own. She never doubted the Lord's love again.

Within a week of that revelation, Carlos's condition improved dramatically. They had successfully defeated death once again. They both enjoyed a brief remission from their illness. It was the last time for Carlos. He developed a rare form of meningitis two weeks ago and never came home again.

Link took Nicola's arm. It was time to go to the cemetery. She smiled up at him and Mama Ophelia. From the very beginning, when Carlos had his first AIDS-related illness, they had been her rock through the whole ordeal. Jonathan escorted little Cisely out the church.

When Jonathan arrived in Florida to attend the funeral, Nicola really leaned on him. She, Carlos and Jonathan had all become very good friends over the years. Jonathan was now a successful infectious disease specialist. Thanks to the medications, he was still enjoying good robust health.

His book for teens, that he started writing after he discovered he was HIV positive, *Just Say No, and If You Can't, Wrap It Up*, was scheduled to be released in a few months. The revealing tell-all book advised young people to practice abstinence and if that wasn't possible, then safe sex was the only intelligent alternative.

Jonathan helped Nicola plan the ceremony. He requested that the presiding reverend read the poem "Footprints." Its message, that the Lord carries you when you have long lost the will and power to stand on your own, had often inspired him in times when he felt hopeless in regards to his own diagnosis.

After the reading, the soloist sang the "Sparrow" song a capella as gravediggers covered Carlos with dirt. Then…it was all over. Family and guests returned to their cars.

Link and Ophelia offered to help Jonathan, Nicola and Cisely back to the limo. They all refused. This was the last time they would all be together. They just wanted a few more minutes alone.

All three of them sat together in silence, holding hands. Out of nowhere, three small birds flew on top of Carlos's gravesite. Were they sparrows? Jonathan, Nicola nor Cisely knew. All they did know was that somehow things would work out for them.

Whatever life had in store, they could face. For the

Lord was carrying all three of them. He was watching over them just like He watched and cared for the tiny little birds, whether they were sparrows or not.

A smile fell across their faces. They rose up, arm in arm, and together they walked away from Carlos's gravesite toward the waiting limo.